LEAVING
for a DREAM

LEAVING
for a DREAM

MB Kelly

Mill City Press

Mill City Press, Inc.
2301 Lucien Way #415
Maitland, FL 32751
407.339.4217
www.millcitypress.net

Printed in the United States of America

ISBN-13: 978-1-54562-572-9

This book is dedicated to the road less travelled, and to all of God's creatures who brave the journey.

May you remain steadfast in your search to uncover its most treasured secrets, and remember to always believe in your dreams. They are the stuff life is made of.

"Nothing happens unless first a dream."

Carl Sandburg

PROLOGUE

"**H**ey, Mel! I've got a secret and I want to tell you, but you have to swear you won't tell anybody else, okay?" My best friend, Anthony, questioned me with an urgency to his voice that normally indicated he needed a quick trip to the boys' bathroom. This sounded big! Most of the girls in my second grade class had other girls as their best friends, but I was different; Anthony and I had hit it off in first grade and it stuck. Besides, I had a crush on him, something I kept to myself.

"Sure, Anthony, but I won't swear," I replied firmly. "If Sister finds out, she'll make me go to detention. I'm not her favorite like somebody else I know!" I harrumphed with raised eyebrows.

"Then you've gotta promise you won't tell—cross your heart and hope to die," he threatened.

Now the suspense was killing me! "Okay, okay—I promise!" I said as I crossed my quickened heart.

When Anthony and I were kids we attended Saints Catherine and Anne Elementary School, the local Catholic school in town. Back in the old days when nuns ruled a Catholic child's universe, each grade was assigned to one nun who taught almost all subjects to fifty or more kids. The same group of kids followed each other every year to the same classrooms—a lot of very strong bonds were formed during those years. The nuns were smart, accomplished, hard-working women, but for the most part they were a tough crowd. They demanded a lot from their young charges. A few possibly bordered on sadistic, but, nonetheless, you always respected them—some might say you feared them. It didn't matter. You wouldn't dream of going home and crying to your parents if Sister yelled at you in front of the class for something you didn't do, or pulled your hair just for the hell of it, because you'd get punished again by Mom and Dad for embarrassing them in front of Sister with your bad behavior. In our first year at Saints Catherine and Anne, our classes were taught by Sister Michael Eileen, a five-foot-tall bundle of bad mood who kept a keen eye on the six-year-old miscreants that were her cross to bear for another school year. I learned very early on, as did most of the class, how to placate Sister with my stellar behavior and uncanny ability to sense her every want or need. The less fortunate among us suffered the ruler, the face slap, and other various and sundry methods of discipline whenever she perceived a transgression.

Anthony and I lucked out in the second grade with Sister Laurence Michelle—she was one of the good ones! I sometimes imagined her to be an angel that God had sent down from heaven just to teach our class. While she wasn't above giving out the occasional detention slip when it was warranted, she was always fair and even kind. I wasn't alone in my feelings for her—all the kids loved her. Anthony happened to be our class clown—even then, I couldn't resist a guy who could make me laugh! I don't know what his secret was, but I think Sister got a kick out of him because he didn't seem to spend a lot of time in detention, even though he was always cutting up. Either that or she simply didn't know what to make of him. I didn't know any boys that looked like Anthony; he had an olive complexion, brown eyes, and dark blond wavy hair, the front of which was pomaded to form a large curl across his forehead. And he wore a pinky ring—in the second grade, mind you! I could just see my younger brothers coming home wearing one of those and our dad catching sight of it—they would've been lucky to keep their pinkies after he got through with them.

"You're not going to believe it, Mel—I found fairies in my backyard!" Anthony exclaimed. Anthony was the first person to call me Mel, a truncated version of my full name, Marian Elizabeth. It was a nickname that stuck with me for the rest of my life.

"You what?" I shouted, my heart practically jumping out of my parochial school blazer.

Anthony, peering about furtively, quickly shushed me. "Shut up, stupid, or someone will hear you! I saw them, I swear—I was playing in the backyard and I saw them!" he repeated, sounding stupefied.

Spellbound, I whispered, "What did they look like, Anthony?"

He looked around to make sure the coast was clear before lowering his voice, as though he were about to impart the secret to immortality. "It was just like in the movies, Mel! They were real tiny and sparkly, and they were flying around the flowers like little bees! I tried to catch one in a jar, but they moved too fast," he explained with eyes as wide as saucers.

Imagine that—real live fairies in his own backyard! Since we lived right down the block from each other, I figured the creatures must be in my backyard, too. Just then, the bell signaled the end of recess. As we walked back to class I determined to come up with a foolproof plan; I was going to catch one of those little fairies if it was the last thing I ever did.

I could barely contain myself when Saturday finally arrived! I snuck out of the house before the rest of my family woke up. It was a soft spring morning and the sun was just starting to break over the eastern horizon. It was becoming light enough outside that I would be able to catch sight of the pixies' sparkly little wings as they danced from flower to flower. With glass jar in hand, I positioned myself on an overturned pail and began my fairy vigil. Hours passed—the sun was by now high overhead. I heard my mother calling to me from the kitchen window.

"Marian Elizabeth, what in God's name are you still doing out there? You'll miss breakfast if you don't get in here!" Mom hadn't taken to calling me by my newly acquired nickname; she thought it un-Christian.

"Coming, Ma," I answered dejectedly. No fairies today. I picked up my empty jar, kicked the pail in frustration and headed back to the house. At least Anthony had gotten to see them.

Must have been the damn pinky ring . . .

CHAPTER 1

The family Morrison consisted of our dad, John, who was a fireman; our mom, Julia, a homemaker, and their four children. While we were raised to identify ourselves as Irish Catholic, we were born from both Irish and Scots lineage, the Scottish genes being introduced into the mix by my father's side of the family. The big family secret was that my father's mother, a God-fearing Roman Catholic, had, over the mighty protests of my great-grandparents, married a Presbyterian! Despite fears of their only child spending eternity in hell for committing such a grievous sin, my grandmother's world did not come to an end. By all accounts, my father's mom and dad enjoyed a successful married life with the most joyous result of my grandmother's fearless act being the birth of my dad. My mother was born to first-generation Irish-American parents, both of whom stuck to the game plan of marrying only into one's faith, and it worked out for them as well. My mother and father were the only children of parents who were, themselves, only children. We grew up without aunts, uncles or cousins, which made our family stand out a bit amongst the other Irish Catholic families we knew that grew to be the size of small island nations due to their and their relatives' ever-expanding families. We

1

didn't mind; our parents instilled in us from a very early age that our little family was perfect just as it was. The only relatives we had growing up were my mother's father and mother; my father's parents had both passed on before Mom and Dad were married. How we adored our grandma and grandpa! And besides, we were part of a much larger family, the New York City Fire Department.

I, Marian Elizabeth, was my parents' first-born child; next in line was Hugh Robert, followed by Brendan Andrew, or Bam-Bam as we used to call him for his hilarious antics. Once, when Brendan was about four years old, he got his head stuck in the slat of a chair and my mom couldn't get him out. Oh, how he screamed and carried on—I thought my mom was going to have a heart attack! Dad had to rush home from work with one of his buddies to free Brendan from his self-imposed prison, but by the time they got there, little Brendan had fallen fast asleep, his head still caught in the chair! He never lived that one down.

The last of us was the baby, Bonnie Maureen. Brendan and Bonnie are what are referred to as "Irish Twins," meaning they were born less than a year apart, a not-uncommon occurrence in Irish Catholic families at that time. My siblings were, respectively, three, five and six years younger than me. Dad called me his best girl, knowing he could always count on me to watch over the others, and I never let him down. There had been one miss for my parents, a baby boy that was born eighteen months after me but passed away while still in my mother's womb. My parents never stopped mourning that poor babe – they had named him Ethan, in memory of one of my father's best friends who had perished during the war. But before they could take in all his stillborn perfection, the doctors whisked him away and that was that.

All in all, four robust kids in six years: not bad, nothing for my mom to hang her head about. My family represented what would come to be referred to as a post-WWII nuclear family: the dad who ruled the roost and the mom who stayed at home to raise the kids. The Holy Trinity was God, Family, and Country; the American Flag was always flying outside our front door, holiday or no. There was one automobile per family: Mom didn't work so Dad got the car. A Catholic education was mandatory, no questions asked. When the school year had ended and Dad was home on one of his rare days off from work, we might be treated to a day of sun and surf at the town beach, but when Dad went back to work and the family was car-less we took to our bikes and headed to the local playground. Instead of being kissed by the warmth of the sun and caressed by the gently lapping ocean waves, we encountered that shimmering oasis of burning-hot metal and broken concrete wherein all the neighborhood's warring adolescent gangs converged to lay down their cudgels for a few hours of peaceful playtime.

Once I had finished the fourth grade, I had my parents' permission to go to the playground unsupervised, with the caveat that I was required to bring my younger brothers along (not the baby, though—Bonnie was always at my mother's side), and God help me if anything happened to them while they were in my charge. The implicit understanding was that if we all came home without a major injury, I had done my job. Cuts, scratches, bruises, none of it counted—you just offered that suffering up to God and be done with it. We had no bike helmets, the playgrounds all had cement floors, and, although there must have been the odd child here and there that sustained a major injury, I don't remember any of us having had one, at least not under my watch.

In keeping with Catholic tradition, the weekends always started with a fish dinner on Friday night (unfortunately for me, never a fish lover, pizza parlors had yet to make their way to our neighborhood). If you had made your First Holy Communion you attended confession on Saturday, then fasted from Saturday night till Sunday morning in preparation for the Communion wafer at Mass. Each weekend spent immersed in religious ritual was made palatable because it culminated in the big dinner Mom cooked on Sunday afternoon. She spent the better part of the day preparing what Dad called a "square meal": meat, potatoes, and a vegetable, and maybe dessert if we were good—we always tried to be extra good on Sundays! After playing outside all day, in good weather and in bad, we were hungry by dinnertime. We had never heard of the concept of dieting—no problem there. Looking back, there was no such animal as an overweight kid. My mother could whistle, a whistle that could be heard a mile away, signaling not only to the Morrison children but to all the kids on the block that playtime was over, and it was time to come home for dinner. Everyone came running when they heard that whistle!

When our father came home from the war, he continued the FDNY tradition like his father before him. We were very proud of our family tradition of firefighting. Dad always marched with his firehouse in the annual St. Patrick's Day Parade that was held every year in New York City. Mom would get us dressed up for that special day in our Irish plaids and wool sweaters and drew little shamrocks on our cheeks with her green magic marker. We'd be at the sidelines screaming, "Dad, Dad, over here! That's our dad!" We excitedly waived our little American flags as he marched by, waving back, looking so proud and handsome in his uniform! We weren't afraid of anything bad happening to our dad because of his job, dangerous though it was—at least it wasn't like being a police officer. There always seemed to be a news story about a policeman getting shot or killed. One of

the families on our block had a dad who was a policeman—
he was shot in the line of duty responding to a robbery. The
family moved away not too long after that. Besides, our dad
was tougher than any fire, that much we were sure of!

Because our father had the car most of the time, our
level of interaction with the outside world pretty much
ended where our street ended. We almost never played with
the children who lived on a different street from ours—the
kids on the other blocks in the neighborhood might as well
have lived in a different state. The thirty houses and their
inhabitants that comprised our little fiefdom defined our
young lives. If you dared venture outside of its perimeters,
you chanced being beaten up by the kids who lived on the
street you were trying to infiltrate. One's turf had to be
safeguarded against all intruders—they would have met the
same fate in our little neck of the woods.

There existed one glorious exception to that rule:
Halloween! Happy Halloween! Hooray for Halloween! Had
God ever invented a better holiday for kids? Well, some
might argue for Christmas, but my personal runner-up
was Easter, another candied Christian holiday. There was
a caveat to that holiday, though: the Easter Bunny aside, it
was serious business as you had to survive the Lenten season
beforehand. The forty-day season of Lent symbolizes our
Savior's suffering on the cross before His death on Good
Friday and resurrection on Easter Sunday. In preparation
for Lent, Sister sat you down in class and made you list your
favorite things on a piece of paper, things you were expected
to readily part with during Lent, an act which symbolized
one's taking Christ's suffering upon themselves. You were
instructed to bring your list home to your mother to have
her sign it, then bring it back to Sister the next day so she
knew that she and your mother were on the same page
about your sacrifice for Jesus.

Because we didn't have many extras, a lot of thought went into our lists. What could you give up for Lent when there were no such things as designer children's clothes, video games, or cell phones? I usually gave up watching my favorite cartoons on Saturday morning, and that was hard. We weren't allowed to watch much television, so Saturday morning cartoons were a real treat! We were also required to put our weekly allowance into the big jar that sat atop Sister's desk every Monday morning during the Lenten season to help feed the starving children overseas. My weekly allowance was five cents; I'm ashamed to admit it, but I missed that nickel—it meant no trip to the candy store on Saturday for the whole month of Lent, and a nickel bought a lot of candy in those days.

The same went for our first Sacrament of Confession, the sacrament that we had to get behind us before we could move on to our First Holy Communion. First Holy Communion is the Big Kahuna of sacraments where the girl gets to wear a beautiful white dress and veil, as she is now a bride of Christ, and the boy gets to wear a little suit with a big ribbon on his arm, much like the winning jockey at the Kentucky Derby. Afterward, your parents throw a party for you where you get presents and money. It almost made the Sacrament of Confession worth the fear we children had to endure while waiting our turn to enter the confessional booth. For months prior to the big day, we practiced again and again:
"In the name of the Father, and of the Son, and of the Holy Spirit," we would solemnly intone as we made the sign of the cross. "Bless me, Father, this is my first confession, and these are my sins."
I believe I can humbly speak for the legions of eight-year-old Catholic children who, knees knocking, stepped into the confessional booth for the first time: that dark, scary place where an innocent child was forced to admit

to committing sins that, for the most part, had to be made up in order to placate the priest sitting behind the grilled window, face hidden in shadow. How sinful could a child that age be? "I hit my brother four times (well, I might have smacked him once or twice, but hitting him four times sounded better), I disobeyed my mother three times, I lied two times, I cursed once." Sounds about right—that should satisfy Father this week. I wasn't sure about God, though—wouldn't He know I had made them up? Wasn't that a sin? No matter, I'd done my Catholic duty.

But Halloween? Now THAT was a holiday, pagan though it may have been. Our mother sewed wonderful homemade costumes for us that she made from scraps of old clothes and curtains. We were allowed to venture out and roam the neighborhood to trick-or-treat without our parents if one of the kids was considered old enough to supervise the younger ones (usually the "fourth grade rule" applied). Sweet freedom! All the kids in the neighborhood made a truce on that one special day of the year—what kid could stop themselves from raking in the mountains of candy and coin that could be foraged from the next block? If Halloween landed on a weekday, you really had your work cut out for you because you only had a couple of hours to accomplish your mission before it got dark. We were given large paper bags that Mom had saved from the grocery store and we made it our goal to get as many goodies into those bags as humanly possible. After each foray, we would come back home, dump our treasure onto our beds, then head out for more. No crusader could have been more intent in his search for the Holy Grail than we were in our search for Halloween loot.

Many of the fathers on our block were civil servants of one kind or another: policemen, firemen, sanitation men. The salaries back then weren't much and with ever-growing families, there wasn't a lot of money to spend on candy and the like, so we took our trick-or-treating very seriously. There were only two rules for Halloween that had to be followed, and if they weren't, you could be the recipient of a serious spanking. Rule number one: you had to be home before dark. Rule number two: no egg throwing. Frequently, the second rule got broken, and usually, if done properly, you didn't get caught. But you never broke rule number one and you made sure you got home on time. As fun as Halloween was, it could get kind of scary for us young kids after dark. And anyway, if some neighborhood ghoul didn't get us, Mom would have!

CHAPTER TWO

My mother was a classic Irish beauty. She was the proud owner of long, wavy, dark brown hair that she kept back from her face in a French twist and was made even more striking in contrast to her fair, flawless complexion. Her eyes were so green they took you by surprise—and she had freckles, the cute kind. Out of the four children, I had inherited my mom's green eyes, but my hair color was somewhere between hers and my baby sister's red hair. My brother Hugh was a tow-headed lad, while little Brendan was dark, like our mother. Unlike me, they were all blue-eyed like our father. Even as a very young girl, I knew my mom had a lot going for her. I would watch her intently as she made herself up for a night out with Dad; she was as beautiful as any one I had ever seen on TV or in the movies. When I brought a new friend to the house, upon meeting my mother they would inevitably say, "Your mom is so pretty!" It made me wonder what their own mothers looked like. Mom was also a devout Catholic who held no quarter for the kinds of misbehaviors a child might be tempted into as set forth in our Baltimore catechisms. My mother was a mystery to me: she was stern so much of the time, especially with me, yet I would sometimes watch her with my father and her manner would change; she would become softer, almost like a younger version of herself, or at least what I'd imagined her to have been like as a young girl. What magical powers did my father possess that could bring such a change upon her? I didn't know, but whatever it was, I was glad Dad had it!

My father wasn't a big man, perhaps 5'10" tall in his prime, but he seemed positively gigantic to us kids. He sported a mane of full white hair and had piercing blue eyes. He carried himself with the quiet, assured, yet slightly menacing air of the hero in a great Western movie. My friends had an interesting reaction upon meeting my father. "Gee, I wouldn't want to get in his way!" they would say under their breath. While he wasn't an angry man, his demeanor spoke for itself. He'd had it tough growing up during the Great Depression. My father's parents passed away within six months of each other when he was only seventeen years old, his grandparents having long been gone. He was very much on his own. After his mother died, he left high school to join the Marines during the Second World War. Mom said that Dad's hair was dark brown when he went overseas to fight; when he came back, it had turned snow white. He was as tough as nails and his word was final on all subjects, but we knew he loved us and that he was proud of his little clan. If my mother had had enough of us kids horsing around, all she would have to utter where those immortal words, "Just wait till your father gets home!" and we'd all run for cover. Once, while Hugh was trying to get a stranglehold on me, I yelled, "Get off me, Hugh—you're such an ass!" Now, that might sound like a rather mild exclamation today, but all Hugh had to say was, "I'm telling Mom you said 'ass'!" and I hid under my bed for what seemed like hours, not coming out again till I was sure Dad wasn't looking for me.

Mom and Dad met a few years after the war ended; he was twenty-five and she was barely out of high school when they got married after dating for only six months. My father, ever the tough guy, could be quite the romantic when the mood struck him and would say, "We knew we were right for each other the moment our eyes met!" My mother, ever practical, would retort, "Why, he practically stole me from my cradle!" We knew Mom and Dad loved each other, yet they rarely displayed openly strong emotion or physical affection toward one another; they had both been raised in the Irish Catholic tradition of the strict observance of propriety while in the presence of others, even their own family. Nevertheless, their love seemed to hang suspended in the air between them. I vividly recall a rare occasion when we were privy to one unguarded moment: we had just finished cleaning up after dinner and were watching television in the den when our parents walked to the couch, hand in hand. Mom sat down, and Dad lay with his head in her lap. She lovingly stroked his white hair as he gazed into her green eyes, smiling, while their children played contentedly nearby. I will hold that memory very close to me, always.

My grandparents held a very special place in our family, made all the more so because we had no other relatives. How excited we were every time they visited! Grandpa would bring comic books for us to read and Grandma would provide all her grandchildren with new underwear. My grandmother and grandfather were first-generation Irish-American, born in the United States. My grandma's mother was born on a farm in County Clare, Ireland, and immigrated to the United States during the late 1800s. She came here on a ship, all by herself, barely a woman. She had a cousin who gave her lodging until she got employment as an upstairs maid for a wealthy Protestant family. It wasn't until many years after her passing that a closely guarded secret was revealed: she had been an indentured servant for that family for a number of years before she was able to marry my great-grandfather. (I did some research on the subject and discovered, to my surprise, that the laws allowing for indenture were not removed from the New York State statutes until 1923, almost sixty years after the end of the Civil War and subsequent abolition of slavery.) She eventually met and married a fellow immigrant, my grandma's dad, then settled into the Irish tenement community in New York City. Their marriage produced three children: my grandma, a boy who died in infancy, and my grandma's little sister.

It was on one typically steamy New York City summer night that my great-grandparents retired to the rickety fire escape of their tenement to try to find some relief from the unrelenting heat and humidity that was a common misery at the time in the long summer months. At some point during the night, my then ten-year-old grandma awoke to screams: her little sister had fallen from the fire escape to the sidewalk below and to her untimely death at three years of age. My grandma never spoke about it—my mother found out about the tragedy from a friend of the family. My mother had always described her grandmother as very tough, not given to displays of affection, but it seemed to me that she needed a spine of steel to weather the storms that she had to endure all her life! After my grandmother's little sister died, my great-grandmother held very tightly to her last surviving child and expected her to be, after the passing of my great-grandfather, a spinster daughter. However, later events were to prove that my grandma had other plans.

My grandfather was known around his neighborhood as a lucky Irishman, but he was no stranger to heartache. My grandpa was born and raised in New York City, the eldest of five children. After his father died when he was only eleven years old, he became the major breadwinner in the family and worked hard at anything and everything that came his way to help put food on the table. By the time he was fifteen, he was working as a runner for a large brokerage firm in Manhattan and doing quite well for a teenager of such humble beginnings. But the larger world called to him, and at seventeen he left home to join the Army's Fighting 69th Infantry Division and fought in France during the First World War, earning a Purple Heart in the process. When he returned home, he started to come around to my great-grandmother's house, asking her permission to court my grandmother, whom he'd known for years from the neighborhood. She wasn't too happy about his proposal, as she had striven to keep my grandmother under lock and key, but grandma had her own ideas and before long she and grandpa were dating. They kept company for a while but the wild "Irish Rover" in my grandfather missed the adventures that beckoned to him from far-off lands and decided to re-up and joined the Navy. Upon completing his second tour of duty he returned home, not knowing what fate had in store for him. Well, my grandmother had him firmly in her sights, and before my grandpa knew what hit him, he was a married man! My mother came along the following year.

My grandfather, being the handsome, affable Irishman that he was, had little trouble finding employment after his two stints in the military. In fact, he found a rather nice position as the doorman for a posh uptown apartment house where he stayed on for almost forty years. He was always a softy, a kind man who made sure he had a little extra in his pocket to put down on the bar for the friend or stranger who couldn't afford a pint. My mother was my grandparents' only child and my grandfather doted on her by her own account. Even during the Great Depression, my grandfather made sure his little family had whatever they needed and maybe a tad more. Given my grandfather's generous nature in temperament as well as pocket, I figured that my grandmother was pushed into being the parent who doled out the discipline in that household, although I couldn't imagine my mother needing any. But if she had, Grandma had the backbone for it, of that I was sure—strong women tend to run in the family! I so looked forward to their visits; my grandfather would enthrall us with his war stories and my grandmother would recount her mother's stories of her years as a little girl growing up on the family farm in Ireland.

I suppose that because I was the oldest child and a bit of a tomboy ("You remind me of my grandmother—a tough little Mick, you are!" my mother would sometimes remark), my father and mother bestowed upon me the role of protector of my younger siblings. I remember one boy who was about my age and the neighborhood bully—he wouldn't stop picking on my brother Hugh. I was eight years old at the time, Hugh five. One day, Hugh came into the house, crying, with a red mark on his face. Through his tears he told Mom that the bully had hit him again while he was playing with his friends. My mother took me aside and, in a conspiratorial tone, ordered me to take the bully down and to leave him no doubt that he was never to bother my little brother again. I solemnly nodded that I understood what had to be done. The next day, I waited in the bushes outside of the house about the same time the bully usually rode his bike down our sidewalk. Then I spotted him: as he neared the bushes I rushed at him, grabbed him by his shirt, yanked him off the bike and proceeded to beat the crap out of him. As instructed, I warned him never to touch my brother again or he'd be the worse for it. He got back on his bike and rode home, whimpering. Mission accomplished! That bully would never bother Hugh again. I turned and looked at our house; my mother was looking out from its big picture window, a tiny smile tugging at the corners of her mouth.

Good times . . .

CHAPTER 3

To some, Labor Day weekend portended a somber ending to summer's optimistic sentiments, but to me it heralded a new school year and all the exciting possibilities that lay ahead. I had just begun my freshman year at Bishop McDonald High School. I loved the uniforms at Bishop McDonald—they were a navy blue and gold plaid pattern; much better than the dull brown and beige uniforms we were forced to endure at Saints Catherine and Anne. I decided that I looked pretty good in navy blue—it accentuated my hair, which was now streaked with blond highlights from the summer sun and had grown down to my waist.

It was great fun starting the school year with so many of my old mates and making new friends with some of the kids who had transferred in from other schools. When the sisters weren't watching I, along with most of the girls at school, would hike up my skirt a couple of inches above my knees at a vain attempt at being fashionable. We had lookouts at every turn, making sure the hems came back down as soon as a nun was spotted scurrying down the hall, wimple flying. There were a couple of totally cute guys I'd pass in the halls on my way to class and I'd see them watching me; I wasn't allowed to date yet, but I could still hope for the future. My teachers seemed nice enough; I had only one mean nun, Sister Agnes, who taught freshmen science on Wednesdays and Fridays. The class was torture—we were all under the impression Sister might be a tad crazy. But all in all, I was quite pleased with my new freshman life.

I adored the fall season, and it was an especially fine day, holding all the promise of many more beautiful fall days to come. The sky was an immaculate blue and the sun, a shining, golden disc hanging amidst white puffy clouds. The air carried a brisk autumnal smell reminiscent of burning leaves. It was a Wednesday; I remember because we were in the middle of Sister Agnes' science class when an announcement came over the PA system: "Will Marian Morrison please report to the principal's office?" Well, that couldn't be good! Had I been caught rolling my uniform skirt above my knees? I asked Sister's permission to leave class and she nodded her consent. I walked down the hall, starting to feel a panic rising in my chest. I had never gotten into trouble at school before—what could I have done to have Father Meehan calling for me? I approached the principal's office and timidly knocked on the door.

"Come in," instructed the woman's voice on the other side of the door. As I walked in, I could make out a man in a uniform sitting in Father Meehan's office.

"Marion Morrison?" asked Mrs. Solan, Bishop McDonald's ancient school secretary, as she peered at me from behind bottle-thick eyeglasses.

"Yes, Mrs. Solan," I answered meekly.

"You may go in, Marian. Father is expecting you," she advised me, pointing to the large oak door behind her.

I tread quietly into Father Meehan's office and curtsied. "Good afternoon, Father," I said reverently.

"Marian, please, come and sit down. Mrs. Solan, hold all calls and keep my door closed. Thank you," he instructed. I looked more closely at the man in the other chair wearing what I could now see was a fireman's uniform.

"Marian, this is Chief Inspector Walker—he works with your father. He's come to take you home. There has been an accident, I'm afraid," Father Meehan said gently.

"An accident? What's happened—is it my dad?" I asked in alarm, my heart pounding with fear. I heard blood rushing through my ears.

"Yes, my child. You need to get home—your family is waiting for you. Our prayers are with you and your loved ones now," Father Meehan replied compassionately as he stood up. He placed his hand on the top of my head, blessed me, and made the sign of the cross over me. I left the office with Chief Inspector Walker holding my arm. I wanted to ask more questions, but I couldn't find my voice; I was terrified. The chief was quiet on the drive home—I think he was grateful for my silence. When we arrived at the house, I walked in and was immediately surrounded by a sea of fire department uniforms. I made my way to the den to find my mother and siblings sitting on the couch, a priest standing close by, the sound of our television set droning in the background.

"Mom, what's going on? Is Dad okay?" I asked as I rushed to her side, my voice quivering. She slowly raised her face to mine—her beautiful green eyes were glistening from a steady rain of tears. My brothers and sister were so quiet, holding on to our mother like ballast as if to stop her from floating away.

"Marian Elizabeth, come—I need my girl. Your father is gone," she cried out in anguish. Her voice came to me as though wafting through a dense fog. Daddy is gone? I must have fallen asleep during science class. This is a dream, a nightmare—why isn't Sister waking me up? She would never stand for this kind of behavior in class. Where did Dad go? It was then that I became aware of the voice coming from the television: there had been a five-alarm fire in Queens earlier that morning. Two firemen had not made it out of the burning building: Lieutenant John Francis Morrison and Fireman James Michael Wheeler. An investigation was ongoing as to the cause of the fire.

"Mom, I'm here . . . I'm right here," I murmured reassuringly as I knelt down beside her, trying to stay calm. What should I do? I was only fourteen years old. Then the answer came to me: I had to step up and be the tough guy again, protecting my younger siblings from the neighborhood bullies—this time around, my mother as well. I couldn't cry—I had to hold it together. I would cry later, when Dad walked through the door to tell us it had all been a terrible mistake. I would run to him and throw my arms around him, feeling safe, knowing that only he could protect me from the bad guys.

The priest intoned, "We'll pray the rosary now." The whole room knelt in unison as we started praying in one voice: "Our Father, who art in heaven, hallowed be Thy name, Thy kingdom come, Thy will be done, on earth as it is in heaven. Give us this day our daily bread; and forgive us our trespasses, as we forgive those who trespass against us. And lead us not into temptation, but deliver us from evil. For Thine is the kingdom and the power and the glory, forever. Amen."

"Hail Mary, full of Grace, the Lord is with Thee, blessed art Thou amongst women and blessed is the fruit of Thy womb, Jesus. Holy Mary, Mother of God, pray for us sinners, now and at the hour of our death. Amen."

"Glory be to the Father, and the Son and the Holy Spirit, now and ever shall be, world without end. Amen."

"Oh, my Jesus, forgive us our sins, save us from the fires of hell, and lead all souls to heaven, especially those most in need of Thy mercy." Father then concluded the service. "And may the souls of the faithfully departed rest in peace. Amen."

I started to get up off my knees; I don't remember what happened next. I came to on my bed, my grandmother holding a cool damp cloth to my head, holding my hand—I was still in my school uniform. I wasn't sure what day it was. I stared into my grandmother's eyes; I started crying, quietly at first. When she took me in her arms my crying took on a life of its own. I sobbed into her chest, wracked with a young girl's grief for her dead father, her hero, her Superman. My memories of that day are vague but never far from me: my family, numb from shock, the constant prayers, the reassuring presence of the clergy, the never-ending stream of firefighters and neighbors, Grandma and Grandpa. Thank you, God, for Grandma and Grandpa. I love them so.

As the oldest child, I was expected to hold up under the weight of the events that followed: the two nights of wake, the funeral Mass, and the burial. And I did. Hugh was now the man of the house at age eleven, an eerie reminder of our grandpa's heart-wrenching situation at the same age. Brendan and Bonnie were just little kids—they were scared more than anything else. Mom was stoic through it all; she said we all had to be strong—Dad would have expected no less. Mom aged in the days following the fire, but even in her mourning she was still Dad's beautiful bride. She clung to my grandfather and he stood steadfastly by her side through it all.

Grandma called the Mass and burial a "grand thing"; the funeral procession from the mass to the cemetery was miles long. The fire trucks were draped with flags and bunting, their lights flashing and horns blaring, providing safe passage to our sad destination. Even the police department had cars posted every few miles en route to the cemetery with their chase lights swirling, offering their condolences. I realized then how many people loved my father almost as much as I did. The story of the fire and its bleak aftermath ran on the front page of the newspapers for days: my dad had died a hero, trying to save two of his men when a ceiling caved in on them during the fire. One had survived, one did not. The survivor, a young man by the name of Glen Eoin Larkin was at the funeral, having missed the wake because of his injuries. He stood as still as a soldier through it all, supported by his crutches and brother firefighters. Glen Eion presented the American flag to my mother after the military ceremony at the cemetery. When it was over, the FDNY Pipe Band, playing "Danny Boy," led us out into the brilliant orange-emblazoned October afternoon. We went back to my dad's firehouse afterward where an Irish wake awaited us. The first wake had been a solemn affair—this one was to celebrate the life of John Francis Morrison, not his untimely death.

There was plenty of food and drink, people laughing, telling stories of my dad and the practical jokes he loved to play on his buddies in the fire house. I wandered through the throngs of people, being stopped occasionally by a well-meaning friend of the family asking if I was okay. "Marian, you're becoming such a lovely young woman—why, you're beginning to look just like your mother! You've been so brave. Is there anything we can do help? Is there anything you need?" They were only being nice, trying to be kind. But there was only one thing I needed, and no one could help me with that now.

CHAPTER 4

Time passed . . . our lives somehow went on. Mom started volunteering at the rectory at Saints Catherine and Anne; she said it helped toward school tuition, but it kept her busy and she was able to keep an eye on Brendan and Bonnie. Brendan was twelve years old now and preparing for his confirmation. He and I had spent many an hour pouring over the saints' names in the family bible, looking for just the right one, just as I had done with Hugh two years before. Hugh had taken the saint name Francis for his confirmation after St. Francis of Assisi and in honor of our dad. Brendan finally settled on Michael, after St. Michael the Archangel. Brendan continued his shenanigans, but he was a good kid. I was beginning to see our father's sense of humor emerge in him. Brendan was the only person I knew who could always coax a smile out of our mother. It was a good thing.

As for Bonnie, she wasn't a baby anymore—she was becoming quite the little beauty. Mom doted on her. No matter how old Bonnie got, she would always be our mother's baby girl. Hugh, now fourteen, was entering the freshman class of Bishop McDonald. He had shot up in height so much in the time since our dad's passing that he tried out and was chosen to play for the frosh basketball team. He was also becoming known as quite the ninth-grade lady-killer while I was now being referred to as Hugh Morrison's older sister. That was okay with me—I was proud of my little brother. He had had to grow up fast after Dad died.

I had now entered my senior year at Bishop McDonald. My last year of high school—here so soon?

I still had the same friends I'd had since the first grade; I couldn't have gotten through the past three years without them. They were my bedrock, my life raft, unchanged in all the years we'd been together. But I had changed. Unlike most of my friends, I had worked since I was eleven years old, mostly babysitting for the neighbors' kids when I wasn't looking after my younger siblings. One year I recall spending many a Saturday morning cleaning a neighbor's house—I cleaned the whole house for her for five dollars. She would wipe her finger across the tables in inspection after I had dusted them. My father thought it was good for me to work, to learn responsibility. I got a real job as a cashier in the local supermarket when I was fifteen. So, between my responsibilities at home, working part time, and homework during the school year, there wasn't a lot of time left over for hanging out.

While most of my friends had their parents' permission to start dating in their freshman and sophomore years, I had been held to a higher standard: I had to wait till my junior year. As my luck would have it, I didn't get to go to my junior prom with my friends—I didn't have a date! By the time we started our junior year at Bishop McDonald, my friends were already veterans of the high school dating scene and had boyfriends, but I didn't have a clue. They felt sorry for me, but they wouldn't have understood. I kept my strict upbringing a tightly held secret—I always had an excuse for why I couldn't do this or go there. I didn't know how to go about flirting with boys; my mother never talked about such things with me. I was becoming a young woman, but either she didn't see it or didn't want to see it. If my father had been alive, he would have balanced my mother's stern views on dating and boys with his Irish good humor and she would have softened, not have been so hard on me.

I started to view my teenage years as a kind of prison, not the carefree time of life my friends seemed to enjoy. As time went on, I started to become withdrawn—I didn't want to be set apart, to be different from my friends. They weren't bad kids; in fact, they were good kids. My friends weren't doing anything wrong, they were just acting like normal teenagers. Those times were relatively innocent: a major offense would have been getting caught smoking a cigarette in the girls' bathroom at school. Even all these years later when we get together and reminisce about the old days, my friends laugh about all the funny escapades they got into and they'll say to me, "Wasn't that hilarious, Mel?" I just smile and laugh along with them knowing that most of the time I wasn't even there.

I attempted to date during my senior year but wasn't very successful. I did manage to find someone to take me to my senior prom—he was a boy from another Catholic high school that I had met at a basketball game. I thought he was kind of cute and he had a great sense of humor, a big plus. I loved being with someone who could make me laugh out loud, something I found harder to do as time went by. I bought a beautiful emerald green gown with shoes dyed to match that I paid for with what I had saved from my part-time job. I was a little jealous of the slinky, strapless numbers so many of the girls were buying but I knew Mom would never let me out of the house wearing one. I looked good, nonetheless. A few of us went in together to pay for a limousine so we could show up to the prom in style. On prom night, my date arrived at the house looking rather dashing in his rented tuxedo, holding a boxed corsage in his lightly sweating hands. To my surprise, Mom was a pretty good sport about it all, even allowing my date to pin the small spray of flowers onto my prom gown. As we were leaving, I turned to wave goodbye. "Be a good girl, Marian Elizabeth!" my mother instructed, waving back. I cringed, hoping my date hadn't heard her. Quickly, I hustled him down the porch steps and into the waiting limo where we joined a party that was already in full swing – our friends had smuggled in enough beer to open a small distributorship! I had started drinking beer in my senior year of high school; a good beer buzz gave me the illusion of freedom and an illusion was better than nothing.

The prom was a resounding success, as was the after-prom party held at a local pub. The gang headed for home at about 1 a.m. My date and I were the last couple to be dropped off. Left to our own devices (and our raging teenaged hormones), we went at it in the back seat of that limo like the world was coming to an end. Somehow, despite the gallons of beer I had drunk that night, I managed to stop myself from going all the way with my very disappointed date. With almost Herculean strength, I pushed him off me, only moments away from losing my virginity. I had just turned eighteen years old and I wanted to be free, and he wanted to set me free. I was desperate to know what it would be like to just let go and let my freak flag fly! But my mother's admonition to be a good girl, like the tolling bell in a church tower, kept ringing in my head and I couldn't stop it. The limo pulled up to my house and my date kissed me goodbye—I knew I would never see him again. When I walked in the door it was going on 2 a.m. My friends and I had planned on going home to change into our shorts then head to the beach to watch the sun come up on the last day of our senior year. As I stepped into the living room I found my mother sitting in the dark, waiting for me.

"Marian Elizabeth Morrison! Where have you been? It's two o'clock in the morning!" she exclaimed as she turned on the light.

"Hi, Ma," I replied evenly, trying to hide my shock at her unexpected early-morning ambush. "You didn't have to wait up for me—everything went fine. You should go back to bed and get some sleep, Ma. I'm going upstairs to change. Tracy Lynn will be here soon," I said as I headed for the stairs.

My best friend, Tracy Lynn, was picking me up in a half-hour to take us to the beach in her new yellow convertible, a graduation gift from her parents.

"And just where do you think you're going at this hour of the morning?" my mother demanded.

"To the beach. I told you about this a week ago, remember? The whole class is going," I reminded her as I quickened my pace in a pathetic attempt at escaping her vigilant watch.

"You'll do no such thing, Marian Elizabeth. I think you've had enough fun for one night," she commented icily.

I stopped midway up the stairs, feeling as though my feet were becoming mired in quicksand. "Mom, you can't be serious—we talked about this. Everyone will be there," I countered.

"You're not everyone," she retorted testily.

"I can't believe you're doing this to me. I'm eighteen years old, for God's sake! Haven't I sacrificed enough for you?" I asked angrily as my eyes started to well with tears. Suddenly, I felt old beyond my years and very tired.

"Don't talk to me about sacrifice, young lady. I'm still your mother and you'll do as I say. I'll not have you setting any bad examples for your brothers and sister. You've had your fun, now get upstairs and go to bed. When she gets here, I'll let Tracy Lynn know that you won't be joining them," she stated firmly, her words cutting me like a knife.

I wanted to run out of the house, run all the way back to the beach in my prom dress and keep running, never looking back. Instead, I walked to my room and dropped onto my bed, not bothering to remove my clothes. Almost instantly, I fell into a deep sleep. I started dreaming, a dream that turned into a nightmare. That early morning in June marked the beginning of my nocturnal battles with vampires, a battle that would last for fifteen years.

I dreamt that I was in an unfamiliar place but somehow I knew it was our home. Vampires were surrounding the house, their terrifying screeches echoing through the dark, their razor-sharp talons ripping the house apart, breaking through its locked windows and doors. I frantically searched for my brothers and sister but couldn't find them anywhere; I knew then that the vampires had gotten to them. I had to find a way to escape, to survive. I came upon a transom window and forced it open. As I started to climb through its narrow enclosure, I felt myself becoming weightless, floating through it instead. No longer of this world, I flew away, searching, into the ink-black night. A lost girl.

CHAPTER 5

"So, Mel, are you coming to the party or what?" It was Tracy Lynn calling again. She was having a surprise birthday party for her boyfriend, Chris, on Saturday and I hadn't gotten back to her about whether I was coming. I was feeling a bit ambivalent about the affair: the party fell on the anniversary of my father's passing and I wasn't feeling particularly celebratory. Mom had planned on having a special Mass said in memory of his death five years earlier, then dinner afterward at the house.

"I guess I could swing by later, after dinner. I might have to miss the birthday cake, though," I replied vaguely.

"That's fine—I understand. I told you that there are a bunch of guys coming from St. Xavier's, right?" Tracy Lynn reminded me. She was always trying to fix me up with one of her boyfriend's pals from the local Catholic college. Chris and Tracy Lynn had been going out since junior year in high school and were now planning their engagement. Chris was one of the good guys: very easygoing, lots of fun to be around, and he seemed to genuinely love Tracy Lynn. She was nuts about him and had had her sights set on him since the eighth grade. Chris didn't seem to mind being locked in at such an early age. Isn't it awesome when the universe cooperates like that?

"Yes, you've reminded me – a few times," I answered, a tad sarcastically. My love life had not gone as smoothly as my friend's. Our shared high school memories of loves' siren call had not yet dimmed in our collective unconscious, and my continued lack of a serious relationship weighed heavily on both our minds.

"Okay! We'll see you later, Mel. You'll have fun, I promise," Tracy Lynn guaranteed.

I wasn't so sure about that. As much as I tried, I never seemed to be in lockstep with the group of us that remained friends after graduation. Two of my closest pals had gone away to college and I had so desperately wanted to join them. All through high school I'd imagined myself attending an ivy-covered college in upstate New York or perhaps New England, strolling through the campus green, arms laden with tomes filled with the musings of the great minds of higher education.

With classes done, I would attend the football and basketball games and the inevitable after-parties, draped glamorously on the arm of the team captain. But, alas, that dream was not to be. My mother needed me closer to home, so I got a job with an accounting firm located fifteen min-utes from our house and I registered with the community college for night classes. Tracy Lynn was the only other member of the group who chose to go to school locally. She wasn't about to go away to college and leave Chris to his own devices. She needn't have worried. Chris was quite content with his hometown life and wasn't going anywhere. Ah, young love . . .

"Hi, Mrs. Hessian, I'm here," I called out to Tracy Lynn's mom as I took off my jacket and hung it up on the ornate hall tree. "Boy, something smells good! What are you cooking in there?" I asked.

"Hello, Mel. I'm just heating up the chili. Go on—everyone's downstairs," she yelled from the kitchen. It was just like Mrs. H.—she wouldn't think of her daughter's guests being fed paltry chips and dip under her roof. I was sure the scrumptious-smelling chili was just the first course in an evening full of home-cooked goodies. It was the main reason for Tracy Lynn's house being given the honorific "Party Central". That, and her very cool parent's seemingly limitless stock of beer in the cellar, which they didn't mind us raiding from time to time – as long as we behaved ourselves. As I descended the basement stairs, I took in the worn paneling on the walls that showcased framed memories of parties past. My eyes lingered on one of my favorites: a photograph of Tracy Lynn, me, and about a dozen other pimply-faced teenaged beauties throwing pillows at each other at her thirteenth birthday party. Now here we were, all grown up with not a pimple to be found, celebrating her main squeeze's birthday.

"Hey, Mel, over here," Tracy Lynn shouted over the blaring music. The cavernous room was filled to capacity with loud bursts of laughter filtering through its smoke-filled atmosphere.

"Trace, you've outdone yourself—nice crowd!" I commented approvingly as I hugged her hello.

"Yeah, not bad—who knew this guy was so popular?" she kidded as she laid her head on Chris' shoulder.

"Hey, where's mine?" Chris whined good-naturedly as he offered me a cold beer.

"Come here, birthday boy!" I said as I planted a pink, gooey kiss on his cheek. It was only nine o'clock at night and Chris was in no pain, God bless him. My gaze wandered past his compact frame and over the large room, resting on a small group of men I'd never seen before. One stood out among the others: a tall, good-looking fellow with dark hair. "Who is that, Chris?" I inquired.

"Who are you talking about?" he asked. I turned his head with my hands and pointed with my pinky finger in the direction of the tall stranger.

"Oh, that's my buddy from school, Terry Dillinger. Do you want me to introduce you?" Chris offered. "I don't think he's here with anybody."

"Sure, why not? I'm game," I replied.

Tracy Lynn looked over at Terry, then back at me, her eyes dancing with mischief. "Just remember, Mel, if you can't be good, be careful," she warned.

"Why do I have to be careful, Trace?" I asked.

She turned to Chris. "Chris, honey, could you get us some more beers?" she asked sweetly.

"Sure, babe, I could use a cold one, too," he said as he espied his empty beer mug.

As he left to garner more brewskies, Tracy Lynn lowered her voice. "I've heard some things about Terry Dillinger, that's all."

"Like what?" I prodded.

"No big thing. I heard Chris say in passing that Terry had a reputation as kind of a bad boy, that's all. I don't even know what he meant by it." She stopped talking when she saw Chris walking back to us with our libations.

"Ready, Freddy?" he asked.

"Sure thing!" I answered confidently as he took my arm and walked me over to where his friends were standing. As we neared, I noticed Terry covertly staring at me through heavy-lidded eyes.

"Terry, my man, enjoying the party?" Chris asked jovially. "Can I get you anything?"

"No thanks, I'm okay," Terry answered. "Nice party, man."

"Glad you're diggin' it. By the way, this is our good friend, Mel Morrison. Mel, this is Terry Dillinger. We have some classes together at St. Xavier's."

Terry offered his hand as he locked eyes with me. "My pleasure, Mel."

As I took his hand to shake, I noticed his long, muscular forearms covered with just the right amount of curly, dark hair. Just what is it about a man's forearms that can make or break the deal? I could never figure it out, but whatever it was, Terry had more than enough to spare.

"Nice to meet you, Terry," I said as I met his gaze. Terry's eyes were so dark they were practically black, intense— almost unreadable. He was a little over six feet tall, with a head of dark brown hair that he wore combed straight back off his forehead. He stood confidently, his strong arms crossed over his broad chest. *Bad boy?* I wondered.

Chris offered up a lame excuse to beat a quick retreat to afford us some privacy. Sometimes I wish he hadn't been so hasty.

CHAPTER 6

I was not in love with Terry when we married, and I suspect he was not in love with me. Maybe we were in love with the idea of love or maybe we were just in heat. Terry was the first man I'd become intimate with—I didn't know quite what to expect from a serious relationship. After being introduced at Tracy Lynn and Chris' party, he and I spent the rest of the night in a darkened nook in the basement getting to know each other and we found out that we had a lot in common; among other things, Terry was a fireman, just like my dad. Terry and his buddies gave me a ride home from the party and the back seat of the car got pretty steamed up that night. An auspicious beginning to a love affair, some might say. From my perspective, it was just plain bad luck.

Terrence Dillinger was a handsome bloke—Black Irish, they call it. He was tall, with dark brown, almost black hair and eyes; his skin would turn a warm suede brown in the summer sun. He had been a star athlete in high school and retained his formidable build. I was no slouch in the looks department either; I was blessed with very good genes—both of my parents looked like movie stars from Hollywood in its heyday. My siblings and I, from an early age, were somehow aware of our genetic physical inheritance and instinctively knew that in time, and by the GRACE OF GOD, we would be attractive people as well. By the time I was twelve, I had begun to mature into what my father called his "lovely Irish lass."

Terry was the last of five children born to his parents and the only boy. His family doted on him, and that adoration had not diminished in the slightest by the time he reached adulthood. He was used to being treated as royalty – that should have sent up a red flag! Yes, a real prince of a man, that Terry Dillinger! My family were crazy about him, and from their limited perspective, why not be? My mother basked in the attention Terry showered on her whenever the family got together and he never arrived without a case of cold beer cradled in those muscular arms of his. To top it all off, he had those Black Irish good looks going for him and radiated so much blarney he could charm a snake.

Terry and I came from uncannily similar backgrounds: both of us were raised in the Irish Catholic tradition with fathers who worked as firemen and mothers who stayed at home raising their large broods of children. We were good kissers with a fondness for beer—and lots of it. But Terry was in a different league from me when it came to the drink—he was a champion, and I a mere runner-up. And it caused problems, a lot of problems. But we were young and managed, as the young do, to have fun and fall in love despite them. At least we thought it was love.

We looked good together; we were considered by many to be the "golden couple." Most importantly, my mother had bestowed upon us her approval of our union. I was doing my bit to keep the tradition alive by marrying an Irish Catholic fireman. My brothers, Hugh and Brendan, gave me away on our wedding day and Bonnie was my maid of honor. A full Mass was said at Saints Catherine and Anne Church by the fire department chaplain, Father

Peter Wilson, with the reception following at Terry's newly renovated firehouse, Engine Company Number 9. Clichéd? Maybe. Too good to be true? As it turned out, yes.

I don't know what Terry was thinking on our wedding day. Looking back at our wedding album he appears very nervous and pale, nothing at all like the "bad boy" I'd been introduced to back in the day. As for me, sitting at my dressing table on that humid spring morning applying the finishing touches to my hair and makeup, I was wondering why I wasn't marrying an Italian guy. Even though I had never dated one, I had always had a thing for Italian men, which was ironic considering my mother's bias against them. She would never divulge her issues with them, only to once briefly mention that her beloved father had had problems with them when he worked as the doorman of the apartment building, and anyone who messed with my granddad messed with his daughter.

I think my adolescent infatuation with males of the Italian persuasion took hold the first time I saw the actor James Darren in the movie *Gidget* wherein he played the part of Moondoggie, Gidget's love interest. I was, perhaps, twelve or thirteen years old when I first glimpsed James' gorgeous tanned face and big brown eyes on the television screen—I thought I'd just about die! My first teenage crush and a years-long love affair with brown eyes started with that movie. But bring home an Italian guy to meet my mother? Not happening! Trying to make sense of things years later, I thought that perhaps I'd married Terry because he could pass for Italian but, being Irish, was socially acceptable to my mother. In any event, being the dutiful daughter that I was, I locked my dreams away once again and promised to love and cherish my new husband, come what may. God knows, I gave it my best.

I tried very hard to be the kind of wife my mother had been to my dad. I cooked Terry's favorite foods, turned our modest apartment into a home anyone would be proud of, and accommodated my husband's infrequent and tepid interest in the boudoir. Other than Terry's empty promises of a cherished lifetime spent together, what was his reason for marrying me? One night, a few years into our marriage, Terry met me at a local restaurant after coming off his shift. While throwing down one double-scotch after another, he let me in on a secret he had been withholding from me all the years we'd been together: the reason he married me was because his friends thought I was the "perfect girl." So that was it? That was his reason? I guess I should have felt complimented that his friends thought so highly of me, but instead I was hurt and confused. He married me because of what his friends thought of me? What made me the perfect girl, anyway?

Despite popular public opinion that Terry and I were the golden couple, it didn't take long before our marriage had begun to unravel, its slow, tortured descent into heartache evident with each night that we went to bed without a warm touch or a loving word. I looked around and saw my less "perfect" friends settling down, buying houses, and having children. Money was always tight, and neither one of us had the discipline to say no to a night out. The issue of starting a family was becoming problematic: he wanted to and I didn't. Deep down, I must have known that it would have been a disaster. Not long after that night in the restaurant, our marriage began to take on the shallow patina of a relationship that was operating on increasingly distant happy memories.

There was a bigger problem in our marriage than the issue of starting a family: my husband was turning into an abusive alcoholic. After a typical evening of drinking, Terry would pinch me or push me around, all the while protesting that he was "only kidding" and would instruct me to "lighten up" if I got upset. The incidents became more frequent, the pushes and slaps a little sharper with each passing year. Terry was always very careful not to do anything in front of family or friends; like every seasoned mean drunk, he had everyone fooled.

Had I been honest with my family and unburdened myself to them from the onset of the abuse, maybe they would have believed me, even supported me. But I kept my personal life a very closely held secret, so they would've had a very hard time believing me—I had become the great pretender. Only our closest friends had the slightest inkling of what was going on behind closed doors, but they would never have taken sides. In their defense, I don't think they knew what to do. I certainly didn't.

Once we were married, Terry would come home later and later after a night out and always drunk, always belligerent. I would retreat and stay away from him as best I could—I never understood why he was so angry with me. How I missed my dad! He would have seen right through Terry and set him straight, but then again, if my father had been alive Terry wouldn't have made it past our front door.

A game of cat-and-mouse: that's pretty much how our married life played out. I became more distant with each confrontation and Terry got angrier. How things had changed since that heady first night in the back seat of his friend's car! When Terry and I had started dating, sparks flew—we were both great kissers so I figured the rest would just take care of itself. As the subject of sex was taboo in my mother's household, I'd had to hobble together bits and pieces of my friends' conversations to try to figure out what constituted a good sexual relationship. As it turned out, our sex life would never have made it to anyone's top-ten list, but since Terry was the only man I had been with, I didn't know any better.

I kept hoping it would improve with patience and time—it didn't. The physical part of our relationship had become almost non-existent. I couldn't stand him being near me. I was so tired; I was anxious all the time. Unlike the unspoken but palpable affection that had wrapped itself around my parents' blessed union, the air around Terry and I crackled and hissed like the singed atmosphere of a lightning storm hovering overhead, ready to explode at any time.

One evening we threw a party at the house. Entertaining had become one of the few things left that I enjoyed doing with my husband, and having company over gave me a fleeting sense of security as Terry would never try anything around other people. Terry held court with our guests while I kept busy in the kitchen, regaling them with stories from the firehouse. He had to work the next day, so I'd hoped he would go easy on the sauce. No such luck . . .

The festivities went well enough until the end of the night. It was getting late: everyone had gone home and Terry went to bed soon afterwards. I decided to straighten up a bit so that I wouldn't have to face the mess in the morning. As I washed the last of the dishes I heard yelling coming up from the courtyard of our building. Looking out of my kitchen window, I could see my sister conducting a shouting match with our brother Hugh about his questionable taste in girlfriends. Excellent strategy, dear sister! I flew downstairs and managed to get everyone into their cars before the neighbors could call the police. Unfortunately, no good deed goes unpunished, as I would quickly discover. It seems I'd acted in haste trying to straighten out my siblings' problems – the police would have come in handy soon enough. Exhausted from the evening's revelries, I slowly made my way back up the stairs. As I walked back into the apartment, I saw my husband run out of our bedroom and head straight for me, looking like a crazed madman. With all the strength his ethanol-fueled body could summon, Terry proceeded to beat the crap out of me. What in God's name had I done wrong this time? Were the appetizers not to his liking? Was the roast not rare enough?

I tried to defend myself, but he had me pinned to the floor and all I could do was reach for his face and try to scratch his eyes out. I hadn't grown up defending two younger brothers from the neighborhood bullies for nothing—I wasn't going down without a good fight! I didn't scream . . . I had learned long ago not to make too much of things. So, I ripped a page from the Irish Martyr Playbook and offered it up to God, like any good Catholic wife would. When Terry was satisfied with his sadistic show of affection, he sneered at me with disdain then staggered back to bed. I was so badly beaten that I could barely move from the floor to the couch. I should have called an ambulance, but I didn't. Should I have called the police? Most definitely, but that would have brought shame on the family, so I didn't. Should I have called my family, expecting them to believe what Terry had done to me after hiding it for so long, and so well? As always, my inclination to shield my family from any kind of possible harm or loss of standing took precedence over my better instincts, no matter the cost to myself.

The day after the beating and pretending to be asleep on the couch, I watched through heavily-hooded eyes as Terry left for work. I could see that I'd scratched up his face pretty good – there might even be a scar or two left to show off his handiwork. How was he going to explain that away? A crazy night of sex with the old lady? Not bloody likely! To no one's great surprise, and to my immense relief, our unhappy union quickly headed south after that reckoning and we were divorced before our fifth wedding anniversary. Terry remained in the apartment, and I left with my only my clothes and the cats we had adopted during our marriage.

There was nothing else I wanted there. I returned to my mother's house, her disapproval and judgment awaiting me.

Terry would say that we had married too young, that we didn't know what we were getting into, but I think it was simpler than that. He was never going to be Italian and I would never be the perfect girl.

CHAPTER 7

After my divorce I was anxious to get on with my life. I was twenty-five years old with no husband, no kids, no career, and no direction. I had continued to work at the accounting firm during our marriage, but the pay wasn't great and I discovered that secretarial work was not exactly my cup of tea. It just so happened that it was my brother Hugh who came to *my* rescue this time. He, along with our brother Brendan, had continued the fire department tradition in our family and was now happily married with a baby on the way. He had begun to seem older than me, settled, content—the big brother I never had. It's funny how things get turned around as the years go by. Hugh was the one who told me about the court officer job—there was a test coming up and he suggested I take it. I had never been in a courthouse and had no idea what a court officer did.

"They're kinda like the cops for the courts, you know, the security force. By the way, Mel, would you have a problem carrying a gun?" Hugh asked nonchalantly as he turned the page of his newspaper.

Me, carry a gun? I had never had any reason to think about it before. My mind drifted back to my ex-husband's proclivity for knocking me around. "No, Hugh, I don't think I would," I answered as I tried to picture myself wearing a uniform again. "If I could survive twelve years of Catholic school, this shouldn't be too hard!" I reassured him.

"Great! I have a buddy, Eddie Crane, who's a court officer in the city. Just so you know, he said it was the hardest civil service test he ever took. I don't know about that. Anyway, Kathleen and I think you should go for it. You're single now—you've gotta think about a stable job with a pension and benefits," he advised.

I did as Hugh suggested and submitted the application along with the requisite test fee and signed up for a preparatory course as well. I studied like I hadn't done since my years at Saints Catherine and Anne with Sister Michael Eileen standing over me with her steel-edged ruler. It took six months to get my test score back, and when the envelope finally arrived I opened it with the trepidation of someone opening a letter from the IRS. "I got a 95! I got a 95! Thank you, God! Thank you, Jesus! Thank you, Blessed Mother!" I screamed at the top of my lungs. I called my family to give them the good news—they were all so happy for me, but Mom had a little different take on it.

"God help us, Marian Elizabeth, I didn't think you were actually going to go through with it! What man is going to give a divorced woman a second look, and one who's wearing a police uniform and carrying a gun, no less?" she asked with no small amount of incredulity. Mom was old school; a woman held little promise for a happy life unless she was married and at home with her children. My divorce from Terry had been a terrible embarrassment for her—it just wasn't done in a Catholic family like ours. I told her there was a first time for everything. She was not amused.

"I'm kind of excited about it, Ma. I know it's not what you're comfortable with, but it's a good job and I have to look after myself now, you know," I reminded her.

"Won't it be dangerous? Aren't you going to be dealing with all sorts of awful people? I don't need anyone knocking on the front door again like they did for you father, God rest him," she admonished me as she made the sign of the cross quickly over her chest with her ever-present rosary.

"It might be at times, but don't forget, Ma, I helped raise three little kids after Dad passed, two of them boys. I think I can handle the bad guys. Besides, I'm not going to be a police officer. Working inside a court is a lot safer," I assured her.

Knowing she was going to lose this argument, Mom sighed. "All right, Marian Elizabeth, have it your way. But promise your old mother that you'll be careful."

"Ma, you're not old, and I'll be extra careful," I replied confidently.

"Then I'll be saying an extra decade for you," she offered.

"Thanks, Ma, it couldn't hurt!" I said as I gave her a quick kiss on the cheek. I was so excited—it would be the beginning of a new life for me!

I passed all the requisite exams with flying colors: the medical and physical, the background check, the psychological exam (how many ways could they ask me what color sports car I preferred, and what did that have to do with the price of potatoes?). Shortly thereafter, I received the official notification of my starting date in the academy which turned out to be only a week away. I had so much to do and so much to look forward to!

I woke up the following week to the first day of my new career as a court officer and the dream of a better life. I jumped out of bed before the alarm clock even had a chance to ring, dressed in the business suit I had laid out the night before, guzzled my protein shake then re-checked my duffle bag for my workout gear. I ran down the list of requirements I'd received from the academy one last time – everything seemed to be in order. I said a quick prayer, kissed the kitties goodbye, then hopped on the train for the ride that was going to deliver me to the steps of my awaiting destiny – the New York State Court Officer Academy!

"Give me twenty push-ups!" barked the drill instructor.

Twenty push-ups! I had never attempted one push-up in my life, never mind twenty. This wasn't mentioned as one of the qualifications for the job. From my seat on the rock-hard, dusty gym floor, I looked up at the sergeant, his whistle clenched between his teeth, hands on hips, double chin set in gritty determination, and decided I had better learn. I wanted this job, bad. "Be careful what you wish for," I thought to myself as I got into position and started the first painful steps to becoming a court officer. Ten minutes later, soaked in perspiration, the class was instructed to turn to the cadet to their right and introduce themselves, as this person was to be their gym buddy for the duration of the academy.

"Hi, I'm Mel," I said to the woman standing next to me as we shook hands.

"Hi, I'm Val. Nice to meet you, Mel. So, what do you think?" she asked as she surveyed the hot, dank room that was to be our prison for the next three months.

"I didn't know I was signing up for boot camp!" I replied in dismay.

"Me, neither! But I'm in it for the long haul. I need this job," she said. Val was a little taller than me with hazel eyes and hair almost the same color as mine. She was attractive, with an open, friendly face and a kind smile.

"I hear ya, Val," I agreed as the whistle screamed for our attention.

"Now that you've all made nice, hit the floor with your buddy and give me thirty sit-ups; first one, then the other," the instructor ordered. Val and I gave each other the "what-are-you-going-to-do?" shrug, then proceeded to give the man what he asked for. It turned out to be the beginning of a beautiful friendship. In no time, Val and I became best buds.

Val was only twenty-six, but she seemed mature beyond her years. She was an only child and a change-of-life baby for her parents, who were now well into their sixties. Val had never been married, but was coming out of a relationship that had ended badly after several years. She thought he was the love of her life; he decided the grass was greener on the other side and left her to graze its verdant pastures. When she finally came out from under her stultifying grief, she determined to start over, to go in a different direction. That's what drew her to the court officer job, much like me. Val became the big sister I never had—some people even mistook us for sisters. But where I could be the life of the party when I turned it on, Val was as steady as a rock—that's what I loved about her. When I was about ready to pass out while running up eight flights of stairs to the academy gym after completing a two-mile run outside in the broiling summer sun, Val was right there pushing me on, not letting me give up. I was there for her when a call came, one month into our training: her beloved father had passed away due to a sudden heart attack. It was a terrible time, but I had her back and she persevered and made it through to graduation. The untimely deaths of our fathers were among the many things that bound us together. It's been like that ever since – I have her back and she has mine.

My favorite part of my time in the academy was gun training. Even though I was a novice at target practice, I found it exhilarating! My father had gone hunting with his buddies every winter but never kept a gun in the house. Terry owned a gun but kept it locked up and out of sight, thank God—one of the few times in our marriage when he displayed uncharacteristic restraint. Until the time I actually held a revolver in my hand, I hadn't given much thought about what it would be like, how it would feel to actually fire one. Well, it felt great, and I turned out to be a pretty accurate shot. The range team had us practice on various types of firearms: revolvers, semi-automatic pistols, rifles, and shotguns. I particularly enjoyed firing the shotgun; there was no pressure in attempting a perfect shot—you pretty much hit the target no matter how bad your aim was. I could see how that might come in handy! My least favorite part of training was the damn running we had to do every day on the track at the school across the street, followed by the agonizing climb up the stairs that lead back to the gym on the eighth floor of the academy. I'd never been a fan of jogging—it made my boobs bounce so much it hurt. I had to wear a second bra to keep those bad boys in place, but it was the price I had to pay to wear the uniform, so I sucked it up and kept on truckin'. My boobs, on the other hand, never forgave me.

On the last day of our academy classes, the day before graduation, we were handed "dream sheets" (as in, "in your dreams") on which to list our preferences for placement in the various courts statewide. There was only one place I wanted to go and that was criminal court in the Big Apple. The next day, after the graduation ceremony, I got the best news I'd heard in quite some time: Val and I both got posted to 100 Centre Street and were even assigned to the same courtroom, part AP54—we were going to be a team.

Watch out, Big Apple!

CHAPTER 8

AP54 was an all-purpose part ("part" being more commonly known as a courtroom), hence its designation. At any given time, there would be between eighty to a hundred cases on the calendar and the noise level in the courtroom could be almost deafening. The judge in AP54 was The Honorable Ethel Lucille Streistein, a tiny terror; the mere mention of her name would send the faint of heart diving for cover into the darkest recesses of the building. As I was to discover only too soon, the court officers in the part weren't just responsible for securing the courtroom and handling prisoners: they interacted continually not just with the public but with the DA's office, the attorneys, the interpreters, the court clerk—pretty much everyone and everything. Another important part of an officer's duties was handling the bridge—the area in the courtroom where the judge is seated. The bridge officer is much like the conductor of an orchestra; it is their responsibility to keep the cases moving as seamlessly as possible throughout the day by making sure all the parties have their act together before calling the case into the calendar. Sounds easy enough, but just try to get the judge, the judge's law clerk, the assistant district attorney, the court reporter, the plaintiff and

47

defendant and their attorneys, and possibly an interpreter to all appear before the court at the appointed time – not so easy. But by far, the most important function of the bridge officer is to bring it all home by quittin' time!

On my second day on the job, the old-timers in AP54 thought it would be funny to assign me to the bridge. I thought they were joking—they weren't. The only problem with their nefarious scheme was that about the only things I had learned the day before were the difference between a plaintiff and a defendant and which hallway was the quickest way back to the locker room. Val had gotten lucky and had been pulled out of the part that morning to walk a patrol and had escaped her hazing.

Tremulously, I stepped up to the bridge and, with sweaty hands, picked up the first of the eighty-five cases to be read into the record that day. I proceeded to stumble, mispronouncing the names on the first docket, then the second— after that I lost count. I had no idea who represented whom or the name of the assistant district attorney assigned to the case, or how to get in touch with the finicky court reporter who kept taking breaks whenever we went off the record. The one thing we were not taught in the academy was how to work the bridge—a minor omission, to say the least.

"Officer, what's going on here? Don't you know what you're doing?" the judge thundered from the bench in a voice that could be heard in outer space. No, your judgeship, actually, I have no idea. I could barely hear myself think over the constant rattle and hum of the predilections of the accused and their counsel bouncing off the walls of the cavernous courtroom. The judge yelled at me and admonished me in front of the audience at regular intervals throughout the day, shaking her head in constant amazement at the poor excuse of an officer she had been forced to put up with. Surely, heads would roll over this debacle! My fellow officers thought the whole thing hilarious.

The calumny continued until the part finally went down at four-thirty—I felt as though I had gone ten rounds with Tyson. I slowly trudged down the long, empty corridor that led to the locker room, my head hung low. How had the promise of a new life come to such an ugly end, and so quickly? How could I show my disgraced visage in the part again after such a public humiliation? In the depths of my despair and out of the corner of my eye, I noticed a small, lone figure striding down the hall opposite me, long black robe billowing in the wind as though flying through darkened storm clouds. It was my nemesis, Judge Streistein—the Wicked Witch of the West had nothing on old Ethel! I tried to keep myself tiny, almost invisible; I hugged the dingy wall as I quietly crept along. She started to pass by me. I silently exhaled an immense sigh of relief when suddenly the judge stopped dead in her tracks and did an about-face. This was it. I was finished.

"You there, Officer!" she called out in her distinctive voice, a voice that could send shivers up the most hardened spine. I turned and looked at her with terror-filled eyes.

"Yes, Judge?" I managed to croak.

"You did a fine job out there, Officer—it was a tough day. Keep up the good work!" she commanded magisterially. I watched in stunned surprise as she turned on her heel and sped off into the setting sun of another day in criminal court. It seemed there would be a tomorrow after all.

The door to AP54 swung open and Officer "Cheech" Cavaliere sauntered in, just in time to sign out for the day—I hadn't seen him since we broke for lunch. Cheech had been a court officer for some twenty years when I met him. The command seemed to leave him alone, almost treated him with kid gloves. When I first got to criminal court, I was told that even though there were no stripes on his shirt, Cheech was the go-to guy. He was a shadowy figure and a tough character to pin down. If you asked where he was, most of the time your inquiry would be answered by a shrug of the shoulders. Cheech moved stealthily from one part of the courthouse to another carrying nothing with him but the daily news.

After I had been in the part for a while, it occurred to me that I never saw him wearing his rig. I thought it odd because Cheech was never on the rotation for pen duty, which was the only time an officer wouldn't be carrying his firearm (exactly what precluded Cheech from ever being assigned to pen duty was another unsolved mystery). One day I cautiously approached him and asked why he never wore his gun—the part was down at the time and it was just the two of us in the courtroom. Cheech quietly gestured for me to come around to his side of the desk. Putting his finger to his lips to ensure my silence, he lifted his pant leg to expose a snub-nosed .38 caliber pistol strapped to his ankle; hardly standard issue for a court officer. This guy had pull.

As a rookie, you get told a lot of things—some true, some not. The line I was fed was that Cheech was the one-man welcoming committee for the new officers. When we met, I got the feeling he was giving me the once-over. I wasn't concerned that Cheech was interested in me in an unsavory way; I had been told he was a family man and that he was strictly a work-church-home sort of guy. I think he was just trying to get a handle on me, seeing as we were going to be working together. I guess I had passed muster because he trusted me enough to show me his secret weapon. I'd never heard the name Cheech before, so I asked him what kind of name it was. He explained that it was Italian slang for his given name, which was Frank, but that no one had called him Frank since he was a kid.

Cheech gave me some very sage advice once. He told me there were only two rules you had to follow to stay under the radar: the first was never to complain about anything because it wouldn't get you anywhere and you might get someone pissed off, in which case they could make your life a living hell. Find a way around the problem. Second, never rat on a fellow officer no matter how bad the situation looked. When I asked him what to do if I found out about a possible breach of duty involving another officer, he referred me back to the first rule. I reassured Cheech that he didn't have to worry about me.

I was a great-granddaughter of the IRA.

CHAPTER 9

"Vivienne, is that you?" I called out to a woman I thought I recognized who was conferencing in the hallway outside of my courtroom. I walked closer to her—I couldn't believe my eyes! There stood Vivienne Gable in all her finely-tuned fabulousness. Vivienne hailed from the old crowd; we hadn't seen each other in years. We had come to know one another when I was dating Terry; Vivienne's boyfriend, Billy Gable, was Terry's best friend. She and Billy had gotten divorced the year before Terry and me.

"Oh my God! Marian Dillinger, just look at you! I'd ask what you're doing here, but the uniform and gun speak for themselves—they suit you! So, how are you?" she asked breezily as she gave me an air kiss. Same old Viv: perfectly made-up, her long brown hair still straight and shiny, her slender frame garbed in a designer career suit, monogrammed leather briefcase in hand. How could I sum up my new life in the few minutes I had left in my lunch break? I wasn't 110 pounds anymore. My once waist-length, straight and shiny auburn hair was now cut well above my shoulders, something I had decided to do when a female perp pulled out a fistful of it while I was trying to get her into handcuffs for her court appearance. Luckily for her she didn't break one of my nails—that shit could've gotten real ugly.

"I'm doing great, Viv!" I answered with the enthusiasm of the leader of the high school pep squad. "By the way, I'm going by Morrison again," I said as I pointed to the name tag above my shield.

"Oh, yes, I see . . . " she commented obliquely as she crooked her head to one side, her eyes narrowing. It became obvious that my mundane story was boring Viv as she quickly resumed her much more interesting narrative. "Perhaps you hadn't heard, Mel, but I'm hyphenating now. My last name is Clarke-Gable, for my daughter's sake, you understand?" she asked with forced patience as though dealing with the village idiot.

"Oh, sure, of course, Viv—it makes perfect sense," I replied, struggling to sound sincere. It was coming back to me why I could never stand old Viv. "Anyway, you can see what I do for a living. I have a nice place over the bridge in Brooklyn that I love. What's new with you? What are you doing here in court?" I asked.

"I'm an attorney now, didn't you know?" she asked. Vivienne appeared somewhat taken aback at my poor observational skills. Why Vivienne would think I had heard about her career choice was anyone's guess, but I wasn't surprised—the shoe fit.

"No, Viv, I wasn't aware, but, you know, it has been awhile," I replied, struggling not to betray my annoyance at the fact that I started this inane conversation.

It's funny, the things you remember about the past. It had dawned on me one night while we were hanging out in her future husband's backyard downing beers that she had quite a crush on my future husband. I'll never forget it: right in the middle of the usual Saturday night goings-on, Vivienne turned to Terry and asked in a voice loud enough to be heard over the booming stereo, "So, Terry, why didn't you ever ask me out?" That was a conversation stopper, I can tell you! All eyes were on my boyfriend, everyone breathless, dying to hear the answer to the question. Thinking for a moment, he answered, "Gee, I really don't know why, Viv." You could almost feel the inaudible, collective sigh of relief that flew around the backyard. Good lad, Terry, dodged that bullet! She made out better on her deal than I did. Terry had started pushing me around while we were dating which escalated into spousal abuse after we got married. I don't think I saw Billy even try to push an opinion on Vivienne— smart girl. Vivienne and Billy had been forced to get married. In fact, they missed our wedding because she was about to give birth to their daughter—two months early.

Vivienne quickly brought me up to speed on her new-and-improved situation. She was now seeing an older man, whom, she said, looked just like the actor Ian Connery (of course he does, Viv!). She had decided after her divorce that becoming an attorney was the way to go (the woman doesn't miss a beat!). Vivienne had heard through the grape-vine about Terry's and my divorce—so sad, of course, but at least there were no children involved, THANK GOD! Her daughter was doing exceptionally well considering every-thing: honor roll in school, travel soccer, lots of friends. Vivienne had gotten the house in the settlement agreement so their daily routine hadn't changed much. Loves being a lawyer. Can't complain, really.

I agreed with Vivienne that yes, THANK GOD, there were no children whose lives would have been shattered because of Terry's and my ugly divorce, and no, I wasn't seeing anyone at the present time. Did Mr. Connery per-chance have an available twin brother? She laughed at that one, a little too quickly if you ask me. No complaints, Viv, thanks for asking, and sooooooo happy to see how great you're doing, really . . .

I checked my watch: it was time for the part to go back up for the afternoon session. Vivienne and I hugged and promised to keep in touch, a promise I was reasonably certain would not be kept by either one of us. As we said our goodbyes, I suddenly remembered why Vivienne and Billy had gotten divorced—the story had traveled far and wide. Billy had come home early from work one day and found old Viv and her lover making nice in their daughter's bedroom. She got that bedroom along with the rest of the house in the divorce settlement.

I got a black eye. Go figure . . .

CHAPTER 10

Not long after Val and I got on the job, the sergeant's exam came up. I took the test and scored high enough on the list that I went on to be promoted quickly. I was given the option of working the evening arraignment part and grabbed the opportunity as it meant pulling in the night differential in addition to the raise in pay and I needed every penny I could get my hands on. Val was pretty much in the same boat I was, single and dependent on one paycheck, so when a spot opened up in arraignments for an officer she took it and we've been the A team ever since.

"Mel, would you shut them up out there? I'm not taking the bench until they do!" ordered the judge.

"Sure, Judge, no problem," I answered. In the spirit of a spit-and-polish Marine snapping to, I left the judge's chambers and entered the courtroom. Turning to the audience, I slammed my hand down hard on the side of the judge's bench and announced in my loudest "I'm not taking any shit from you people" voice, "Come to order! Arraignments Part 1 is now in session! Please be seated. The Honorable Geoffrey M. Lefftwing is now presiding."

Like fifth graders being cowed into submission by the threat of a good crack in the head by an eraser thrown with unerring expertise by Mother Mary Discipline, the attorneys and their clients took their seats and did, in fact, come to order. The judge, with a dramatic sweep of his black robe, his long silver hair perfectly coiffed and gleaming in the bright courtroom lights, ascended the bench like a seasoned actor taking the stage. You had to hand it to the guy—he could be such a diva, but he really pulled it off every night. For a guy in his late sixties, he looked good and knew it.

"Officer, you may call the first case," instructed the judge. T.J., this evening's bridge officer, proceeded to call in the first of the hundred or so cases choking the court docket. It was going to be a busy night. Luckily, Val and I had called in some markers the week before and were leaving early for some fun and frivolity at the neighborhood watering hole.

"Hey, Val, check it out—look who's going to be visiting with us tonight!" I exclaimed as I looked over the calendar. The infamous rap star, Mama Wanna Rap, was making an appearance in our courtroom on charges of disorderly conduct and possession of narcotics.

"Holy shit! Isn't that the rap star that got busted for possession at the airport?" she asked.

"Yeah, that's her. Hey, you want to bet I'm gonna get her autograph?" I challenged.

"Okay, big talker. I'll put a five on that bet. I heard she was a bitch back in the pens," Val commented.

"All righty then, watch and learn from the master," I coolly replied.

T.J. yelled out over the noisy courtroom, "Calling docket number 17664 of 1993: The People of the State of New York v. Robinson. Parties step up and give your appearances for the record," he instructed.

The defendant in the case, who was known professionally as Mama Wanna Rap but was formerly Monique Robinson from East New York, sauntered up to the table with her attorney. She looked more like Monique from the hood than Mama: hair all messy, nails unpolished, no makeup, and wearing only jeans and a T-shirt. My sistas in uniform were a hell of a lot more glamorous than that.

"Dorothy Gaille for the people, Your Honor."

"Niles G. Lynde for the defendant, Your Honor."

Mel Morrison for an early retirement, Your Honor . . .

"Ms. Gaille, Mr. Lynde, sidebar," ordered the judge.

While the judge, the ADA, and the attorney discussed the merits of the defense (none, as Mama was filmed strolling through the airport toking on a doobie the size of a cigar) and a possible resolution (can she pay the $1,000 fine or not?), I walked over to the bridge, leaned over the table, and whispered in my sweetest voice, "Ms. Rap, could I trouble you for an autograph? Please? Cause, damn, Mama, I really dig your shit!" I proclaimed.

With a look that could melt a rock, but realizing I carried a loaded weapon at my side, she replied in *her* sweetest voice, "Sure, Officer, anything I can do for a fan." I love my job.

It was coming up on nine o'clock in the evening, and after another highly satisfying night of listening to one newly graduated law school student after another trying to make a case for their unfortunate clients, our replacements showed up and Val and I headed for the locker room—we'd heard enough for one night. After you've worked in a court-room for a while, you learn the art of discerning what you must pay attention to in order to get through the day. It is an absolute necessity in our line of work because if you didn't learn it, you would be going home every night with a headache that no amount of booze or drugs could kick. Some of what you hear is hard to listen to, such as cases involving murder, child abuse, and rape. But, occasionally, you luck out and you want to pay attention. Tonight, we hit the jackpot!

In addition to being entertained by Mama Wanna Rap, we were treated to the spectacle of yet another hapless contestant in the criminal court's coin-toss contest. The plaintiff in the action was a mattress store manager: a bald, chubby little man who continually wiped his sweaty, substantial forehead with a worn-looking handkerchief. His complaint accused the defendant in the case, a striking redhead with a butt so big you could balance a large TV on it, with second-degree assault for attacking him in his store with a knife after a failed sales negotiation. She counter-charged that he had incited her behavior by failing to deliver on their sales agreement and then trying to forcibly throw her out of the store when she demanded his compliance with same.

According to Big Red's sworn statement, the store manager agreed to give her a free, queen-sized, top-of-the-line matched set if she agreed to sleep with him on it. She went on to state that she'd kept up her end of the bargain but he did not, so she decided to take matters into her own hands. After some discussion among the attorneys (including the all-important question of who was going to handle the Super Bowl pool) and with longing glances being exchanged between the plaintiff and defendant, the ADA agreed to dismiss the charges. And we have a winner, folks!

Some men will never learn.

"All right, my friend, pay up! You owe me five," I boasted as I proudly waved the autographed adjourn slip from Mama Wanna Rap in Val's face as we walked into the locker room to change into our civvies.

"Okay, you win. How about I buy us a couple of cold ones when we get out of here?" she offered.

"I'll tell you what, Val—make it a 'tini at Baldini's and we're square," I replied jauntily.

Just as every cop has their neighborhood watering hole, we court officers had Baldini's, a dark, slightly fatigued-looking place that was a safe three blocks away from the courthouse. It was close enough to walk to but not too close for an encounter with a judge or, God forbid, a reporter; reporters were always nosing around, looking to score a news item about something going on that day in court. Friday nights were always hopping at Baldini's. They had a great house band that could play just about any request and would occasionally invite someone from the crowd to come up on stage and jam with them. I turned out to be one of their more frequent guest performers: as long as the crowd wanted to hear me sing and I had enough liquid encouragement in me, I could get up there and belt them out with the best of them, a talent I seemed to have inherited from my father.

From time to time, Val and I would call in our markers and get someone to cover for us in arraignments so we could head over to Baldini's while the party was still going on—this was one of those nights. Nick, the owner, was an elderly gentleman who had been in that spot for some thirty years. He always greeted us with a big smile and a friendly kiss on the cheek—and why not? Besides being easy on the eyes (once we ditched the uniforms) we, along with about a hundred other court officers, gave him steady, reliable business. Being a civil servant may not be glamorous, but it's a steady paycheck that buys a lot of drinks.

"Hello, my gorgeous girls! Good to see you! Want to arrest me tonight?" Nick asked with his old-world charm, his arms outstretched in playful anticipation of being handcuffed.

"It would be our pleasure, Nick. But first, can you get a dry vodka martini for me—three olives—and a tap beer for Val? Then we'll arrest you," I promised. He never tired of that routine.

"No problem, my gorgeous girls. I've waited this long, another coupla hours ain't gonna kill me."

We sat down at the bar, checking for the familiar faces of Friday night at Baldini's. Sitting in one of the booths was a man I hadn't seen before and, believe me, I would've remembered him! A woman was sitting in the booth with him, but I couldn't make out who she was from my position at the bar. Even though he was sitting down, he appeared to be tall, with dark hair and a good build and he was wearing an expensive-looking suit.

"Shit! What's an attorney doing in here? Isn't anything sacred?" I grumbled to Val. Still, my curiosity got the better of me. "Val, with your best hold 'em or fold 'em, check out the suit in the second booth," I said as I cocked my head in mystery man's direction.

She looked over my shoulder. "He's a looker—I don't recognize him, though. He's sitting with that court reporter who transferred to district court a while back. We worked with her a few times, remember? I think her name is Rita," Val remarked.

"I think you're right. She left after she married that cop. They bought a house in the suburbs or something."

"I wonder what she's doing so far from home. Anyway, Mel, are you interested in "Tall, Dark and Handsome" or not?" Val asked.

"I'm not dead, Val, just in a slump."

"So, what are you waiting for? Go over there and do something," she demanded.

"What if he's, you know, with Rita?" I replied as I felt myself starting to chicken out.

"Well, if he is, I don't think her cop husband would be too happy about it," Val smartly observed.

"Oh, all right. What should I say?" I asked, feeling a bit like a thirteen-year-old at her first school dance.

Val was losing her well-worn patience with me. "Do I have to hold your hand, Mel? What's wrong with you, anyway? You can walk into the pens and handcuff a guy twice your size with a rap sheet as big as a phone book, but you don't know what to say to *that* guy?

That last one brought me around. I took a long gulp of my drink, arose from my perch at the bar, and walked toward the booth with as much confidence as one martini would allow.

"Hey, Rita, how are you?" I asked, trying not to stare at Tall, Dark, and Handsome. "I haven't seen you in here for a while. Last I heard you were in district court."

"Hi, Mel. What's doing? Yeah, I'm still in district," she answered. "By the way, this is Ritchie Gianelli. Ritchie, this is Marian Morrison."

Be still, my heart—he's Italian!

"Hi, Marian. Are you a court reporter, too?" Ritchie asked, his slightly rakish smile revealing row after row of perfectly straight white teeth. He offered his hand to me in greeting.

"Goodness, no!" I replied with a slight giggle, trying to project feminine. I shook his strong, tanned hand and suppressed a shiver. "And you can call me Mel. No, I'm a sergeant in night arraignments. Rita and I used to work together on occasion. Do you practice here in criminal court? You don't look familiar."

Ritchie gave a quick laugh. "Wait a minute—you think I'm a lawyer?"

"I thought you might be," I replied, slightly embarrassed at my apparent faux pas.

"Hell no! I don't usually dress up like this. I went on an interview today for the sergeant's spot that's open here. Who knows, Mel? Maybe we'll be working together soon."

"Maybe we will! Okay, well then, best of luck with the interview. I'll let you guys get back to your dinner," I said with the biggest smile I could manage without looking like a loon. "Bye, Rita. Bye, Ritchie."

"Nice meeting you, Mel," Ritchie answered with a smile, his pearly whites glistening.

Gee, he even has big brown eyes, I thought to myself as I walked back to my bar stool, giving thanks that I had decided to wear a short skirt and my only pair of stilettos to work this evening. When you wear black Oxfords at work five days a week, you can forget how a nice high heel will force your body to move in a way that, while unnatural, is totally hot.

"So, what happened? What's his name?" asked Val eagerly.

"Ritchie . . . Ritchie Gianelli," I replied dreamily, his name practically rolling off my tongue.

"An Italian Stallion—your dream come true!" Val shrieked.

"Just drink your beer," I ordered, looking around to see if anyone had heard her. Thank God it was so noisy. "Anyway, it appears he might be joining our little court family. He had an interview today for the empty sergeant's spot in JP18. He seemed nice. Sure is good-looking. And he has brown eyes! You know me, Val, brown eyes are always a deal breaker," I sighed.

"Yup, the James Darren syndrome strikes again!" she joked.

"I didn't find out why he was with Rita. They could have something going on—you know how this place is," I said conspiratorially as I took another sip of my martini.

"This is true . . . if he gets the job, we'll find out soon enough. Look, I'm starving. Can we get some dinner so I'm not too hungover tomorrow morning? I've got a busy day ahead of me. George and I are looking at houses."

"This is starting to sound serious, my friend. What gives?"

"Don't get all freaked out, Mel, but we're thinking about moving in together, maybe even getting married."

"Freaked out? I'm thrilled! You guys are great together—I totally mean that. I love you guys!" I said as I leaned over and gave Val a warm hug.

"That's what I'd hoped you'd say. I know how you feel about the whole marriage thing. I wasn't sure how you'd react."

"Well, I'm tickled about it and that's the truth. I think you and George are going to be one of those rare species of human being that will actually grow old together," I replied sincerely.

"There's one other thing," Val said, screwing up her face. "Don't hate me for this, but I put in for a transfer to days. I won't need the night differential once we've moved in together, and George wants me to be home more."

"Hate you? What kind of talk is that? But I'm gonna miss you like crazy! How am I going to deal with those creeps without you?" I asked, wondering if I could. We had been a team for four years now.

"You're gonna be fine. If anyone can deal with them, you can!" Val answered confidently.

"I say, this calls for another round!" I yelled above the noise of the crowded bar. "No, wait, I'm buying a bottle of champagne. Screw the cost—we're celebrating!"

As we turned to our menus, Rita and Ritchie started to get up from their booth. Passing our table on the way out of the restaurant, I could swear I saw James Darren wink at me. I gestured to the bartender. "Hit us again, my good man. This time, bring over a nice bottle of champagne and some tall glasses!"

CHAPTER 11

I hated Mondays, especially if I had to work the weekend before. This was one of those Mondays. "Mel, phone call!" Gloria, the part clerk, yelled over the noise of the courtroom as she passed me the receiver.

"Sergeant Morrison," I answered gruffly, sounding as disenchanted as I felt.

"Hi, Mel, it's Ritchie," announced the sexy baritone on the other end of the line.

Suddenly, Monday started looking a whole lot better. It was Ritchie Gianelli on the phone, the Italian Stallion himself! Ritchie had gotten the promotion to sergeant and even though he worked days and I worked nights, we always managed to squeeze in the time to catch up with each other as he was leaving and I was coming in. After a while, Ritchie would sometimes hang out in my part after his shift ended, waiting for me to take my break. I didn't know what to make of it at first; I had heard through the grapevine that Ritchie had been dating someone when he came aboard the criminal court love boat, but it seemed like all he wanted to do was talk.

It was during those talks that we found out we had a lot in common: we had both endured tortured marriages that ended in acrimonious divorces, we didn't have children,we loved the same kinds of music and we loved the beach and football. We'd spend hours ruminating over what went wrong with our marriages and how it colored our outlooks on life and love. We had come to the realization that our divorces had made us wary of relationships, but yet we never stopped thinking about *IT*. The heart is a very resilient organ; it can be broken again and again—who needs that? The only thing then is to turn away from romantic love and fill up your life with other things to distract you from its incessant calling. Our job was good at helping us do just that; dealing with murderers, rapists, and child molesters every day had a way of making one wary of committing to a life complicated by the love of a good man or woman.

There was one problem: we were attracted to each other. Big time. We had managed to keep those feelings at bay due to Ritchie's ongoing relationship and because I was never able to completely shirk my strict Catholic upbringing. What was that commandment again? Something about not coveting your neighbor's whatever. If I remembered correctly from my religious education, coveting Ritchie would've cost me some heavy time in purgatory. He had confided to me that he loved his girlfriend but was not in love with her, and that they were of the same mind when it came to the subject of marriage. Ritchie said they had agreed to keep things simple; I wondered how agreeable she actually was with all that simplicity. He never mentioned her name and I didn't ask, but I did ask him about his dating philosophy.

"I've heard that phrase before, 'I love her but I'm not *in* love with her,' but it's never made any sense to me. What do you mean when you say that?" I asked Ritchie one day, curious to hear his explanation.

"It's just that we've known each other a long time. It's not that "thing" that happens when you've just met someone, and a bomb goes off—it's comfortable. At this point, we're good friends more than anything else."

"What if you wanted to date another woman?" I inquired casually.

"What about it?" he countered.

"Wouldn't she be hurt? Wouldn't you be hurt if she wanted to see another man?"

"See, that's just the thing, Mel. We have an understanding—if either one of us was interested in seeing someone else, the other person would be cool with it. We're not tied down to each other like that," he answered confidently.

"Gee, Ritchie, that's very sophisticated of you. I don't think I could ever be in a relationship like that. I'd never be that understanding," I admitted.

"That's good to know," Ritchie replied, as though making a mental note of my opinion on the subject.

Clearing my head, I brought myself back to the matter at hand; there was a hot guy on the phone talking to me! "So, Ritchie, what's going on?" I demurely inquired.

"Not a whole hell of a lot—just doing my bit to uphold truth, justice, and the American way," he righteously intoned. "By the way, are you going to Sylvester's retirement party at Duffy's Tavern on Friday night?" he asked.

"Yup! I got someone to cover for me—I wouldn't miss it. Are you going?"

"Sure, I'll be there. Sly went out of his way to help me figure things out when I first got here. This place won't be the same without him."

"I know what you mean. It's always the good ones that retire while they can still enjoy life instead of hanging on like leeches, sucking the life out of the rest of us."

"Good analogy, Mel. Says it all. I'll see you Friday night then. I'll have a cold one waiting for you. Wait—make that shaken, not stirred," he said with a wry smile in his voice.

He remembered! As I hung up the phone, I felt a flutter in my gut. "Shake it off, Morrison," I said to myself. "Shake it off."

Sylvester's retirement party at Duffy's was a resounding success! We sent Sly out in style, which meant we got him stone drunk and he had to be carried to the curb and dumped into a taxi at the end of the night. At one particularly rowdy point during the party, the crowd hoisted me up on the stage and, with the assistance of a couple of shots of bourbon, I belted out a bar favorite with the house band that garnered us a standing ovation! Sometimes I just couldn't get over how much confidence I had gained since I had become an officer—just a few short years ago I wouldn't have been caught dead talking in front of crowd, much less singing in front of one! At the end of the evening, Ritchie was nice enough to offer to drive me home to Brooklyn, an offer I found hard to refuse.

"Geez, you were really something on that stage tonight, Mel! Where did you learn to sing like that?" he asked as we drove over the Brooklyn Bridge, the night sky awash in starlight and indigo.

"I don't know . . . maybe it's in the genes. My father used to get up at parties and sing "Danny Boy" at the drop of a hat—he never had to be asked twice. He was really good, too!" I replied, smiling at the memory of it. We talked shop and shared a good laugh over the new lieutenant in the building.

"You heard what he did at his last post, right?"

"Nope. So, what's the story, Ritchie?"

"The word on the street is that when he was the sergeant there, he took out his gun after a liquid lunch, waved it around the locker room, and screamed, 'This is my effing kingdom and if any of you has a problem with that, you can kiss this!' pointing the gun at his ass cheeks. Then he gets a round off into the wall as everyone's ducking for cover. You know the drill: he gets rewarded being such a wack job, and lands the lieutenant spot here," he replied, shaking his head.

"Richard, I've been thinking," I mused.

"Uh oh!" Ritchie glanced over at me with feigned alarm.

I gave him one of my "Don't mess with me. I'm a female with a gun!" looks. God, he was sexy – and tall, dark and handsome – the triple threat! My thoughts started wandering down the wayward road to sex. "Ignore your baser instincts, Marian Elizabeth Morrison—dare not stray from the path of righteousness!" directed my moral compass. I dug my fingernails into the palms of my hands and forced myself to get back on track.

"As I was saying, we're going about our careers the wrong way. What's the point in coming to work on time, day in and day out, performing our sworn duty, yet never getting ahead when all we have to do to get promoted and make some real money is to practically kill somebody?" I hypothesized.

Ritchie laughed out loud. "Just keep reminding yourself that it's a steady paycheck and bennies, Mel. This job is no road to the high life, that's for sure," he asserted.

"That's another thing that gets my Irish up—that saying, something about money not making you happy," I mused. "That's just something rich people say to keep the goods all to themselves, the bastards!" I postulated. Ritchie vigorously nodded his head in abject agreement with my keen observation on the state of rich versus poor.

When we got to my apartment, Ritchie insisted on walking me to the door. Before I could get the keys out of my pocketbook, he grabbed me with those long, strong arms and kissed me. Suddenly, all thoughts of hell and damnation flew out of my head. I had so successfully cut myself off from my emotional life that I couldn't have prepared myself for how his kiss would make me feel.

"Dear God," I silently and fervently prayed, "has anyone ever been so lonely that one simple kiss could make them feel like they've been resurrected from the dead?"

God answered with a resounding "YES."

Thank you, God. Normally, I was a strict adherent to the Three-Date Rule: no sex until the third date, assuming there was a third date. There would be no three-date protocol with Ritchie—we couldn't make it upstairs fast enough. James Darren, move over! We just about fell off the bed in the midst of our ardor. Nothing, not even the image of my dear, disapproving mother warning me that I was heading straight for the fires of hell was going to stop me this time.

As the days and weeks went by, Ritchie and I spent more and more time together. From the get-go, there was almost nothing about him that didn't turn me on; he had a mildly sardonic sense of humor that perfectly complemented my somewhat sarcastic view of life, and our physical attraction to each other bordered on the combustible. Until that first night with Ritchie in my Brooklyn bed, I just didn't know, couldn't have known, what passion even meant. The best that could be said about my previous sexual experiences were limited to my marital relations with Terry: can you say "Wham, bam, thank you, ma'am"? When I got involved with Terry, I didn't know anything about sex other than what I'd read in *Cosmo* or picked up from my friends; anything that even *hinted* at something of a sexual nature was simply not discussed around my mother. The closest she ever got to addressing the issue was when I got my first period. While she couldn't bring herself to talk to me about my life-changing experience, she did allow me to attend a film on the subject (and its attendant implications) that the local recreation center was featuring as part of their "Push for Personal Hygiene" campaign. After my marriage fell apart, I'd shied away from getting too involved with another guy, and the pickings were getting slim—anyone approaching "decent" was either in a steady relationship or married. The dating pool had almost dried up by the time I was ready to take another dip.

Ritchie changed all that. Besides resembling my dream lover with his big brown eyes, dark brown hair, and a physique to die for, he possessed an out-sized personality that could fill up any room the second he walked through the door. His kisses belonged in the kissing hall of fame! I was, simply put, crazy about him, and he was crazy about me—he told me so! He said he was crazy about my auburn hair and green eyes; he called it a "killer combination!" I was trying with all my might to keep a lid on my escalating feelings for Ritchie, given the *laissez-faire* standard we had decided to hold our relationship to, but he made it really, really, hard. My mother would have called him a charmer, which, coming from my mother, wasn't necessarily a compliment. For once, I didn't give a wit about her neurotic obsession with Italians. Never mind—Mom would never have understood my feelings for Ritchie.

All I knew was that I didn't want to have to toe the line this time. I wanted, for once in my life, to just let go, but as hard as I tried, I couldn't leave the Catholic girl in me on the shelf completely. One night over dinner, almost holding my breath, I asked Ritchie about the girl he'd been seeing before we started dating—he hadn't mentioned her once since we started going out. He assured me that he had told her about me and that she was cool about it. In fact, he said, she agreed with him that it was probably time for them to start seeing other people, as they were becoming little more than good friends. I started to exhale for what seemed like the first time in weeks. Ritchie and I never mentioned the word love—we were both too smart for that, but it sure felt something like it, and that was good enough. Even though we hadn't been dating long, we had even talked about moving in together, something that I'd never thought I'd have the nerve to do. And anyway, hadn't God answered "YES"? Unfortunately, Val was not a fan of Ritchie's. She had worked with him a couple of times and wasn't mad about him—she thought he was a player. When I first told her about our being together she almost hit the roof, which was not like her.

"Mel, what's wrong with you? Everyone knows he's got a girlfriend!" she chastised me.

"He said he broke it off with her, and, anyway, we're practically living together, or didn't you get the memo?" I retorted. "Look, Val, I know I'm letting things move fast with Ritchie and this isn't like me at all, but I'm sick of being so careful all the time. Everyone I know, including you, are falling in love, getting engaged, getting married, and here *I* am, Miss Goody Two-Shoes! I'm not a freaking saint, Val! And why not Ritchie? You're acting like my mother, for crying out loud." I felt my chest tightening as I held back the anger I felt at . . . what?

"Whoa, there, cowgirl! I'm not holding you to some ridiculous standard, but I am your best friend. I'm just putting it out there. I don't think he's good enough for you! Did he actually break up with her? Do you know it for a fact?"

"He told me he did and that's good enough for me. Besides, we're spending all of our free time together—we work in the same building, for God's sake! I think I would know if he was still seeing her. I want to trust him, Val. Am I wrong?" I asked plaintively, looking to her for guidance.

"I'm sure he's crazy about you, Mel—that's not the point. What's not to be crazy over? Here's something: how come you guys never go out in public together? We haven't even double-dated," she asked.

"It's kind of hard when he and I work different schedules, Val. And we go out on the weekends. Why would I lie?" I asked defensively.

"You're right, I'm sorry. I shouldn't be getting in your business like this," she apologized half-heartedly.

"Don't worry, Val. We're still in the honeymoon phase of our relationship—we don't want too much interruption from the outside world until we're a little more settled," I answered as though reading from an article in *Metro Style* magazine.

Val looked annoyed. "Do you really believe what you're saying? If you ask me, he sounds more like a married man keeping a mistress," Val stated firmly.

I could tell she needed more convincing. "You'll see. We've already planned to go to the opening day softball game together, the key word here being 'together,'" I said confidently.

"Okay, Mel, you win," Val replied, throwing her hands in the air. "Listen, I hope I'm wrong about Ritchie—you've been lit up like a 150-watt bulb lately. I hope it works out. Just promise me you'll try to keep your wits about you."

"Scout's honor!" I promised.

Ritchie and I went to the ball game together, as a couple, and made it through without incident. No strange woman skulking in the bushes, no whispers among the crowd about his old girlfriend. In fact, everyone seemed to be happy for us, including Val. At the picnic afterward, while Ritchie went off to get some more beer, Val and I talked.

"I was wrong, Mel. I have to admit it—you guys do seem to be good together," she observed.

"I knew if you'd just give him a chance, you'd like him," I replied, a bit smugly.

"Don't get carried away! I haven't conferred my complete seal of approval on him just yet. I'm only giving him one thumb-up. But you seem happy, so I'm happy for you," she replied honestly.

"He wants us to move in together," I confided, not looking directly at her. Richie and I hadn't been dating for very long. I expected a tongue-lashing; instead, Val sounded exasperated.

"Mel, you're a big girl now. Whatever makes you happy, I'll support you," she stated.

"Who's better than you?" I asked, raising my plastic cup.

"Nobody!" she answered enthusiastically as we tapped our plastic cups together in a toast.

"To Mel and Ritchie!" we sang in unison.

"Hey, you guys, get your asses over here!" yelled Margaret Dolores, the courthouse's version of the President of the Olympic Committee. "We need two more bodies for volleyball," she barked.

"Coming, coach," I yelled back as we stood up, weaving slightly. "Let the games begin!" I roared.

Ritchie and I had passed the test; he moved in with me about two weeks later. We were now a bona fide couple. Gidget and Moondoggie, together at last.

CHAPTER 12

I t was the first Friday of the month and time to meet up with the Friday Night Dinner Ladies.

I always looked forward to what had become our traditional kick-off to the start of a new month: getting together for a nice meal and some juicy gossip with the girls. We had all worked together in the court system at one time or another and became close friends in the process, so we decided it was a good way to keep in touch. Our little group represented a microcosm of the court family at large: different races, different ages, but the same problems, the same joys. My fellow gastronomes were Val; Isabel, who was a Spanish interpreter; Gloria, my part clerk; Carole Anne, a court reporter; and Jaycee, a judge's secretary. Each month, one of the group would pick the restaurant where we would meet, and this Friday was Gloria's turn. She emailed everyone her choice:

"FYI—Friday Night Dinner Ladies: I found the cutest bistro over by the seaport called Chez Janine. It just opened and I hear it's getting rave reviews. Meet you at #176 South Village Avenue at 8 p.m. with bells on!"

The restaurant was just a short walk from the courthouse. I changed quickly into my civvies and got there just a little after eight and, by the looks of it, everyone had been able to come. Luckily, Gloria had the foresight to book a reservation—the place was packed. We sat at our table and perused the lush menu while the waiter filled our water glasses and took our orders—that was the signal to start dishing.

"Wait till you guys hear this!" Carole Anne was barely able to contain herself. "You know that trial I've been working on? I swear, I thought I was in Bizarro World today! I'm typing away, and right in the middle of the doctor's testimony I hear snoring. I'm looking around, trying to be casual—I thought it might be a juror, not that I could blame them. Good grief, if I have to take down any more crap on that doctor's description of a healthy thorax, I think I'll scream!" she declared, her voice rising in exasperation.

"Go ahead with your rest of your story, Carole Anne," Gloria prompted her. "Mel only has an hour for dinner."

"Oh, yeah, sorry, Mel. Anyway, the snoring is getting louder and louder till I realize it's coming from the bench. I look up, and there is the judge snoozing away, right in the middle of an expert witness' testimony! Then, suddenly, he wakes up—like out of a sound sleep. He starts apologizing to the jury—he doesn't even direct me to go off the record, so I just keep typing." Carole Anne proceeded to imitate the judge's nasally voice: "'I apologize to the members of the jury and to the witness and I ask your indulgence. I am fighting a cold and took some medication this morning. It appears that it is making me a tad drowsy, so don't be concerned if you see me nod off from time to time. I assure you that I am paying attention when I need to be. You may resume your testimony, Doctor.'" Carole Anne continued her hilarious narrative: "This is all on the record, mind you. I can't wait for a request for a read-back of that transcript," she laughed.

"And who said justice never sleeps?" Val interjected. "But I think I can top that," she declared.

We all leaned in closer: she always had a funny bit about the courtroom and the crew.

"I had just gotten in tonight . . . I was on my way to the locker room to change into my uniform and I hear the phone in the part ringing off the hook. I check out the number and it's coming from the command. I figured I'd better answer it, even though I'm still off the clock. So, I answer the damn thing and it's the captain telling me we have a 'situation' in chambers and to go check it out, ASAP. I should've just kept on walking to the locker room—you'd think by now I'd know better, right?" Val looked around the table at the heads nodding in agreement at her astounding lack of good judgment.

"So, I head for chambers and when I walk in there is the lieutenant, the chief clerk, and a couple of guys from engineering just standing there and staring at something on the floor, like they're hypnotized. I asked them what the 'situation' was that was such a big emergency that I had to be summoned there, and they all point to a fish on the floor—and it's just lying there, motionless. It was the judge's giant pet piranha; somehow it had jumped out of that smelly-ass fish tank that he keeps back there and died. It was probably trying to escape from the other one that was always attacking it. Since everybody was just standing there with their hands in their pockets, I had to pick up the damn thing with a newspaper, go back outside to the big dumpster and toss it – all before I had my coffee. What did they think I was gonna do—shoot it? It was already dead! Gee, I wonder if I'll get a commendation at the next awards ceremony for "Bravery in Action". What do you think, guys?" Val asked as she took a swig of her beer.

"Wait a minute. You're saying the judge keeps piranha fish in his chambers?" Carole Anne asked incredulously.

"You betcha," answered Val, as I nodded in agreement. "If you can believe this, he thinks they help young children relax when they go back there for in-camera interviews— you know, like they're sitting at the dentist's office waiting to have their braces adjusted," Val commented drolly.

"What do you think the poor fish was trying to do, Val?" Carole Anne asked innocently.

"I don't know—commit suicide?" Val answered patiently, trying to hold her sarcasm at bay with poor Carole Anne. We were all roaring our heads off—it was stories like those that kept us coming back to our jobs day in and day out.

I looked around the table at the friends who had become so important to me over the last few years. For a while after my divorce, I had no real friends. I had committed a grave error after getting married in that I took my husband's friends as my own and neglected mine, something my mother had done after marrying my father. Friendships that had once seemed solid as a rock were now reduced to little more than the once-a-year exchange of Christmas cards. Tracy Lynn and I have stayed close, of course, but once she and Chris got married and started their family we didn't have a lot of time to hang out together. I love her children, but not having any myself limited what we had in common. In time, Tracy Lynn seemed to be only half-listening to my latest escapades, and for my part, I could only listen to so much baby talk. That, plus the fact that she and Chris had stayed in touch with Terry and his new wife put some distance between us. I had to admit that their staying friends with the man who had beaten me emotionally and physically hurt me to the core, but I couldn't be too harsh with them about it—they were caught in the middle of that mess.

So, despite our die-hard allegiance to our friendship, we, too, drifted apart. Still, we always make it a point to get together for our birthdays, and I never miss the kids' birthday parties, even if it is just to pop in to drop off a present and a have a bite of cake. There are always big hugs and kisses awaiting "Auntie M," as her kids call me, and Tracy Lynn and I always make sure we profess our love for each other, no matter what life throws down the path of our friendship. And so, here I am tonight, dining out with friends from a different life; not any more beloved than friends of old, just the newest additions.

I watched Carole Anne as she spoke and thought of the misconceptions people make of others based solely on their appearance. Carole Anne was the archetype blonde bombshell, with huge cornflower-blue eyes, her beautiful smile revealing teeth like little white pearls, and a pert, turned-up nose. She was in her mid-forties, but could pass for thirty. She didn't dress provocatively, but didn't have to; Carole Anne had a figure that would leave most women out of the running. She spoke somewhat breathlessly, her words coming out faster than she could sometimes manage. Maybe that was a by-product of sitting for hours on end, listening intently to someone else speak, and having to transcribe even the most mundane musings of the average litigant. I didn't know how the court reporters did it day after day: wanting, but not being able, to stop some bald-faced liar in the middle of their testimony and scream at them, "Who the hell do you think you're kidding with this crap?" then hitting them with their steno machine. But most importantly, Carole Anne was a friend to all. She never forgot a birthday or anniversary, and had a gracious smile for everyone she met. She would say, "I always try to say something nice to people even if they don't seem deserving of a friendly gesture—you never know what kind of burden they're carrying." Indeed, she seemed a woman to be envied, and many did.

What many people didn't know about the beautiful blonde court reporter was that she had been married in her early twenties, and very happily at that. Carole Anne had married the love of her life and they had one child together, a son, upon whom the sun rose and shone even on the rainiest of days. One Saturday afternoon, after returning home from a full day of shopping at the mall with her friends, she retrieved an urgent message on her answering machine from the police department. When she called them back, they wouldn't speak with her over the phone and asked her to come down to the station with a friend or relative. Of course, that would normally have been her husband, but as she would come to learn later that evening at the police station, that would not have been possible.

Earlier that day, her husband and their eight-year-old took their boat out for a father-son excursion, something they did together on a regular basis. The father had sailed all his life and the son was fast earning his sea legs. They made quite a handsome pair in their matching caps and Macs! When they shoved off from the dock, a cloudless blue sky welcomed them. Two hours into their sail, the skies turned ugly, the waves grew immense, and the once calm sea opened its great maw and swallowed them—their bodies were never recovered. Carole Anne will forever hold my steadfast admiration and friendship just for surviving that unspeakable horror.

A couple of years after her world crashed down around her, she met Paul. Paul was the new IPS driver for her neighborhood. He seemed like a very nice guy and, for the first time in a long while, she found herself looking forward to his coming to her door and their friendly chats. She felt as though there was a kinship between them, though she couldn't understand why. They were basically strangers and their talks had never really progressed beyond the topic of the day's weather. But on the third anniversary of the death of her family, as she lay in bed, blanketed by the leaden weight of her sadness, she felt that if she didn't talk to someone right then, she might take her own life. The savage vigor of her melancholy was finally overtaking her frail will to live.

Like an answer to a desperate prayer, the doorbell rang. At first, Carole Anne wasn't going to answer it, as the simple act of getting out of bed was almost beyond her endurance, but something compelled her to go to the door. She peeked through the blinds; the light snowfall of an hour before had turned into a raging snowstorm. Paul was standing huddled under the small overhang outside the front door, trying, without much success, to keep the blowing snow off the packages in his arms. For the moment, she shook off the comforting allure of the promise of never-ending sleep, opened the door, and asked Paul if he would care to come in and warm up a bit. Would he like a hot cup of coffee? He answered quickly that, yes, thank you, he would love a cup of coffee; it had been a difficult day for him, what with the snowstorm and all.

Sitting down at the table in Carole Anne's tidy kitchen, Paul slowly opened up to her. He admitted, somewhat shyly, that he liked her, and that he always looked forward to seeing a package addressed to her in his truck. He hoped she wouldn't think he was acting out of line when he said he thought she was very pretty. He thought she was kind; he didn't get to meet many kind people on his route, he explained. Most were too busy or too caught up in their own lives to show kindness toward a delivery man, like her asking him in for a cup of hot coffee on a wintery day. Carole Anne felt herself blushing; Paul started to warm in her presence.

He confided to her that he had been married once, to his high school sweetheart. They had a beautiful little girl together, a nice house in the suburbs, everything they had ever hoped for or dreamed about. They were so happy. Until the day a demon thief, a drunk driver, snatched their precious lives from the world, cutting Paul's heart out from him, devastating him. Today happened to be the third anniversary of their passing. The previous two years, while driving his old route, he had taken the day off in memoriam, but this year was different somehow—he felt as though he must go to work, that he had to get out of the house. He couldn't explain the feeling, the urgency of it. He hoped he wasn't boring her with his story. For some reason, he thought she might understand.

Paul stayed for coffee that day and never left. He and Carole Anne were married not long after their talk in the kitchen on that cold winter day—that was fifteen years ago. They went on to have two beautiful boys together and all is well. "Fairy tales do exist," I thought to myself as my gaze wandered over to Jaycee, who was carrying on a lively conversation with Gloria.

"Say what? Are you tellin' me that you ain't had sex with yo' man for a whole six months? Damn girl!" Jaycee exclaimed, her long fake eyelashes batting with disbelief. "Whuz up with that, Day-Glo?" Jaycee asked as she leaned back in her chair, crossing her arms over her substantial bosom, which was quite noticeable in her low-cut leopard-print blouse.

"For God's sake, Miss Thing, keep your voice down, please! I don't want the whole restaurant to know my business!" Gloria retorted, looking flustered. Lowering her voice, she tried to explain her predicament while the rest of the table huddled toward her. Did we hear her right? Gloria and Cliff hadn't had sex in a half-year? Weren't they the picture of the "perfect couple"?

"Look, all I'm saying is that after two people have been together as long as we have, after raising a family and all that goes with it, the relationship becomes more like a good friendship instead of a hot romance. We can't all be like you, Jaycee," Gloria commented defensively, referring to Jaycee's very busy love life.

Jaycee was the brown sugar to our coffee klatch. She was larger-than-life, and not just because she was a plus-sized woman: Jaycee took over any room she walked into; she was always dressed to the nines, impeccably made up, her hair done just right. She had a booming, infectious laugh. Jaycee was the walking, talking embodiment of the slogan "Black is Beautiful." She had worked her way up from filing for a clerical service to becoming a judge's secretary in just three short years. Her love life sizzled; it seemed like every few months or so there was an ever-younger, hot new man waiting in the wings just to do her bidding. We didn't know where she got the energy! What I loved most about Jaycee was her openness and the fact that she was never afraid to take responsibility for her actions, good or bad, unlike so many other people I knew. Like what she did when she was sixteen years old and eight months pregnant.

Jaycee was being raised by her strict Baptist grand-mother when she found out the result of her fling with a twenty-year-old from the neighborhood. At sixteen, she already had the figure of a grown woman and her periods were always tricky, coming one month and not the next, so Jaycee didn't pay much attention when her clothes started getting tighter and her periods went missing. She figured she was just filling out more, pretty much the way she had been doing since the age of eleven. One day, after experi-encing what she thought were severe menstrual pains, she ran to the bathroom and proceeded to go into labor. When she saw a baby emerging from her private parts, she pan-icked and tried to flush it down the toilet. How would she explain this to her very religious grandmother, the woman who had rescued her from her crack-addicted mother to give her a decent home and upbringing?

She might have succeeded in washing her sin away had not her God-fearing and suspicious grandmother followed her and witnessed her baby's inauspicious beginnings. She promptly shoved Jaycee off her throne and rescued the poor child from certain death. Her grandmother called an ambulance and got them to the hospital in time to save the baby's life, but not his right leg, which had to be amputated below the knee because of injuries he sustained during his traumatic birth.

With time, and with the help of her devoted grandmother, Jaycee grew to be a good and loving mother to her son, a handsome boy who himself grew to be a good and loving young man and a college graduate. I've had the pleasure of being with them on occasion and I've seen with my own eyes how strong their bond is. Their relationship is a testament to the power of love and forgiveness. I didn't know too many people who would be so brave as to own up to such a thing as what Jaycee tried that fateful day, but she did, and I admired her tremendously for it. That, and for her fashion savvy; she always knew how to put together an outfit with just the right amount of bling and everyone sought out her sartorial know-how. Jaycee was the courthouse's resident diva who could speak the King's English with the best of them but fell into the vernacular when dishing the dirt with the girls.

"Girl, you got to step up yo' game!" Jaycee warned Gloria. "Tell you what—I'll take you over to Vicky's Cache and we'll check out their new lingerie line. Just give me yo' credit card and I'll set you straight up—you be crack-a-lackin' in no time, girl!" Jaycee interrupted her pep talk for a second to check her look in the wall mirror. "You got to get yo' freak on, Day-Glo, or I'm telling you, yo' man gonna be findin' hisself some new tail in a New York minute. Clifford at that dangerous age now, you know—kids gittin' growed up and all," she advised as she touched up her bright red lipstick.

Gloria looked disgusted and tired; clearly, she needed to vent. "I know, I know . . . it sounds bad, but I don't know what to do! I don't know that Cliff even cares that much anymore. God, I'm so sick of the whole *sex* thing. It's always being shoved down your throat—you can't get away from it! And I worry about what it's doing to our children: how is it shaping their views on relationships? Do they think you must be sexed-up 24/7 and looking like a hooker, otherwise you're done for? What happened to love? Don't get me wrong, girls, I still want to enjoy the occasional roll in the sack with my husband, but he hasn't asked in a while. Anyway, that still doesn't mean I have to be assaulted by pornography on a minute-to-minute basis to feel like a viable woman!" she declared.

Gloria stopped her tirade long enough to take a deep gulp of her white wine. Putting her goblet down, making sure the cocktail napkin was square with the glass, she continued her heated commentary: "I don't care what anyone else thinks, I think sex has become highly overrated! I won't even read the fashion magazines anymore—can you believe that? Imagine the nerve of those snot-nosed queens that pass for designers who have no desire whatsoever to explore the contours and crevices, the BEAUTY of a grown woman's body, yet thinking they have the wherewithal, THE POWER, to instruct her on how to be thinner, sexier, more desirable, more everything! And women go along with it. The joke's on us, ladies!" she announced to the table.

Carole Anne looked perturbed. "Gloria, I'd appreciate it if you didn't use such a derogatory term for homosexual—my brother is gay, you know," she responded protectively.

"Oh, for God's sake, Carole Anne, get off the PC wagon, will you? I've heard your brother call himself a queen—and a lot worse!" Gloria shot back. Carole Anne looked around the table for support, but she was on her own this time; Gloria was on a high-octane, estrogen-fueled rollercoaster ride that would just have to run its course. She looked around the table then crooked her slender, manicured finger, inviting her dinner companions to come closer.

"Girls, don't fool yourselves into thinking that men have "evolved" and that they've become more understanding of the "fairer sex". That's total bullshit! All it ever really comes down to is the guy who's standing next to them at the urinal—who's got the bigger dick and all that crap. Why do you think some nitwit, a MAN, invented Viagra? For a woman's pleasure? I don't think so! It's never been about what women want," Gloria argued as she stabbed at her salad then continued her discourse of all things anti-woman. "And while I'm on the topic of Big Pharma and the medical profession, the other day I had to go for a mammogram—I hadn't had one done in a few years and my doctor was really starting to get on my case about it. So, I gave in, thinking it CAN'T be the same procedure I'd gone through all those years before – you know, that machine they squish your boobs into till you think you're going to faint from the pain?" Everyone at the table vigorously nodded their heads in agreement, wincing at the very thought of it. "Well, I'm ushered into a room, given a gown to change into then the technician comes in and motions for me to step up to the VERY SAME GOD-FORSAKEN TORTURE CHAMBER!!! I couldn't believe it—I thought my head was going to explode!!!" she shrieked.

I motioned to her to keep her voice down.

Her face flushed in supreme indignation, Gloria picked up the wine menu and started fanning herself with it. Not skipping a beat, she went on with her tale of modern medicine's version of the inquisition. "Trying, and not very successfully, I'm afraid, to keep from screaming at the poor technician, I said to her, 'Are you kidding with this? If men had to put their balls into this contraption to be tested for testicular cancer, it wouldn't exist!' I did manage to pull myself together long enough to tell the poor woman that I wasn't blaming her, that she was just the messenger." The Friday Night Dinner Ladies exhaled a unanimous sigh of relief for that small blessing, but Gloria wasn't done just yet. "And on top of everything else, especially during this time of my life, I'm still faced with dealing with uninvited competition from other women just when I thought I was getting to the age when I could relax a little, maybe even count on other women to be simpatico—present company excluded, of course, ladies. And in competition for what, I want to know? The chance to change my husband's Depends when he's ninety? Jacycee, honey, you know I love you dearly, but when you get to be my age, then you can tell me how I should act. I'm telling you now, menopause ain't for sissies!" she warned her dinner companions as she finally sat back in her chair. Gloria's long, elegant fingers tapped on her wineglass, telegraphing her supreme dissatisfaction with her current state of affairs. She took another gulp of wine, the three-carat Harry Winston adorning her left hand sparkling furiously as she did so.

Gloria had the polished look of a woman who had married well. She was the oldest of the group and approaching fifty but she fought the good fight and kept the crow's-feet and sagging skin at bay with regular visits to her plastic surgeon. She was currently experiencing a brutal bout with menopause, for which she had our utmost sympathy. Gloria's clothes were never off-the-rack, and her jewelry was all top-shelf. She kept her slim figure in check with weekly games of tennis at the club and had her perfectly manicured nails and chin-length, blunt-cut, unobtrusively highlighted light brown hair maintained at the exclusive Tres Chic spa salon every week. Gloria hailed from an upper middle-class family who expected her to marry into money. She had entered the court system and become a clerk after trying college for a while and not finding it a good fit. People in the know told her that a woman like herself could easily land a lawyer for a husband if she played her cards right, and that the pickings were pretty good at the courthouse. As it happened, Gloria was an excellent card player. It all turned out for the best; she loved being a clerk and met her future husband in the bargain and, while being a court clerk wasn't the most glamorous of careers, it gave Gloria a sense of self. It afforded her an identity apart from that of just being the wife of a famous lawyer and the mother of his children, although when pressed, she had to admit she didn't mind the perks that went along with those titles.

When he and Gloria met, Cliff was an up-and-coming attorney who was well on his way to establishing what would become one of the most sought-after law firms in town. He was the complete package: young, successful, and as handsome as Gloria was beautiful. They fell in love during jury selection for the trial of one of Cliff's clients and subsequently married. They had beautiful twin girls, both of whom were currently attending law school.

Cliff and Gloria had always taken their marriage vows seriously, but now, after a quarter of a century together, it was becoming harder. The kids were getting older and had their own lives to lead and it had created a vacuum in their relationship which they were both finding harder to fill, and despite all the attempts at keeping the sexual spark alive after so many years, their love life had grown somewhat stale. Still, Gloria could turn a head or two when she walked into a courtroom and Cliff had maintained his boyish good looks while maturing into a self-possessed man sporting a full head of hair with just the right amount of grey at the temples, not to mention being very rich.

So far, they had managed to keep temptation at bay; after all, they still had their health, their wealth, and a fine family to show for all their hard work and the occasional sacrifice. They enjoyed what anyone would consider the good life. And yes, they did still love each other, if not as passionately as in years past. But the dinner ladies tended to agree with Jaycee's assessment of their precarious situation. So far, their marriage still seemed to be working, but for how much longer? There was plenty of temptation to be found lurking amongst the nooks and crannies of the courthouse, even for the most stalwart of spouses, but most especially for the husbands. The pickings were so plentiful, the joke went, that a man twice Cliff's age with no hair and none of his money could practically trip over a willing partner if he wanted it badly enough. Despite all her convincing arguments, was Gloria really willing to take the chance of losing it all when maybe all it took was a menopausal booty call?

Val, always the voice of reason, attempted to broker the disagreement. "Jaycee, I can understand Gloria's frustration. What she's trying to say is true—our society is disintegrating. All you need to do is turn on the television any time of the day or night to watch people sleeping with just about anybody or anything so they can grab their fifteen minutes of fame. And who's at home in the afternoon watching this stuff unsupervised these days? Kids! And what's going to happen when those same kids grow up and become the adults who run this world? It makes me sick just to think about it," Val sighed in disgust.

"Well, ma baby boy never sat home watching that shit and that's why he goin' to medical school!" Jaycee proclaimed, working her head from side to side like a giant bobblehead doll. "But that ain't what we're talking about now, is it? We're talking about Miss Gloria here making sure her man don't stick his dick into some hoochie mama's honey pot," Jaycee declared.

Isabel added her Mexican-spiced mix to the debate. "Aye, momi, thas no lie. My seester in Miami, her husband left her for a twenty-year-old seex month ago. He tole her that she was too old for heem, that son of a beech! After all dos years together, for some gran puta? Bastardo! I'd like to cut off heez cojones pequenisimos for what he did to my seester!" Isabel spat, her dark eyes ablaze with passionate thoughts of bloody revenge for her sister's pain.

Isabel was every inch the proud Latina woman, with fiery eyes that matched her temperament and jet-black hair that fell in satin waves all the way to her tiny waist, but there was a twist to her story. Isabel was the descendant of grandparents who fled mainland China just prior to the Japanese invasion in the 1930s and found their way to Mexico, being unable at the time to enter the United States. They found a home in the Chinese expatriate community in Mexicali and eventually opened a Cantonese restaurant there. While they continued to honor their Chinese heritage, the Han family embraced their adopted Mexican culture. Like her mother before her, Isabel was raised speaking fluent Cantonese and Spanish, with a smattering of English, and attended the local Catholic schools where she became immersed in her surroundings. While attending university, Isabel had the opportunity to lodge with a family in the northeastern United States as an exchange student and wound up staying on. Like the rest of our group, she found out about a job opportunity with the courts, specifically as a Spanish Interpreter. Imagine the look on peoples' faces when the part called for an interpreter on a case and the petite and demure, decidedly Asian-looking Isabel showed up speaking flawless Spanish! We still got a kick out of it when she would go off on a rant about something, like she was doing tonight—she was truly a study in contrasts when she got going!

For the past few years, she has been living with Carlos, a fellow Spanish interpreter. Carlos was very handsome; a big, hungry man, his tastes always ran to the extreme—that is, until he met Isabel. She had somehow tempered his ravenous appetite for life—he liked to say that he now purred instead of roared. Isabel and Carlos were, by any standard, a match made in heaven—fiery temperaments aside, they almost never fought. They were staunchly committed to the integrity of their relationship, yet each had their own friends and interests and never took issue with one of them taking a trip without the other or making dinner plans with an old friend, even one of the opposite sex. They had given some thought to tying the knot, but Carlos and Isabel decided not to mess with a good thing. I had given some thought to someday being in a relationship much like theirs—it would have been a burst of fresh air infused into my rather mundane ideas of romance. Was my love affair with Ritchie the litmus test?

"Hey, Mel, you been awful quiet tonight, girl. Whuz up with you and that hot man you got?" Jaycee inquired as she tried in vain to lather her roll with a rock-hard pat of butter.

"I'm just listening to the fascinating discourse at the table, Jaycee," I answered blithely, though in truth, I *was* a little quiet tonight. I had tried unsuccessfully to get Ritchie on the phone before leaving for the restaurant—that had been happening a lot lately.

"So, Momi Mel, how's eet going wiz you and that gorgeous hunk of man-meat, eh?" Isabel winked at me, her almond-shaped black eyes dancing with mischief.

"We're fine, Isabel . . . taking it easy, no hassles. Keeping it real, know what I'm saying?" I wasn't even sure I knew what I was saying.

It hadn't been that long since Ritchie and I, embraced by a white heat, began our torrid love affair, but lately I was spending more and more nights alone in a cold bed as Ritchie worked longer hours with the second job he had recently taken on. Regardless of our quick decision to move in together after only dating for a couple of months, I thought I was being smart about love this time. I had tried to pattern my relationship with Ritchie on Isabel and Carlos' affair, with all its attendant ease and grace, but it didn't have the same feel. No, despite its auspicious beginnings, our love affair was turning out to be anything but easy. It was beginning to feel more like a supernova that explodes in the night sky, only to become a distant, dying star, its light fading in the morning sun. That familiar, persistent feeling of impending doom was tugging at me, keeping me in an almost constant state of anxiety. I kept my feelings under wraps—I hadn't even talked to Val about it.

"I forgot to tell you, Mel, I saw Ritchie the other night," Carole Anne remarked.

"When was that?" I asked.

"Tuesday night. I was at the store getting something for dinner and saw him getting in his car," she replied.

I thought back to Tuesday—if I remembered correctly, Ritchie said he was working in the city that night. Or maybe it was Monday night I was thinking of? He was working so much overtime lately I was having trouble keeping track of his schedule.

"Are you positive it was him? I'm pretty sure he had to be in the city that night," I commented. Something else didn't jibe with her story; Carole Anne lived on Long Island, a long way from the city. What would he have been doing there?

"Well, I thought it was him, but it was getting dark—I could be mistaken. He didn't answer when I called out to him," she answered.

"Yeah, I think you mistook him for someone else. That happens," I said as I slowly moved the food around on my plate. I was getting that tight feeling in my stomach again—or was it was just the duck?

I got home from work around midnight. I carefully opened the door to the bedroom and switched on the small night-light near the dresser. Ritchie was already asleep, snoring soundly. I tiptoed over to his side of the bed and sat down, taking in the hunk of man-meat before me. Even in sleep, Ritchie's body pulsed an electro-magnetic field of testosterone. Forget Viagra. If I could find a way to package whatever it was Ritchie had and sell it, I'd be a billionaire! "Lucky Ritchie," I whispered as I touched my lips to his smooth face.

He roused slightly. "Hey, babe," he mumbled as he turned to his other side.

I wasn't giving up. All that talk at dinner about sex got my mojo working. I got into bed and slipped my arms around Ritchie's waist, pulling him close. I could feel my heart pound against his muscular back, stronger, more insistent with each beat. Ritchie reached around and pulled my arms away from him. "Not tonight, babe, okay? I'm tired. Tomorrow night, I promise," he murmured. No sex tonight; that would make the second night this week.

"Okay, hon," I answered, my mojo slowly deflating like a badly worn tire. No, in fact, it wasn't okay, but I wasn't going to beg. How had things begun to change so quickly for us? Just six months ago, we couldn't keep our hands off each other; I thought back to all the times we caught a quickie in the janitor's closet in between our shifts. We had so much fun together—we loved the same music, the same food. Not that we didn't now, but something was different: I couldn't put my hands on it, but it was there, like the subtle change in the air when summer begins its inevitable decline into fall. I slid under the blanket, my eyes suddenly becoming heavy with sleep. I turned over and uneasily drifted off, awaiting a visit from the vampires.

CHAPTER 13

Val was the one person in the world I could call when I happened upon the evidence: the love letters ("Dear Ritchie, I never stopped loving you. Where do we go from here?"), wherein the little home-wrecker drew a heart around their intertwined names, and the box of condoms. Dear God . . .

"I knew it, I just knew it! He's been screwing around on you with that slut! Damn!" Val practically spit the words out.

"Val, please, if you care about me at all, you'll stop. I can't handle the I-told-you-so rap right now," I pleaded with her.

"I'm so sorry, Mel! What a dick! I could kill him!" she hissed. So very sweet of her to offer . . .

"Ritchie told me that he was visiting his mother in New Jersey yesterday, said she needed help with her car or something. He got home late last night and I was already asleep. He went out again this morning to run errands. I found the stuff in a box under the bed in the spare room when I was vacuuming," I lamented.

"You poor kid—do you want me to come over?" Val asked, the concern for me evident in the tone of her voice.

"No, that's okay. I need to get my head together before he gets home. I'll call you later, Val, and thanks for listening," I sighed.

"Mel, I'm a phone call away if you need me, and please, will you do me a favor?" she asked.

"Sure, what is it, Val?"

"Just promise me you won't kill him till I get there. That way I can testify I saw the whole thing and that you did it in self-defense!" she declared, half-jokingly. She was trying to lift my spirits, but she may have been more concerned about real bloodshed than she was letting on. She needn't have worried. My breaking heart had sucked me dry of the energy to want to murder Ritchie for his betrayal.

"I promise. Anyway, I need time to think about this," I murmured as I slowly hung up the phone.

I waited a whole week to confront him—as cool as a cucumber, was I. Over time, one develops a strong sense of reserve working in a courtroom—he had no clue what he was in for. Ritchie's heart had been reclaimed by Rita, the ace court reporter. How could I not have known it was her all along? Why hadn't I seen it coming? Even their names screamed it out: Ritchie and Rita, Rita and Ritchie! My world had just imploded, yet here I was, standing at the kitchen sink with evidence in hand, as seemingly at ease as if I were just waiting to call the next case on the calendar.

Ritchie came out of the spare room and ambled into the kitchen, surrounded by an air of Walter Mitty-like self-absorption. He snapped out of his reverie, startled to see me standing there. Whom did he expect to see?

"Hey, Mel. You're still here? I thought you'd be out shopping or something," he mumbled as he picked up the day's mail and leafed through it, trying not to make eye contact with me.

Yeah, or something. Oh, yes, honey, I just got back from screwing our next-door neighbor – what's new with you? I looked at him standing in the doorway, framing it with his tall, muscular body, so handsome, so unkind.

"Hi, honey," I greeted Ritchie as steadily as I could, trying hard not to dissolve into a pool of teary anguish. "Gosh, you are a busy boy! You've been locked up in that room all morning. Something got your attention?" I asked, not wanting to hear the answer.

"Yeah, well, you know how it is with the computer. Once you get started, it's hard to stop," he replied, still averting his gaze from me.

"Right . . . speaking of which, just how is Rita doing these days?" I queried with as much nonchalance as I could manage. As Ritchie's face drained of color, a deer-in-the-headlights look came over him. I didn't recognize this Ritchie—where had his bravado gone? "Let's sit down," I advised him. "You look a little faint." I needed to sit as well; the floor beneath me seemed to be moving. In the space of a couple of minutes we had gone from live-in lovers to strangers on a plane—we could barely look at each other. My hands started to shake . . . I struggled to breathe.

"H-h-how did you find out?" Ritchie stammered.

My hands stopped shaking. "How did I find out?" I asked, my voice rising as my face suddenly flushed with anger. "I'm no P.I., Ritchie, but you didn't exactly go to much trouble to hide the evidence. My guess is that you wanted me to find out!" I threw the love letters and condoms on the table. "Nice penmanship, by the way, and I really dig the artwork, but my name's not Rita and I'm on the pill, remember?" I almost shouted. I wanted to scream!

Ritchie stiffened in his chair. "I'm really sorry, Mel. I'm sorry you found out like this. I honestly don't know what to say."

"I don't think honesty is your strong suit, lover boy," I snapped. Like a seasoned trial attorney ready to pounce on her prey in the witness stand, I stood up from the table and started pacing the kitchen floor. "Just how long have you and Rita been, for lack of a better word, boinking each other?" I felt myself grinding my teeth.

Ritchie didn't answer me. He must have been paying very close attention to the goings-on in the trial parts he had been covering the past year: never offer information that's not expressly asked for; keep your answers short and simple; appear naive, even stupid if you have to; but most importantly, wow the jury with your movie star good looks! "Members of the jury, the defendant has been screwing the co-defendant and lying about it to his loving and loyal girl-friend, almost destroying her in the process. Plaintiff recommends twenty-five years to life!"

"Last I heard, Rita had a husband. Did that change?" I asked.

"She was going to tell him. We've been discussing how we were going to tell the both of you. We were just waiting for the right time," Ritchie said as he stared down at the table.

Look me in the eyes, you coward—that's the least I deserve. "How good of you, Richard! Why don't I nominate the both of you for the Nobel Peace Prize while we're at it!" I yelled again, my voice overflowing with sarcasm.

"Look, Mel, I am truly sorry for what's happened, but let's face facts: we haven't exactly been on the same page lately. I mean, when was the last time we had sex? A month ago?" Typical defense tactic: try to deflect the blame back onto the victim. "Your Honor, she isn't putting out. I'm just a normal, red-blooded male. I have needs!"

"And it's my fault that you took a second job?" I asked. A couple of months before, Ritchie told me that he had been offered a part-time security job in the city for a movie company that was filming there at night. Ritchie said he wanted to take advantage of it and that he had to give them an answer right away. I gave him my full support. I thought he was becoming more responsible, possibly even planning a future for us. Stupid, stupid, stupid! "Let me guess, Ritchie. Rita's husband was working nights too, so she had some time to kill and just happened to be in the city when you ran into her?" I asked, mockingly.

"Okay, okay, you got me! You won your case, counselor," Ritchie shot back. It felt like he had slapped me in the face.

"Why did you do this, Ritchie? I haven't even looked at another man since we've been together. Why didn't you talk to me if you were so unhappy? I love you." It came out of my mouth, just like that . . . I loved him.

"Mel, I thought we felt the same way about this. Look, we had a great time, didn't we?" Suddenly, he was speaking of our time together in the past tense. "I loved you, too. I still care about you—a lot. But you knew what you were getting into when we moved in together. You knew how I felt about commitment. I thought you felt the same way."

"Moving in together wasn't a commitment for you? I thought our issues were with marriage. Have I ever put any pressure on you for that?" I asked, searching his face for some show of affection, of love. Ritchie shifted ever so slightly in his seat, not enough to give anything away. I had always loved Ritchie's energy, the way he could take over any room he walked into with his out-sized personality and physical prowess. Now I was beginning to see what a cool character he really was.

"I thought it was over between Rita and me. Remember the night at Balducci's when she introduced us? We'd met there for dinner after my interview to talk about where things were going. It was hard to meet near district court— we were always afraid that someone would see us together. And her husband's a cop—his precinct isn't too far from the courthouse. Anyway, we broke up not too long after that. The truth is, I wanted her to leave her husband but she wouldn't do it. She wasn't ready to break up her marriage for me," he confessed.

I started to recall our talks about commitment and marriage and his relationship with his girlfriend, who now had a face and a name, the girlfriend who was so okay about everything. In truth, she wasn't ready to leave her husband for Ritchie. She was the one who didn't want to take the chance.

"You tricked me, then? You were using me to pass the time until Rita made up her mind?" I challenged him, my voice twisted in anger. I started pacing the floor again, trying not to panic, trying to picture myself walking out the door, not Ritchie.

"I don't think you'll ever believe me, Mel, but I swear I didn't get into this with the intention of using you. I believed what we had was real. I'm not a bastard, I'm just human."

Suddenly, I stopped pacing. Wasn't I human, too? I stared at Ritchie's face, already trying to commit it to memory, my eyes filling with tears. "Why, Ritchie, why?" I begged.

"Rita needs me," he answered plainly as he turned his face away from me.

A few nights after our break up, I had the most beautiful dream. I was sitting on a chair in what seemed to be the lounge of an elegant hotel. Val was sitting in the chair next to mine—we were waiting for someone to arrive. I saw a man walk into the room – he was very handsome. As he started walking toward us, I recognized him. It was my father! I turned to Val to tell her my father had come back, but she wasn't there anymore. I looked at him again—he seemed so young. A golden glow was emanating from him, surrounding him like a halo. My father came over to me and held me. "Hello, Marian, my lovely Irish lass," he greeted me softly. I was safe again.

He took me by the hand and led me to a door that opened onto a large apartment. We stood in the doorway together, his arm around my shoulder. The rooms were lovely, already furnished and decorated. Someone lived there. I noticed photographs set in silver frames that were placed throughout the apartment; the pictures appeared to be that of a young family but I couldn't see their faces. I could faintly detect the sound of children's laughter nearby. My father said to me, "This will be yours, my beloved daughter. Everything will be made right again," he promised.

I closed my eyes as he took my face in his hands and kissed me gently on the forehead. When I opened them, he was gone. I didn't want to wake up—I wanted to be in heaven with my father, for surely, he was an angel. But, as the alarm clock began its daily assault on the quiet of my room and I slowly opened my eyes, I saw the light of early morning peeking through my bedroom window and heard the birdsong heralding a new day.

Life beckoned to me, but I couldn't answer its call.

CHAPTER 14

I had failed, again. How was I going to face my mother after this? I didn't go with my gut, didn't trust my instincts about Ritchie—I'd let my heart rule my head, something I swore I wouldn't do. In my line of work, that could really cost me. Even worse, I didn't heed the advice of my best friend. I was an abject failure at love and possibly at my job. I was a mess! How could I go back to work like this? The "Powers That Be" might think I couldn't handle my responsibilities, take my guns away from me and stick me in some godforsaken post with a dunce cap on my head. How could I face anyone in court? Everyone would know, even the evening janitor. Ritchie had taken off after our confrontation, not telling me where he was going, but he didn't have to. I fell into bed, pulled the covers over my head and didn't come out for three days. I finally emerged from my tomb, but not into a luminous white light—more like the gray glare from a bare light bulb swinging from the ceiling, casting a long shadow over me.

Sitting down at the kitchen table, I swirled my tea with a silver spoon, staring at the amber-colored vortex in the cup coming to life. I took a long sip, letting the rising steam from the hot tea warm my face. I started waking up to the nightmare that was now my life. The tough Mick in me wouldn't let me fall apart completely. I didn't care about myself anymore, but the cats still had to eat, and I had to keep a roof over our heads—at least they still needed me. A question kept running through my mind: why hadn't Ritchie wanted to take care of me instead of Rita? Should I have pretended to be a needy female? I guess I could have tried, but let's face it, a woman who carries a gun for a living, no matter how pretty or sexy she is, doesn't project needy.

I started to dread going to sleep. I would crawl into my now half-empty bed and slip toward a dark abyss that wouldn't let me live or die, just grieve. Those familiar feelings that had dug such an empty hole in my life, the ones that I thought I'd left behind when I met Ritchie, were now burrowing their way back into my soul. I thought I had outsmarted love this time, but I was wrong. My heart was breaking. Would Ritchie think I was needy enough now?

I put a request in with the command to take a week off. Captain Murphy, in his grumpy way, was surprisingly understanding and granted the leave. I left the apartment for a day while Ritchie moved his things out. When I finally returned to work, I got in as late as I could manage to avoid the rush of court personnel leaving the building for the day. I sneaked up the back staircase that led to the women's locker room hoping—no, praying—that it would be empty. I heard the bathroom door open.

"Ooh, girl, welcome back! Where you been at?" It was Josephine, the singing court officer. She broke into song whenever the spirit moved her. She had the gift of making the sun come out on the rainiest of days with her voice. I was relieved to see it was her.

"Hey, Miss Josephine. Just took some time off to chill," I lied. Bad news travels fast—it's one of the principle rules of physics. I knew she would be up on the latest court gossip, but I was able to relax a bit because Josephine was a very cool lady. Over the years, we'd had many a soulful talk and a lot of laughs together. I lay down on the locker room's ancient, cracked leather couch, feeling so drained that I didn't bother to check it for water bugs or spiders.

"Now you listen to me, Miss Mel! You got nothin', and I mean nothin', to be hanging your head about up in here. Praise Jesus, that good-for-nothing Casanova is gonna get his. Just you remember this: if the hat don't fit, it ain't cause yo' head's too big, you just gotta get a better hat, you hear?" she instructed.

"I hear ya. Thanks, Josephine," I said as I managed a weak smile. "You always know the right thing to say."

"Well, my momma didn't raise no fool! I feel some praise coming on." Josephine, in her strong contralto, broke into one of her daily supplications to the Lord, "How Great Is Your Glory."

"Do I hear an Amen?" she sang.

"Amen, Miss Josephine!" I answered.

"All right, then. Have a good night," she said as she walked out the door humming.

"You, too," I called after her. As she left the locker room my radio crackled.

"Unit 5 to Unit 7."

"Unit 7, go," I responded.

"Captain wants to see you in the office before he leaves."

"Got it. Over." My worst nightmare realized; the captain was checking up on me to see if I was still in one piece. I took the back elevator to the captain's office. As I approached, I lightly knocked on its paint-spattered window.

"Come in," boomed a male voice. Carefully closing the door behind me, I turned and saluted.

"Good evening, Captain Murphy."

"At ease, Morrison. I trust you had a nice vacation."

"It was fine, Captain, thanks for asking."

"Glad to hear it. I need someone in that part that doesn't have shit for brains."

He was putting me on notice not to melt down. "I can handle it, sir," I answered steadily. I stood in front of the captain's desk as though my feet were stuck in cement, staring at the wall, grateful for its effortless, dingy gray-green color.

Looking up from his newspaper the captain asked, "Anything else, Sergeant?"

I blinked, not knowing why I was still standing there. Maybe I was waiting for him to tell me to get on with the rest of my life. "No, sir," I answered.

"You're dismissed," he ordered.

He couldn't have been more right.

CHAPTER 15

The light on the answering machine was blinking; I half-heartedly hit the play button.

"Marian Elizabeth, this is your mother calling. I haven't heard from you in a while. Please return my call as soon as you get this message," she directed in her best "because I'm your mother and I said so" voice.

I exhaled a defeated groan. "Dear God," I prayed as I started dialing my mother's number, "please give me the strength to endure what surely will follow." Since my breakup with Ritchie, I had been avoiding the family. It was two weeks before Thanksgiving and I was facing yet another holiday season alone. I sat upright in my bed and determined to project a stolid comportment when she answered the phone.

"Hi, Ma, how are you?" I asked chirpily when she picked up. "Sorry I haven't called lately, but I've been kind of busy at work," I fibbed. She wasn't buying it.

"It's that Richard person, isn't it?" she asked with undisguised irritation. Even though I had not told my mother about his leaving me, I didn't have to. She possessed a radar-like ability to pick up on my unspoken misery.

"But you can call him Ritchie, Ma," I answered evenly, trying to keep emotion out of the conversation.

"What's going on, Marian Elizabeth?" my mother demanded.

"We broke up, Ma, that's what's been going on. Are you happy now?" I replied testily.

"My happiness has nothing to do with it, young lady. All those vowels in his name! I told you, but you wouldn't listen. You had to have it your way!" she remarked imperiously.

"And the names McNamara, Greeley and Scully, just to name a few, don't end with vowels?" I shot back, feeling a tad victorious.

"You always were a hard one, Marian Elizabeth. 'Stick with your own kind and you won't go wrong,' I told you. Isn't that what I said?" she parried.

"Are you saying Terry was right for me, Ma?" I replied in disbelief. There was a slight pause on the other end of the line, but it only took a second or two before my mother resumed her tone of upright indignation.

"I'm not saying anything of the kind. You know exactly what I'm talking about," she answered brusquely. I knew there would be no truce in this battle.

"Have it your way, Ma. Can we just get off this subject, please? I'm starting to get a headache. What else did you want to talk about?"

"Are you coming to your brother's for Thanksgiving?" she inquired. "He's offered to have it this year seeing as your sister is too far along to handle it." My little brother Brendan and his wife, Bernadette, had just bought a house and offered to have the holidays there seeing as Bonnie was about ten months pregnant with her first child, who was beginning to look like a Christmas baby.

"Yes, I'll be there," I answered, without much zeal.

"I'll need you to pick up your grandmother. Can you do that for me?" she asked.

"Of course I'll bring Grandma!" I replied without hesitation, my grim disposition brightening up a bit at the mention of her name. I so looked forward to seeing my grandmother; I could always count on her to help me clear a path through the thickets of my tangled states of affairs and get me back on the straight and narrow.

Thanksgiving Eve found me driving down the familiar roads to my grandmother's apartment. After my grandfather passed away, she sold the home they had shared for so long and moved into a beautiful assisted living facility. She was getting on in years and couldn't deal with the responsibilities of the house anymore. I suspected it may have had more to do with the absence of the man she had spent fifty years of her life with than the occasional leaking faucet. I visited with her regularly. I could talk to my grandmother in a way I never could with my mother. She had even met Ritchie once—he came with me on one of my visits and we took her out for dinner. I'll never forget how she flirted with him, showing him old photographs of herself as a young girl on the beach in her swim dress. Ritchie flirted right back. She didn't care a whit that he was Italian. I forgave Ritchie much for his good-humored indulgence of my grandmother's flight of fancy that day.

We had a routine on my visits that almost never varied: I would pick Grandma up precisely at eleven o'clock in the morning at her apartment (which was always as neat as a pin); that would give me enough time to get us to the eleven-thirty Mass exactly on time. With my grandmother, you got to Mass before the priest entered with the processional and didn't leave until after the Mass had ended. There was no skipping out of church after taking Communion, no sir!

Grandma wasn't a gossip by any means, but every now and then she would lower her voice and complain to me about Mrs. Greene next door and her habit of leaving her apartment door open for everyone to see; how she would prance around in her slip with her clothes lying about. "Doesn't the woman know what a hanger is?" Grandma would sniff.

We would attend Mass at her new church, Maria Regina, and afterward we'd enjoy a pleasant lunch at the local dinette. Grandma always ordered a BLT with extra mayo— and tea, of course. Then we would return to the assisted living facility where, weather permitting, we'd take a walk through the gardens, stopping to enjoy the beautiful flowers and reminisce. Today I met Grandma in the large reception area of the residence then walked her out to the car. I made sure she was buckled in before starting for Brendan's house.

"How are you feeling, dear? You look a little pale . . . your mother said you've been feeling a bit under the weather," she reported as she put on her gloves. Unlike my mother's propensity for calling me by my full Christian name, Grandma always called me "dear", another reason why I loved her so. She also had a gift for turning complicated matters into minor worries.

"I'm okay, Grandma, nothing for you to worry about," I assured her as I pulled onto the highway.

"I know this Ritchie business has been hard on you, dear. Promise me that you'll take care of yourself. You can't be getting sick on his account—that just wouldn't do," she tisked.

"Anything for you, Grandma, you know that. I just hope I don't leave this world without knowing the kind of love you and Grandpa had. He must have been so easy to love."

"And you're not? Don't be going daffy on me, young lady. Just so you know, your granddad was not always the sweet, silly man you came to know in his older years." She leaned closer to me and lowered her voice. "He could be quite the hellion when he had a pint or two in him!"

I looked over at my grandmother in amazement. My dear, sweet grandpa, a hellion?

"Grandma, what are you talking about? Are we speaking of the same person, James J. O'Brien?"

"Your granddad, God rest him, he once came home after a night at the bar and feeling no pain, I can tell you. I remember it like it was yesterday; your mother couldn't have been but two years old at the time. He got it into his head that something bad was going to happen to her. I tried to reason with him, but he wasn't having it. He walked right past me and went straight to her room to check that she was still alive, God help us! He told me that night that if anything were to happen to her, I might as well throw myself into the East River and be done with it and he wouldn't be running to fish me out. Imagine that!" She was shaking her head at the very thought of it.

"Wow!" I replied in astonishment. This most certainly was not a description of the grandfather I knew and loved.

"Indeed! But he calmed down as time went on."

"You didn't want to clobber him after a remark like that?"

"No, I was used to your granddad's ways by then. He would wake up the next morning, give me my kiss and be off to work as though nothing had happened. We married for life back then, dear, for better or worse. And I give him his due . . . he never put a hand to me or your mother, and he brought his paycheck home to me at the end of every week. A lot of women had it far worse, believe me. And we did love each other. Yes, your granddad was the love of my life."

"So, Grandpa was protective of Mom? When I look back, I guess they did seem pretty close," I observed.

"Ah, yes, dear, that they were. He took her everywhere with him. Sundays were special; we'd attend Mass together then come home for an early afternoon dinner. Afterward, while I sat down with a hot cup of tea and put my feet up, your granddad and mom would start out for Boland's Pub where they'd listen to the races from Santa Anita on the big radio there. He'd have his pint and she'd have her Shirley Temple cocktail, feeling very grown-up. In some ways, she was like the son he never had."

I'd forgotten about my grandfather's fondness for a good horse race. "Grandma, are you saying Mom was a tomboy? You're killing me here!"

"Yes, dear, that's exactly what I'm saying. It took me the better part of the morning to get your mother into a dress when the occasion warranted. She would rather have been climbing a tree than wearing a pretty frock."

"No way! I mean, she's so different from what you're describing to me. I can't picture Mom climbing a tree!" For the first time in my life, the thought occurred to me that perhaps my mother and I were not as different as I'd always believed.

"Well, dear, she did and then she grew up, met your father, and that was that," she replied in her staunchly unequivocal way.

I pondered how my mother went from being a tomboy who loved to climb trees to marrying my father with almost nothing going on in-between other than "growing up", as my grandmother put it. But that was my grandmother for you! I got a kick out of her matter-of-fact attitude toward life; nothing was ever that involved or needed too much explanation, and if it did, well, it was left for another time or wasn't discussed at all. I was beginning to see the bigger picture: three generations of women, all seemingly different but very much the same in so many ways. I sometimes preferred my grandmother's uncomplicated world view to the modern-day let's-talk-about-it-ad-nauseam approach to life's problems, or, as my late grandfather would put it, "Too much talk and not enough action."

"I think about Dad and Grandpa all the time," I sighed. "I miss them so."

"Well, at least we have our memories to hold onto, dear. Thank God for those."

"You know, Grandma, when you think about it, all we're really made up of is our memories. Aren't our lives built upon what we remember about the past, good and bad? What we said or did just a second ago is now only a memory, isn't it?"

Grandma had grown quiet. I glanced over at her, looking so tiny in the front seat of my Jeep. I could see that while I was waxing philosophical, my grandmother had left me to step back in time, to remember. I wanted her to come back to me, not to leave me, not even for a moment. I raised my voice a bit: "Grandma, how did you and Grandpa do it? Fifty years!"

She blinked, then adjusted the brim of her tweed hat. "We just did, dear, there was no trick to it. We got married, had children, and hoped for the best. And we prayed a lot."

"I pray a lot, Grandma—I say the rosary almost every day." Apart from Val, my grandmother was the only person I would talk to about Ritchie.

"I know you do, dear. You must never forget that the Blessed Mother is listening to your prayers and is always intervening on your behalf with the Lord. But you must learn to be patient and leave your cares in God's hands. He will answer them in his time, not in yours."

"I'm trying, Grandma. But it's hard—I'm so lonely sometimes."

"Now, now, then," she said as she patted my hand, "we'll be at your brother's house soon and we're going to enjoy a wonderful meal with the family and be merry, maybe even have a glass of wine or two. It's a party we'll be havin'!"

"I love you, Grandma."

"I love you too, dear."

CHAPTER 16

For most of my life I'd owned cats for the usual reasons: their independence, beauty, grace, and, of course, curiosity. They could also be quite affectionate when they chose to be. I loved the Timmeister and Keggers with all my heart and nothing, not even an adorable puppy, could change that. It wasn't that I didn't like dogs—as kids growing up we always had a dog. Our father believed his children should have a dog, that we would learn responsibility by taking care of one. Of course, as probably is the case in most households, it was mostly our mother who wound up taking care of the various dogs we owned over the years. I was familiar with the work that went into having a dog. They had to be walked and trained and picked up after and you couldn't pull an all-nighter or take a last-minute vacation with a dog at home. Dogs were a real commitment, almost like having a child. Cats were, well, easy.

A few days after Ritchie left, I took complete leave of my senses. I looked up pet stores in the Yellow Pages, found the nearest Puppy Palace, jumped in my car, and took off like I was late for a Beatles reunion concert—I literally ran into the store. I was desperate for some unconditional puppy love! And there they were, about a dozen of the cutest, tiniest creatures that God in his wisdom had ever put on this earth. While I was tempted to put them all in my car and damn the price (and my sanity), I spotted a small, fluffy, vanilla-and-black coated puppy in a cage overhead who was fending off the playful roughhousing of an even smaller Chihuahua. There was my Mac—it was love at first sight! I brought him home in his tiny dog carrier, along with bags of toys, treats, and the latest in puppy fashion. My Mac would be the best-dressed dog in the neighborhood! I even lucked out and found a little Irish sweater for him to wear in the cold weather.

As we entered my apartment, I slowly put Mac down on the living room floor so he could get to know his new home. He ran toward the Timmeister and Keggers who both leapt up on the kitchen counter to escape the strange new creature that had invaded their territory. He was a handful for such a little guy! Mac got into everything, and puppy poop was not the first thing I looked forward to cleaning up when I walked through the door after a long night at work. But the happy puppy kisses I was greeted with made it worth every second. I loved the little guy! It took a few days, but by the end of our first week together, along with the help of a small mountain of Wee-Wee Pads and my very understanding landlady, Mrs. Frasier, we became a family.

Mac is my best boy. He saved my life. He has slept next to me since day one and wakes me up in the morning licking my toes. When I talk to him, he looks intently into my eyes, trying hard to understand every word I'm saying—I'm sure he gets most of it. Besides being gorgeous, he's a genius. Everyone on the block loves the Macster. He has a wag of the tail for almost everyone we meet on our walks, but he'll give a low growl and the tail stops wagging if he smells trouble.

I remember as a child being told that there were no animals in heaven, that there was another place they went to when they died. I went to my mother, almost disconsolate. "How could that be?" I asked her tearfully. "Animals are innocent. They don't hurt anyone—they just love us," I cried.

My mother gave me a special gift that day. She replied adamantly, "Who told you such a thing? Why, of course there are animals in heaven! There were animals with the baby Jesus when he was born in the manger and there were animals in the Garden of Eden, so yes, animals go to heaven when they die, just like us," she averred.

As I grow older, I am reminded daily of how much of what I believed to be true and real just a few years ago is now questioned or proven false, or thought to be unfashionable. Sometimes I go to bed feeling that I know less than I did the day before. But I know one thing that will always be true, always be real, and his name is Mac.

CHAPTER 17

"**C**ome on, Mel, snap out of it! You've been hanging out with Mac for almost two months now. We've hardly seen you. How many times can you watch Groundhog Day with a dog?" Val asked.

Believe it or not, more than you'd think. Since the day Ritchie and I had our heart-to-heart (or rather, heartless-to-heartbroken) talk, my waking life had degenerated into the simple acts of getting out of bed, taking care of my furry family, slogging through work and coming home to do it all over again. And watching movies; lots and lots of romantic stories revolving around disastrous relationships that, through the course of all manner of highly improbable twists and turns, become miracles of true love. I couldn't watch enough of the stuff.

"Are you forgetting the kitties?" I reminded Val. "They love watching movies too, you know."

"Don't be such a smart-ass! I am not letting you stay home with the animals for the holidays, do you hear me?" she remonstrated. "We're just having family over, no biggie, and you're coming, even if I have to pick you up myself and drive you over here. George said he'll make the string beans just the way you like them." George was Val's boyfriend:

super guy, down to earth. She loves George and George loves her—really loves her. He even calls her on our girls' nights out just to make sure she's okay. Val met him on a singles cruise wherein I practically had to kidnap her to get her on the boat. Val cringed at the very idea of going. It turned out to be just another week at sea for me, but it was the luckiest thing she ever did.

God bless Val! She knew how hard it was going to be for me to face another holiday season alone. For the first time since my divorce, I had eagerly anticipated enjoying the holidays with my boyfriend at my side, a happy couple like any other, but our untimely break up put an end to those plans. Joining my family for yet another yuletide get-together by myself was more than I could bear. All three of my siblings were now married: Hugh and Kathleen were the proud parents of two beautiful children; my baby sister Bonnie was, at twenty-four years of age, happily married to Finbarr and pregnant with their first child. Brendan and his bride, Bernadette, were still honeymooning a year after their nuptials.

"I have to work Christmas Eve, Val, but thanks for thinking of me."

"Then how about stopping by before work, just for a little while?" Val asked with a hint of sadness in her voice.

I instantly changed my tone from sadness to gladness. "Yes, my friend, I can, and I will!" I couldn't stand to have my best bud feel down on my account.

"Great! See you then!" she replied happily.

A couple years ago, my brother Hugh and his wife, Kathleen, invited everyone to their new house upstate for Thanksgiving. It was a large, beautifully decorated home, with plenty of room for the ever-growing number of family and friends that had been invited to the festivities. Even though another year had passed, and I still had no significant other to enjoy the holidays with, I was nonetheless looking forward to seeing everyone and determined to have a good time. Since my divorce I had become, for all intents and purposes, my mother's table partner. My mother was a relatively young woman when our father died and still turned heads wherever she went. There had been much speculation about her intentions and no shortage of interest from the opposite sex, but she stated in no uncertain terms that no man could begin to fill my father's shoes and that she would remain his wife till the day she joined him in heaven. The clan still managed to enjoy the holidays despite the absence of our beloved father sitting at the head of the table. Besides, I couldn't have passed on the invitation even if I'd wanted to—I was put in charge of bringing the beverages.

That year had begun with me trying to recover from one post-divorce dating disaster after another and, as the holiday season approached, I was struggling to pull myself out of a particularly long dry spell. I thought I had seen it all, that I was well on my way to becoming a hardened warrior in the fight to find Mr. Right, but nothing could have prepared me for what was to come that Thanksgiving Day. On that sunny, chilly, late November afternoon I watched as couple after couple found their way to the festive table, a smile frozen on my face with the help of the half-bottle of wine I had already drunk, my eyes sparkling with the holiday spirit (or was it the champagne?). As I searched the table for my name card (my sister-in-law had become a stickler for dining protocol since moving into the manse), I noticed a man guiding a wheelchair-bound woman to the table. I found my place card; their seats happened to be next to mine. I had not met them before. I waited until the woman's wheelchair had been comfortably secured before I took my seat. Kathleen came over to the table and introduced us.

"Mel, these are our new friends, Nancy and Jeff. Nancy, Jeff, I'd like you to meet Hugh's big sister, Mel. They've helped us feel right at home here, Mel. We couldn't have asked for better neighbors!" she chirped. With the introductions taken care of, Kathleen sped away to wrest control of the kitchen from my mother. I was left trying to figure the Nancy and Jeff thing out, without much success.

"It's a pleasure to meet you, Mel," Jeff said as he stood up and offered his hand for a shake.

"Nice to meet you, too," I answered brightly as Jeff sat down and put his arm around the back of Nancy's wheelchair. "Have you guys lived in the area long?" I asked in a feeble attempt at small talk.

"As a matter of fact, I'm kind of new around here," Jeff replied.

"Jeff moved down here from Vermont just last Friday," added Nancy. "We were doing the long-distance relationship thing for a while, but those ten-hour car trips back and forth every weekend were killing us, so we decided, what the heck, we're in love so let's just take the leap!" she gushed.

I couldn't help but notice the light from the dining room chandelier dance on the surface of what appeared to be a large diamond ring on Nancy's unmoving right hand. I started to feel queasy, like the feeling I got that time in the seventh grade when some freak stuck a tampon in my three-ring binder that fell out onto the floor as I was sitting down to my desk. As I stooped to pick it up, Mr. Prendergast, our math teacher, stopped the class to ask me what it was. When I mumbled, "Nothing, Mr. Prendergast," he walked over to my desk and demanded I hand it to him—I guess he thought it was a crib note. He snatched the tampon from me and when he realized what it was, his face turned a bright scarlet red and he angrily ordered me to dispose of the wretched thing outside of the classroom—he might as well have been sending me to the guillotine. The muffled laughter from my classmates echoed behind me as I slithered to the outside hallway to find a proper receptacle for the offending object. I returned to class and crumpled into a tiny ball in my seat. It was that feeling again, the feeling of being humiliated and wanting to disappear into nothingness.

"Moving in with Nancy was the best decision I've ever made," Jeff continued as he smiled sweetly at his love. "I get to take care of her every day for the rest of my life," he said as he took a brush out of Nancy's purse and began to run it through her hair.

Jeff was not an unattractive man: slightly balding, fit, about six feet tall, bespectacled, nicely dressed. Nancy happened to be a very attractive forty-something blonde who, from what I could discern from Jeff's patiently loving attempts at feeding her, was apparently suffering from some sort of neurological disorder that had rendered her unable to move anything but her head. My eyes started to glaze over; I was having trouble making sense out of what I was seeing and hearing. My insides felt like they were being turned into mush by a sausage grinder, and it wasn't from drinking too much wine—I hadn't drunk enough. Trying to clear my throat, I choked out, "Ahem, Nancy, I hope I'm not being nosy, but are you and Jeff married?"

"You're not being nosy," she replied. " We love talking about it! Well, we haven't tied the knot yet, but we're hoping for a New Year's Eve wedding. We wanted to get ourselves settled into the house before making plans, but then we thought, why not New Year's Eve? Everything will still be decorated from the holidays. I bought the most beautiful dress! It's a stunning, low-cut black velvet number with just a hint of ivory lace at the cuffs. It's so exciting, isn't it, honey?" Nancy giggled with girlish delight, turning her head in Jeff's direction.

Jeff snuggled Nancy's ear. "I can hardly wait, love," he replied. Nancy beamed.

"Would you please excuse me? I left something in the kitchen," I mumbled as I gulped a large mouthful of wine and left the table to search out one of several of the upstairs bathrooms. Finding one, I ran for the toilet, hugged the bowl, and proceeded to vomit like I had invented vomiting.

Can't wait for Christmas . . .

CHAPTER 18

The winter after Ritchie left had been long and dreary. The holiday season held little joy for me, and spring fared no better—it was a wet and listless season. I wasn't looking forward to the warm weather the way I normally would. Val had started getting on my case—she was worried about me.

I had become very comfortable in my quiet life with my furry family. The only times I ventured out anymore were to hang with Val and George or attend the occasional family function—the very idea of having to head into the void again was almost too much to bear. I swore on my life after my depressing, anxious, loveless foray into the singles scene that I was finished—five years of torture was quite enough, thank you very much. Add to the mix the condition I was in over Ritchie's leaving and you had the recipe for one very messed-up lady. Val was only too happy to help me get on with things.

"Look, kiddo, this weekend you and I are going online and sending your fabulousness out into cyberspace," she informed me one day.

"Val, I really don't want to do this. What happened to fate? Besides, we did this back in the old days with the

121

personal ads, remember? It didn't get me anywhere and it's not how you hooked up with George," I protested.

"A new day has dawned, Mel. Internet dating is all the rage now! Do you know Cathy, the legal aid attorney?"

"Yeah, I know her, why?"

"Well, she met her husband online and now they're married with a new baby. And you know Steve, the tall, good-looking officer at the magnetometers? He met his fiancé online and they're getting married next year. Look, what have you got to lose? Just put it out there—you don't have to answer anything if you don't want to. If nothing else, it will help keep your mind off the dickhead," she commented.

"Don't call him that," I said defensively.

"Okay . . . how's shithead?" she replied.

"That's better," I retorted.

"All righty, then! Be at my house at 1 p.m. on Sunday. George will be watching the ball game, so we'll have the whole day to ourselves at the computer."

I dreaded the arrival of Sunday. When the big day came, I felt like I was being forced to walk through a plate glass window when I rang George and Val's doorbell.

"Hey, you made it! I'm so proud of you!" Val exclaimed as she gave me a reassuring hug.

"I need a drink," I replied dolefully.

Val was two steps ahead of me. "No problemo. The bloodies are in the fridge. Help yourself—I'm good," she said. Bloody Marys in hand, we set about the task of presenting that which was *moi* to the Internet dating community. "Don't put too much personal info out there," Val advised. "You want to leave something to the imagination."

"What should I say then? Should I mention what I do for a living?" I asked.

"I wouldn't at first . . . might scare the nice guys off and you don't want to attract any nut jobs. When in doubt, keep it simple," she proposed.

After hours of writing and rewriting, my profile came to read thusly: "My name is Marian Elizabeth Morrison but everyone calls me Mel. I'm thirty years old, divorced with no children. I have reddish-brown hair and green eyes, 5'5" tall and 125 lbs. I'm interested in meeting a nice guy for friendship, possibly leading to more; must like the Beatles, football, the beach, and old movies. A good sense of humor a plus." Not great, but not bad either. I posted a picture of myself taken at Tracy Lynn's house the summer before. I looked good—pretty, but not slutty. I wanted the right kind of guy to answer my profile: no more wife-beaters or skirt-chasers. The responses started coming in the following week and I waded through about ten of them before getting up the nerve to contact "Francis A. Brennan, but everyone calls me Frank."

He described himself thusly: "I'm single, thirty-one years old, approximately 5'8" and I have dark brown hair and blue eyes; weight, about 150 lbs. I love the outdoors and like to think I have a pretty good sense of humor. I enjoy all kinds of music, especially The Beatles. I'd love to take you to a nice restaurant for a delicious meal and good conversation." His picture seemed recent enough, given his age. Hmmm . . . blue eyes and NOT Italian. Oh well, I couldn't have everything. Besides, Francis looked pretty good: not exactly handsome but nice looking in a preppy sort of way. He wasn't as tall as I was used to, but tall hadn't gotten me very far. As Val would say, now was the time to think outside the box and go for something new! Taking a deep breath, I wrote Francis that I would very much like to get together and would like to call him to set something up. Dating Rule #1: never give a strange man your phone number and set up the meeting in a public place. Francis was more than happy to give me his number. I waited a couple of days—I didn't want to appear desperate. Finally, I got my Irish up and called; he answered his phone on the second ring.

"Um, Francis? This is Mel, Mel Morrison," I said, somewhat timidly. I had never called a man for a date before.

"Hi, Mel, how are you? I'm so glad you called!" Francis answered. He had a nice voice—friendly, yet masculine. "And, please, call me Frank."

"Okay, Frank it is! So, I was wondering, Frank, would you like to get together over coffee sometime?"

"That sounds fine, Mel. Where would you like to go?"

"There's a nice coffee shop downtown on Main Street, right next door to Conway's Jewelry Store. How does Saturday sound, say around 2 p.m.?"

"That's perfect! Would you like me to pick you up?" (Dating rule #2: you meet a strange man for coffee in broad daylight, drive to the meeting place in your own car, and you give your best friend all the details in case she doesn't hear from you by the end of the night.)

"No, thank you. Actually, I plan on doing some shopping in the area on Saturday so I can meet you there and that way you won't be inconvenienced. Does that sound okay?" That's good, Mel, gives the both of you some breathing room. You don't want to give the impression you suspect he might be an ax murderer.

"Sounds great, Mel. See you then!" he replied.

An unexplainable, yet pleasant, tingling sensation ran down my spine as we ended our call. For the first time in a very long while I felt the tiniest bit of hope creeping back into my soul. In spite of myself, I was beginning to look forward to meeting Mr. Francis A.Brennan.

CHAPTER 19

Over the course of the three years I spent surfing the singles scene, I met quite an interesting cast of characters; everyone had a game to play, a trick up their sleeve. A man you thought was a decent enough guy would turn into a would-be rapist at the end of your dinner date—I'm sure he wasn't planning on having a hefty dose of pepper spray for dessert! Another charming fellow who gave every indication that he was a single, hard-working man who just wanted to meet a nice woman was married with one kid and another on the way. Of course, you found out about that little white lie when one day you stopped in at a grocery store in the next town and ran into each other in the cereal aisle, he with his family in tow. I'd never seen a grocery cart piled that high take off as though being pursued by the police without at least dropping a loaf of bread—he must have had some practice.

One almost started to look forward to meeting the latest addition to the rogue gallery with a kind of morbid sense of anticipation—what would the BIG LIE be this time around? The "full" head of hair that could be combed with a toothbrush; the "stocky but toned" build that couldn't fit into the seat of an airplane if it was maneuvered in with a forklift; the "gainfully employed" gentleman who turned out to be the neighborhood bookie and carried a concealed weapon ("Hey! A guy can't be too careful, right babe?") Frank was going to be my swan song to the singles scene; I was going to hang ten for the last time. If Frank turned out to be just another jerk, I had determined to enter a convent.

I prayed like I hadn't done in quite some time that he might be the one—I wasn't sure if a nun's habit would be a good look for me. I had stopped going to Mass and saying the rosary for a while after the Ritchie debacle. I didn't think God could hear my cries for help while I was rotting away in that special hell reserved for dumped-on girlfriends. I prayed: "Blessed Mother, I know I haven't suffered as you did, but I have suffered an awful lot. I've been so lonely. I've been a pretty good girl. Doesn't that count for anything? I've offered my suffering up to you. All I'm asking for is someone to love and to be loved in return. I hope I'm not asking for too much. I want to keep believing that true love is possible. Thank you for all the blessings you have bestowed upon me and those I love. Amen."

Saturday finally arrived. I dressed casually in a nice pair of jeans and a plain white shirt, a navy-blue cotton sweater tied around my neck. I didn't want to appear like I was expecting anything special to happen—just meeting a friend for a cup of tea. I got to the coffee shop a little ahead of time, sat down with the paper and waited. I pride myself in always being on time; something to do with good manners, I suppose. I looked at my watch: ten minutes after two, then fifteen minutes after two. I started to get that uneasy, sinking feeling in my gut when, at two-thirty, a small, frail-looking man in a school varsity jacket walked into the shop looking around. I slumped down in my seat. Blessed Mother, please don't do this to me. A school varsity jacket? He said he was thirty-one years old!

As he came nearer to where I was sitting, I peeked over the top of my paper to get a better look at him. What fresh hell was this? Frank was a troll in a varsity jacket! His complexion had the color and texture of paste. What happened to his love of the outdoors? His eyes were sunken so far into his face that I could barely make out their color. He was, as far as I could tell, about as tall as I was and possibly weighed less—his clothes were hanging on him like a scarecrow's. As his myopic gaze continued to search the shop, I felt the familiar feelings of panic and nausea take hold of me as I tried to hide behind my paper, hoping beyond hope that he would think he had the wrong place, or that maybe he had been stood up. But, as I begged God to make me invisible, his eyes locked onto me and he quickly walked over to the table, hand outstretched.

"You must be Mel. Hi! I'm Frank . . . Frank Brennan. So sorry I'm late—hope you haven't been waiting long. I'm usually right on time, but I hit a little bit of traffic getting here. You know, I would've picked you out anywhere. You look just like your picture!" he said admiringly.

Why, you little shit! Whose picture did you send me, anyway—your cuter older brother? The one who loves the outdoors? The one who graduated from college? I had to get my head together—I couldn't believe this was happening to me. Very funny, Blessed Mother. I guess I hadn't suffered enough after all.

"Hi, Frank," I said with as much enthusiasm as I could muster, given that my breath had just been knocked out of me and blown clear to China. "No, I don't mind that you're late—it gave me a chance to read the paper. Please, have a seat," I said. Frank sat down opposite me and ordered a cup of coffee. "Just curious about something, Frank—didn't you say you were thirty-one years old?" I asked, careful to keep the sarcasm at bay.

"Yes, I'm thirty-one. Why do you ask?"

"Well, I guess the varsity jacket threw me a bit," I replied. The understatement of the year.

"Oh, right, the jacket. I never got rid of it. Sometimes I take it out of mothballs and wear it just for kicks," he said cheerily. I wanted to kick his ass.

"What sport did you letter in, Frank?" I queried. My guess was chess, or maybe he was named "Mathlete of the Year".

"I was the manager of my high school baseball team," he answered proudly. God, this just keeps getting better; it wasn't even a college varsity jacket! Maybe Frank thought the jacket was going to impress me. Guess again, Francis! I felt a little sorry for the guy—better than wanting to kill him.

I decided right there and then to ride out the storm, to let it take me where it wanted; kind of like a tornado picking up a mobile home, ripping it to shreds and dropping the flotsam halfway across the state. It couldn't get any worse.

"So, Mel, what do you do for a living?" Frank inquired, moving his seat in closer to mine.

"I'm a court officer assigned to criminal court, a sergeant, actually," I replied with one eye on the clock. This would normally be the turning point in the conversation: either my prospective date would make an excuse for having to cut our date short, or hang in for what they expected to be the ride of their lives.

"No kidding! So, you carry a gun?" he asked excitedly. It appeared Frank might be in the latter category.

"Yes, I do. Not right now, though," I responded with a forced chuckle. Lucky for him.

"That's wild! I've never dated a woman in law enforcement—it must be awesome! Do you like your job?" he asked eagerly. Here we go: he's turned on by women in law enforcement, has a great gun collection back at his house (would you like to come over later and check it out?) and loves dogs, especially pit bulls.

"As a matter of fact, I do—most of the time. Every job has its ups and downs, of course. So far, I guess I've been fortunate in that it's been a positive experience. I work with a lot of nice people and I've learned more than I ever bargained for. I'm one of the sergeants in the evening arraignment part that runs from 5 p.m. to 1 a.m., Monday to Friday. Would that be a problem for you, Frank, my working nights?" I asked, praying it would be exactly the turn-off I needed for a quick getaway.

"It wouldn't be a problem for me. You still have weekends off, right?" he asked eagerly.

I ascertained that Frank was a persistent fellow. "Yes, Frank, I usually do," I replied. I could see I wasn't getting a free pass on this one.

"Then it definitely wouldn't be a problem!" he said cheerfully.

"What about you, Frank? What do you do?" I inquired. He mentioned in his profile that he was a substitute teacher, but I was almost afraid to hear his answer.

"I'm in a transitional period right now," he responded as he shifted slightly in his chair. My eyebrows shot up. "I used to work on Wall Street as a trader, but I left two years ago to finish my teaching degree. I majored in Elementary Education with a minor in English Literature. I've been substitute teaching since graduation, but I'm keeping my fingers crossed that I get offered a permanent, full-time position for the fall semester," he said hopefully.

"That's quite a change, isn't it, Frank?" I asked. Yes, Mel, I used to make five mil a year, had a duplex on Central Park West and a home in the Hamptons, but now that I've met you, I've decided to put that all behind me and just be your average working stiff . . .

"I'd had every intention on finishing college, but somehow I got sidetracked," he replied. "I had a friend who got me a summer job running for a commodities firm on Wall Street and that was the end of college. I became a trader not too long after that. The money was too good to give up and the benefits weren't bad, either, and I'm not just talking about health insurance," he noted.

"Then what are you talking about?" I asked, my curiosity piqued.

"A lot of money attracts a lot of things: women, for one—drugs, for another. I was never a big drinker, but you know what they say, everyone's got their poison and cocaine was mine. I'm not using it as an excuse, mind you, but everyone, and I mean everyone, was doing it. That's where I really got into trouble. I want to be upfront with you, Mel, you know, before we go any further," Frank intoned earnestly.

"Please do," I agreed. By this point in the action, I had also ascertained that Frank was what one would call an optimist.

He took a deep breath. "I'm putting it all on the line here, Mel. The thing is, I got addicted to coke. Bad. That's the real reason I lost my job, and it probably had a lot to do with me and my girlfriend breaking up, but I just didn't want to believe it. You believe what you want to believe when you're using. Anyway, I've been working real hard to straighten out. I've been doing pretty well, but it hasn't been easy. I'd lost a lot of weight when I was using that I'm just starting to gain back. I don't have much money any-more—between finishing school and working as a substitute teacher, my bank account isn't what it once was. I drive a ten-year-old car and sublet a studio apartment. You must think I'm a total loser," he said, not taking his eyes off me, almost challenging me to take a chance with him.

His story explained a lot about his looks. The picture he included with his profile had obviously been taken before he plunged nose-first into his winter wonderland. I took a long, hard look at Frank and replied, "I think you're trying to level with me, and I appreciate it—believe me, I really do appreciate your being honest—it counts for an awful lot with me. But don't you think you could've been a tad more honest in your profile?" I asked.

"Would you have given me a chance if I was?" he countered.

"Right, stupid question," I replied, stating the obvious.

"You must have gotten a lot of responses to your profile. Can I ask what made you pick me?" he asked as he fiddled with his placemat.

I had to think for a moment. They were all similar, but his did stand out a bit among the others.

"My father's middle name was Francis and he had blue eyes," I said.

Frank seemed to be taken off guard at my response. "What do you mean, he *had* blue eyes?" he asked.

"My dad died when I was fourteen," I answered.

"Gosh, I'm really sorry to hear that. I can't imagine losing a parent so young," he responded empathetically.

"Yeah, it was a total bummer," I replied. It suddenly got very quiet at the table.

Frank softened his voice. "I hope I'm not going to upset you by this question, Mel, but it's important that I know the answer," he intoned earnestly.

"Go ahead, Frank, what do you want to know?"

"Were you completely honest in your profile?" The question didn't upset me, but it took me by surprise. I prided myself on being very honest, sometimes to my detriment.

"Yes, I was," I answered somewhat indignantly. "I didn't mention what I did for a living, but other than that, yes, I was completely honest. Trustworthiness is very important to me. Are you trustworthy, Frank?" I retorted.

"I'd like to think so. I've never hurt anyone, at least not intentionally," he answered. Frank paused briefly, then continued. "After everything I've told you, I wouldn't blame you if you got up and left right now, but I hope you'll stay. I'm having a really nice time talking with you, better than I've had in a long time. Hey, are you hungry?" he asked. The course of our conversation took an abrupt turn. "Would you mind having dinner with me? All this talking has made me as hungry as a horse!" Frank exclaimed as he picked up a menu.

"Sure, I could use a good burger," I replied. It wasn't like I had anything else to do. I had to eat and I guessed it was probably a good sign that he had an appetite—it backed up his story a bit. Truth be told, I was beginning to enjoy our little get-together. Once we let our guards down, we recounted the abridged versions of our life stories. Frank had even gone to Catholic school! We had a few laughs over that one.

"Come on, Mel. You have to admit those nuns were a pretty nasty bunch. I could call them something else, but I'm in the company of a lady," he observed as he nodded his head in my direction.

"How very cordial of you, Frank, but I have a slightly different take on it. Agreed, there were those nasties here and there that bordered on psychotic, but could you blame them? While the priests were living in the lap of luxury and being wined and dined by the parish elite, those poor women were toiling day after day for pocket change, educating the masses, serving the poor, and what was their reward? Kneeling on a cold marble floor at the end of an exhausting day to give thanks for their blessings. Most of them were saints, if you ask me."

"You know what? You've got a point—I never thought of it that way. But my ear is still ringing from the slap I got from Sister Rosalind twenty years ago!" he said as he put his hand to his ear as though reliving that awful event.

"No offense, Frank, but I'm thinking you probably had it coming!" I teased.

"Yeah, I was a kind of a smart-ass in school," he admitted. "You know, sometimes I miss the old days," he said with a touch of nostalgia in his voice.

"Me, too," I sighed wistfully.

Before we knew it, the shop was closing for the evening—we had been talking for almost three hours! Our waitress came over to the table; she was about seventeen years old, a cute kid. "Need anything else, guys? We're getting ready to close up," she advised us.

Frank asked me if there was anything more I needed—I told him I was good. "No, thank you, miss. Could we have the check, please?" When Frank first suggested we have dinner I agreed, as long as it was understood that I paid my own way. In any event, I knew substitute teachers didn't make much money, and I didn't want him to feel obligated. But, as soon as the check hit the table, he grabbed it out of my reach.

"Frank, I thought we had a deal about splitting the check," I said firmly.

"What can I say? That's how I was raised. If my dad caught me taking money from a woman, he'd have my head."

"Well, far be it for me to second-guess your father, but I absolutely insist on leaving the tip."

"All right, you can leave the tip—just don't tell my dad."

"Agreed! This was fun. Thank you, Frank," I said with a smile.

"I assure you, the pleasure was all mine," he replied, smiling back.

When the waitress returned to our table she said, "Can I ask you guys a question?"

"Sure, as long as you're not going to ask me how old I am," I jested.

"No way! I know better than that—my mom hates that question, too!" she answered. I looked at her askance—how old did she think I was, anyway? "I was wondering, how long have you guys been married? I mean, you look like you've been together forever, and you seem to have so much fun. I don't see that too much around here."

Blushing slightly, I looked over at Frank and without missing a beat he answered, "To tell you the truth, it feels like we just met!"

Okay, Mel, he might not be James Darren, but give the guy a break—with a line like that he deserves a second chance; in fact, he was beginning to grow on me. As we left the coffee shop, me in my jauntily tied sweater and he in his varsity jacket, we stopped at my car.

"I hope I didn't embarrass you too much back there," Frank apologized.

"Nothing I can't handle. It was kinda sweet, actually," I replied.

"I had a great time tonight. Can I see you again, Mel?"

"Sure. Give me a call during the week," I said as I wrote down my number. "We'll figure something out."

With a smile that could light up a Christmas tree he replied, "Awesome! I'll call you on Wednesday!"

He opened the car door and took my arm as I dropped into the seat. He didn't make any moves on me, not even an attempt at a goodnight kiss. I liked it—it was old-fashioned. I missed old-fashioned; courtesy and respect, good manners, they were fast becoming dinosaurs in the world I lived in. I often felt as though I had been born in the wrong century, that perhaps the eighteenth century would have been a better fit for me. As I drove away watching Frank in my rearview window, waving goodbye, I hoped I was doing the right thing by agreeing to see him again. I wasn't convinced that my broken heart had completely healed. I wouldn't put my worst enemy through what Ritchie had put me through, never mind a nice guy like Frank. But, as Val would often remind me, it was time to rejoin the world of the living.

First thing Sunday morning, the phone rang—it was Val calling. I picked up the receiver, trying to shake off the early morning fugglies.

"Are you up yet? I couldn't wait! How'd it go?" she asked excitedly. Shifting my weight, with Mac nestled snuggly against my side, I tried to pry open one eye to see the time on the alarm clock. Sundays were sacred; no one, not even Val, was supposed to invade my space this early on Sunday morning. I glanced at the clock—it was only seven thirty!

"Geez, Val what gives? You know I need my beauty sleep," I whined.

"I was worried sick! You didn't call last night. Didn't you check your answering machine?"

"Oh, no! I forgot—I'm sorry. I was kind of tired when I got home and went straight to bed. Didn't get much sleep, though . . . had one of my nightmares again. Forgive me?"

"Those damn dreams! You've gotta get some therapy. Okay, I'll let you off the hook this time, but call me back as soon as you're awake," Val instructed me.

I was still groggy but afraid to go back to sleep. "To sleep, perchance to dream." Isn't that what Shakespeare wrote? He must never have dreamt of the undead. I managed to fall back asleep for a little while. When I woke again at nine, I dialed Val's number, knowing she had been downing cup after cup of coffee in anticipation of hearing my recount of the previous day's events. "Otay, Panky, regale me!" she ordered when she answered the phone.

Yawning, I replied, "Well, he seems like a nice guy. Not exactly my type, but not bad, either. We had some laughs over dinner. Actually, it turned out to be a really nice evening," I replied nonchalantly.

"I thought you said you were just meeting him for coffee."

"That was the plan, but it wound up being dinner as well. It was fine. We have tentative plans to meet again next week."

"And?"

"And what?"

"You know what! How was IT?" Val demanded.

"Jesus, Mary, and Saint Joseph! Why are you assuming we did anything? Can't we just have had a pleasant evening and be done with it? And you of all people should know my rules about dating!" I admonished Val.

"I get confused, Mel. Is that date rule #2 or #3?" she retorted.

"Ha, ha, Val, you're killing me – you're such a comedienne. By the way, it's rule #3," I pointed out.

"You mean you didn't do anything? Not even a good night kiss?" she persisted.

"No, Sherlock, we didn't. And it was, in fact, rather nice—no pressure."

"And you still want to see each other again?" she asked in disbelief.

"Yes, we're planning on seeing each other again soon. You can rest easy now, okay?" I reassured her. Val had slipped into big sister mode and I didn't want her to worry unnecessarily.

"I'm proud of you, Mel. Sounds like you handled everything beautifully. Say . . . isn't there a saint in your arsenal that you can pray to for impossible causes?"

"So, I've become an impossible cause now?"

"Oh, come on, buddy, don't be that way—you know what I mean. What could it hurt?"

"You're right, Val, I'm being too sensitive. Let me think . . . I could be wrong, but if memory serves, I believe it's St. Jude."

"Well then, Mel, put those hands together and get going. This one sounds promising!"

"I'm praying, sister, I'm praying!" I averred.

The night before, I'd had one of my vampire dreams. In this nightmare, Ritchie stood at the head of a pack of demons flying closely overhead, fierce and unrelenting in their pursuit. Terrified, running for my life, I cried out to him, "I beg of you, Ritchie, leave me in peace. Please don't let me suffer anymore!" Swiftly and silently he descended upon me, enveloping me, suffocating me. I awoke to the eerie quiet of my darkened bedroom in a cold sweat, shaking. I reached for my rosary on the night stand and prayed to be delivered from the purgatory where my troubled memories of Ritchie Gianelli dwelt.

CHAPTER 20

Frank called on Wednesday, just as he said he would—that scored quite a few points with me. How many hours had I wasted over the years in anxious anticipation of the all-important follow-up phone call from a prospective beau that never came? Too many to count. We both had family commitments scheduled for that Saturday that couldn't be ignored, so we made plans for Sunday. The weatherman reported a seasonably warm June day for Sunday, and knowing Frank didn't have a lot of money to spend I suggested going to a street fair that was being held not too far from my apartment. He had readily passed dating rules one and two, so I agreed that he could come to my apartment to pick me up. This time he wasn't late—that put a few more points on the old scoreboard!

When I answered the door, Frank handed me a hand-picked bouquet of flowers and gave me a chaste kiss on the mouth. *What a difference a week can make!* I thought to myself as he walked through the door. He looked good . . . different somehow. He appeared to have filled out a bit and looked taller, his back straighter; he was wearing a nice pair of jeans with a blue-and-white-striped oxford shirt and a navy blue blazer, which brought out the beautiful blue color of his eyes. His once-pasty complexion now radiated some life. I hadn't noticed the week before what a beautiful smile he had; I think I was too distracted by the varsity jacket, which he had, thankfully, not worn for this date.

"Hi, Frank! I hope you didn't have any trouble finding a parking spot. The flowers are beautiful, thank you. Come on in," I said as I opened the large mahogany door.

"Hi, Mel! Hey, nice place you've got here," he said approvingly as he glanced around. "I didn't have a problem with parking at all—it's a nice day out so I road my Harley here."

I looked askance at this new and improved Frank Brennan—did I hear him right?

"You ride a Harley?" I asked.

"Yeah, sometimes—why?"

"I don't know—you didn't seem the type to me when we met last week and you didn't mention it."

"Well, I guess you didn't have me all figured out, then," he answered as a sly smile crept across his boyish face.

I smiled back. It felt good to smile again. All at once, a ball of white and black fur scurried into the room.

"And this must be Mac!" Frank exclaimed. I had described my four-footed family on our first meeting. Mac came running out of the bedroom where he had been taking a nap. With his little legs pumping he ran up to Frank, tail wagging and holding his favorite toy in his mouth, begging Frank to play with him.

"He's a cute little guy," Frank said as he threw the toy squirrel across the room, Mac running off in hot pursuit of his prey.

"That's my Mac—he's the best!" I said proudly as he came running back to Frank with the squirrel, dropping it at his feet. Frank picked him up and Mac licked is face.

"Doggy kisses—I love 'em!" Frank laughed. The cats, Timmeister and Keggers, came out from their usual hiding place behind the sofa to inspect the new human in the house.

Cautiously, they came over to where Frank was standing, sniffed him, then began to rub up against his denim-clad legs. "You've got quite a menagerie here, Mel!" he observed.

"Oh, God, I forgot about the cats! You're not allergic, are you?" I asked, a tad apprehensively. I was desperate for love, but not so desperate as to give my precious pets away for anybody.

"No, it's fine, I like cats—I grew up with cats in the house," he answered. "I'd have one now, but my place is real small and I'm gone too much. It wouldn't be fair to them, you know?" he remarked as he scratched them behind their ears.

"Well, how about that! They aren't usually this friendly with people they don't know. In fact, they can act like a couple of cowardly lions when it comes to meeting strangers," I said as I thought back to the first time Ritchie stayed at my apartment; the cats didn't come out of hiding for almost two days and pretty much ignored him the rest of the time. The feeling was mutual; Ritchie tolerated them for my sake but there was no love lost between them. This time around, I would pay closer attention to my cats' behavior. So far, Frank was passing with flying colors!

"Would you like to take the tour?" I asked. I loved to show off my apartment and was proud of the work I had put into the place. I scoured every decorating magazine I could get my hands on for new ideas and had been known to spend a whole weekend plastered to the home channels, the occasional drop of spittle gracing my gaping maw as I sat mesmerized by the latest trends in architectural fashion and design. I would sometimes dream of the day I would walk through the large glass doors of the courthouse for the last time and retire to my new career as an interior designer.

"Sure, I'd love to. By the way, I wanted to tell you that you look real nice, really pretty," he complimented.

"Thank you," I shyly replied. Today I had put some extra effort into my appearance and I guess it showed. "You're looking very debonair yourself, Frank." We looked at each other and smiled. It was going to be a good day.

"Right this way, Mr. Brennan," I instructed, leading him into the living room for the first leg of the tour. As we continued through the rest of apartment, I was careful to point out the original glass chandeliers, the floor-to-ceiling windows, the oak floors, the brass fixtures; then I introduced him to my pride and joy, the marbled fireplace. He was duly impressed.

"You've got a great place here; big rooms, lots of light—and check out that fireplace!" Frank remarked approvingly.

"Yeah, these old brownstones are a treasure. I feel so blessed to be living here," I replied as I quickly checked the time—it was already one o'clock. "Well, I guess we'd better be going," I said as I hugged my little tribe and promised not to be home too late. I grabbed my keys as Frank and I left to embark on our first official date.

We leisurely strolled to the avenue where the fair was being held; as we walked, we began to open up more about our pasts. I asked Frank how he had made it all the way to the age of thirty-one without getting married.

"It went by so fast, Mare—I mean, Mel," he quickly corrected himself as his face turned red.

"I'm sorry, did you just call me 'Mare'?" I asked.

"Yes, and I apologize. It's just that I have a habit of making nicknames for people and you're too pretty to be a Mel—that's a guy's name. Marian is beautiful, so I shortened it to Mare. I'm sorry if I stepped out of line."

"No, no, don't apologize. It's just that I've never been called Mare before, that's all," I replied as I silently counted all of the names I'd acquired thus far: Marian, Elizabeth, Bridget (my confirmation name), Morrison, Sarge, Mel, and now Mare. What harm would there be with one more name added to the list? I decided to find it charming.

"It's okay by me," I reassured Frank. "So, you were saying that things went by so fast?" I prompted him.

"Right, where was I? Okay . . . remember I told you I worked on Wall Street? Well, after I was there for a while, I started dating a stockbroker—her name was Donna. God, I was crazy about her! We got really involved, to the point of looking at engagement rings. I thought we were in love."

"What happened?"

"The usual story: boy meets girl, boy loses girl," he replied off-handedly.

"That's it? That's the whole story?" I carefully pressed him.

"No, nothing is that simple, unfortunately. You know, it's weird—it's been almost two years and I'm still a little uncomfortable talking about it," he said awkwardly.

"I understand," I replied consolingly. This was obviously a touchy subject for Frank. "We can talk about something else if you want."

"No, that's okay . . . I want to talk about it," he said as he straightened up, moving his head back and forth around his shoulders as though preparing for a body blow. "Donna and I had been going out for almost a year. I thought she was my dream girl and I thought she felt the same way about me. I came home from work one day real excited—I'd bought the ring Donna said she liked and planned on proposing to her that night over a fancy dinner at her favorite restaurant. It sounds a little hokey now, but I even had the waiter in on it. He was going to make a special desert for her that I could place the ring on, you know, to showcase it when I proposed. Then just like that, out of left field, Donna comes home that night and tells me she's leaving me for another guy—some big shot with a seat on the stock exchange. I couldn't believe it! Here I was all ready to ask Donna to marry me and she was already hooked up with another guy! What the hell was I thinking? She was way out of my league. What made me think she would settle for someone like me? Must have been the cocaine convincing me I was something I wasn't. Anyway, they got married six months later. I read all about it in the society page in the *Times*. That's when I really started going downhill with the drugs," Frank admitted.

"Do you still have feelings for her?" I asked. I was starting to like Frank and I was determined to sniff out any suppressed emotions he might still have for his ex. I wasn't about to walk into that minefield again. At least I knew that Frank wouldn't have to worry about me going back to Ritchie; in spite of the long shadow our failed love affair had cast over my heart, if nothing else, my pride would have stopped me from ever taking him back had he attempted a reconciliation.

"I wouldn't be here with you if I did, Mare. Nope, that train has left the station," he answered with such finality in his voice that I had to believe him . . . it was a good feeling.

"As I mentioned when we talked last week, I've been working toward obtaining a full-time teaching position so that I can make some decent money. Now that I'm almost there, wanting to share my life with someone special has become important to me again. What about you, Mare? What's your story? You seem like the kind of girl who'd be settled down with a couple of kids by now."

"What makes you say that, Frank?" I asked curiously.

"I'm not sure—there's just something about you," he replied with a shrug.

"Is that good or bad?" I persisted.

Frank chuckled. "Definitely a good thing. But seriously, why are you still unattached?" he asked again. I hadn't told him about Ritchie when we first met. He only knew about my marriage and divorce, and I'd made that story as short and sweet as I could. I'd admitted to him that I was more relieved than sad when Terry and I broke up; there was no affection between us in the end, not even friendship—just hard feelings. I didn't quite know what to say about Ritchie and me; it was less than a year since we'd parted company and some wounds take a long time to heal.

"Looks like we have something in common, Frank. I was living with my boyfriend for a while—Ritchie, that's his name. He's a sergeant in the courts also. I thought we had the whole relationship thing nailed; neither one of us was into marriage—we'd both been through nasty divorces and weren't thinking that way. I thought things were going great, that I'd finally gotten it right. He was so different from my ex—he wasn't abusive, for starters. And it wasn't all bad; we had some really good times together. Ritchie had some very attractive qualities, and he had this unbelievable energy! I don't know . . . looking back on it, maybe I fell for him because I thought different would be better, but it wasn't. It was just different. My ex abused me and Ritchie cheated on me. And that's all, folks!" I whooped, trying to make light of the subject.

"Ouch! You're one tough lady! When Donna left me, I was almost destroyed!" he remarked, somewhat aghast at my blithe demeanor.

"Well, it sure hasn't been the easiest thing I've ever had to deal with, but it's kind of how I was raised, you know?"

"No, I don't know—tell me," he prompted.

"It's just the whole 'Tough Mick' thing," I said. Frank nodded his familiarity with the concept. "When my dad died I was only fourteen years old. I had to help take care of my younger brothers and sister, help my mom. Not that I minded," I added quickly. "I love my family. But I missed out on a lot."

"Like what?"

"Like just being allowed to be a normal teenager. My closest friends, almost everyone I knew, in fact, were dating from the time we started high school. Their parents allowed them to hang out, usually at each other's houses, go to the co-ed dances, things I couldn't do until I was a junior. It was innocent stuff, but my mother had this notion that any time we were out together we were planning orgies or something. What a laugh! Most of us were still virgins when we graduated. By the time I had my mom's permission to date, my friends had the whole boyfriend-girlfriend thing figured out. And they knew how to be friends with boys—I didn't. I always thought they were just trying to get me to fool around with them."

"Why did you think that?"

"I don't know, exactly. But I can remember one time, I think I was about fifteen years old, and I was sitting on our front porch keeping an eye on my little sister when a guy I knew came walking down our street. He was a year ahead of me in school, a nice guy. He walked over to me, just to say hello and shoot the breeze. My mother came to the front door and said in a voice that could make your hair stand on end, "Marian Elizabeth, come in the house, NOW!" He looked at me as if to say, "What was THAT all about?" Of course, I did as I was told, almost dying from the embarrassment. I don't want to sound like sour apples, but I think my mom put the idea into my head that I attracted the wrong kind of attention, if you know what I mean," I lamented.

"Speaking for the guys, Mare, it couldn't have been easy behaving around you! Maybe your mom thought she was protecting you," Frank suggested.

"I don't know—it never felt that way to me. She was always scrutinizing me for no reason," I replied. At that moment, a terrible, humiliating memory that I'd buried for years finally crawled to the surface of my conscious mind. At first, I thought it too embarrassing to discuss with Frank, but I so desperately wanted to finally tell someone that I took a chance; he possessed a certain kindness that I found quite comforting. "I've never told this to anyone before, Frank, but I'd like to tell you," I confessed.

"Please, Mare, go ahead and tell me—you seem very upset right now and I promise that I will take whatever you entrust me with to my grave," he vowed.

"Well . . . okay," I replied haltingly. "I'm not comfortable admitting this, but I started to develop physically at a very early age; by the time I turned twelve, I was constantly being made fun of by the boys at school. None of the other girls looked like I did and it was so embarrassing always being different—in that way, especially—I hated it! And it was presenting a lot of other problems for me—I didn't want to go to gym class anymore, if you catch my drift," I said.

Frank nodded his empathy. "Where was your mom in all this? Isn't this something she would have discussed with you, especially as it was causing you problems at school?" he asked.

"That's just the thing. She never discussed anything with me. There was an unspoken line that you just didn't cross when it came to anything involving the physical. I didn't know who to turn to—I had no older sister or aunt that I could go to for advice, so I had to take matters into my own twelve-year-old hands."

"What did you do, Mare?" Frank asked with concern.

"I took my babysitting money and went to the local five-and-dime store where they had bras for teenagers and picked one out that looked like it would fit me, then went home and tried it on. I was so happy when it did—I thought my problems would go away then, but was I in for a rude surprise!" I quipped.

"What happened next?"

"That same day my father was working, so my mom invited our grandparents over for dinner. After we all sat down at the table and started to eat, my mother looked over at me and said loud enough for everyone to hear, "Marian

Elizabeth Morrison, who gave you permission to go out and buy that bra? You go to your room and take it off this instant!" I almost died from humiliation—my poor grandparents didn't know which way to look. I got up from the table and ran upstairs to my room. I never wanted to be seen in public again after that," I sadly reminisced.

"Gee, I don't know what to say, Mare. That's just plain awful! What could your mother have been thinking?" he asked as he shook his head in disbelief. Then he continued: "In no way am I trying to excuse what your mother did that day, but maybe, in her old-school way of thinking, she didn't want you to grow up too fast. Just a thought," Frank added warmly.

"Maybe you're right. And, anyway, I don't think it matters anymore. I haven't had the leisure time to tend to my own heart, it seems," I reflected pensively.

Frank attempted to disarm the darkened mood of the conversation. "You know, Mare, if you resemble your mom at all, there must have been plenty of men lining up outside her door after your dad died. How come she never remarried?" he asked lightly.

"My mother? Get married again? It's more likely that a cow will actually jump over the moon!" I joked. "My father's a saint in her eyes. Honestly, though, it's hard for me to picture my mother with another man. Want to know something, Frank? Now that I'm talking about it, I guess those years did toughen me up a bit. I don't think I'd be too good at my job if I was a wuss," I ruminated.

"I hear you. I always joke that my father was just slightly to the left of Attila the Hun when I was growing up. He was hard on me, too, especially when it came to school, but I survived. Your mom sounds like a tough nut, too."

"She is that!" I concurred. "But I have some good memories of those years. My mother was the one who bought all the Beatles' albums for me when they came out. My father had no use for them; he thought they were bringing about the decline and fall of Western civilization! And when my father had to work nights, my mother would let me stay up late with her watching old movies on TV."

"Hence, your love for the Beatles and old movies," Frank accurately observed. I had forgotten that I put that in my profile.

"Enough about my sordid past, Frank, what about your family?" I inquired.

"They're good—they're still living in the Bronx. My dad just retired after teaching for the past thirty-five years in the city school system," Frank answered proudly, the look on his face reflecting his admiration for his father.

"And now you're following the same path," I noted.

"Looks that way—much better than the road I was traveling down before, wouldn't you agree?" he asked.

"You made the right choice, Frank. I think you'd be great with kids!" I observed.

"Yeah, I'm glad now that I chose elementary education—I like the little buggers. I've found out since substitute teaching that it's a hell of a lot easier teaching third graders than teenagers, that's for sure."

"Do you have any brothers or sisters?" I inquired.

"I have a younger brother, Marty. He's doing great! We're only a year apart in age so we're pretty tight. I keep a close eye on him. I told him I'd kick his butt from one end of the city to the other if he messed up. He finished school on time, has a good job, he even has a steady girl. Ha! Maybe he should have been kicking *my* butt!" he laughed out loud.

We stopped for a moment. The summer wind kicked up, blowing the hair from my face. Frank ran his fingers through the errant strands, his hand lingering on my cheek as he did so. He put his arm through mine as we continued our walk.

"It's sad, isn't it?" I rued. "My grandparents were married over fifty years when my grandfather died. I'm certain my parents would still be together if Dad hadn't passed away—they'd be married thirty-one years. I once asked my grandmother what their secret was and she looked at me like I had two heads. She said, 'There is no secret, dear, that's the secret.'"

"What do you think she meant by that?" Frank asked.

"That you can't out-smart love; you can't make it happen just because you want it to. I think the best you can hope for is that someday love finds you and sticks around for the ride."

"Your grandmother sounds like a very wise lady. I'd like to meet her someday."

"Maybe you will, Frank."

"By the way, Mare, why do you use the nickname Mel? Your real name is beautiful; old-fashioned maybe, but beautiful just the same. Did your parents name you after Maid Marian?"

"Funny that you'd pick up on the Maid Marian thing," I noted. In fact, I was impressed!

"Don't forget, I'm an English teacher, among other things," Frank reminded me with a playful nudge.

"Well, the story goes that my dad was a huge Robin Hood fan, and when I was born he insisted on naming me after Maid Marian, much to my mother's strenuous objections. She said the name wasn't acceptable because it wasn't Irish. But Dad was standing firm so Mom agreed as long as she got to pick my middle name, Elizabeth."

"Are you referring to Henry the VIII's daughter, Queens Elizabeth the First? I don't recall the history books exactly giving her kudos on her relationship with Ireland!" Frank exclaimed.

"No, no," I laughed. "Mom figured she'd get Dad to change his mind when she told him she was going to name me after her favorite movie star, Elizabeth Taylor, whom my dad couldn't stand."

"Her reverse psychology didn't work then?"

"Obviously not. My parents were both thick as mules, so the name stood. Anyway, a kid in grammar school started calling me Mel and it's stuck ever since, just not with my mom, who's always called me by my full name. It drives me crazy."

"Maybe that's why she does it."

"I don't think so. I think she likes the formality of it, or maybe it just reminds her of my dad and his head-strong ways."

"I really hope you don't mind me calling you Mare. It just kind of slipped out and it felt right."

"I don't mind at all, Frank. It's a nice change from Mel, actually."

"You know, I think we've done all right for ourselves, Mare. We're both healthy and it's not like we're living on the streets. Hopefully, I'm going to be a full-time teacher soon and you've got a good job that you love. I always tell myself that things could be worse," Frank observed.

"I tell myself that too!" I said in agreement.

"Well then, I guess great minds do think alike!" he responded with a warm smile. I was beginning to find Frank's smile very inviting.

We walked some more then decided to stop at a charming neighborhood café to get a bite to eat. Frank pulled out my chair and held it for me as I sat down. He ordered a cheese and bread selection and a bottle of white wine. I sipped my drink, relaxing in the ivied and brick ambiance of the restaurant, taking my measure of Frank. I had never dated a man like him, yet he seemed so familiar to me. I was enjoying the day, enjoying being in his company. It wasn't like being with Terry; Frank was a light drinker and would never hit or abuse a woman, of that I was sure. And while we hadn't known each other very long, I was certain that, unlike Ritchie, lying and cheating weren't his forte. He had gone through a bad spell and was coming out of it on the right end of things, and that took courage. I admired Frank for that.

I decided right there and then to go in a new direction: I was going to become a friend to Frank, a true friend, and give our relationship a chance to grow into something strong and real before becoming lovers, if that's where things were headed. I thought of the successful relationships I knew: Val and George, my parents, my siblings and their spouses, my grandparents; their love for one another had not only made life worth living, but it helped them survive the hardships and disappointments of daily life and it all hinged on the friendship that anchored their love. I looked at Frank and wondered what he was thinking. Did he feel as I did? His heart had been broken, too. We finished our meal and Frank asked for the check. This time, I didn't offer to chip in.

"It's still early, Mare. Do you want to get an espresso? I know a nice place just around the corner."

"The whole day has been wonderful, Frank, but I'm afraid it's got to be an early night for me."

"Why?" Frank asked, sounding disappointed. "I thought you didn't have to go to work tomorrow until five."

"I'm not working tomorrow—I have to go to requal."

"What's requal?"

"That's court officer lingo for firearms requalification. Once a year we have to go to the range to requalify on our firearms to make sure our guns are in working order and that we still know how to use them."

"It's hard for me to picture you with a gun in your hand—you're too pretty. You only have to go once a year?"

"That's the official requirement for the job, but I like to go a few times a year to a range out on Long Island for extra practice. Most court officers will never have to take their guns out of their holsters except to requalify, but you never know. I'm friends with the owner, Pistol Pete, and he gives me ammo at no charge. I qualify as a sharpshooter now, but I'm hoping to make it to expert this time around. We'll see what happens tomorrow. Wish me luck!"

"Good luck, Mare! It's nice to know I'm dating someone who can protect me from the bad guys."

"Funny thing . . . I've been looking for that person most of my life, too," I replied quietly.

Frank took my hand in his. "Don't worry, Mare. I'll protect you," he promised.

Frank and I walked back to my apartment and lingered in the doorway, a soft light shining on us from the street lamp. I didn't invite him to come in. It had been a perfect day: no drama, no unfulfilled expectations – just a very pleasant time spent with a very nice guy. It was not at all like what I had ever experienced before with a man. I wanted to go to sleep that night taking it all in, making sense of it.

Frank asked, "May I kiss you good night, Mare?" I couldn't believe my ears—he was asking my permission to kiss me. No lunging, no grappling! Without answering him, I moved closer and offered my lips to his. Fireworks didn't exactly light the dark sky over our heads and bells didn't peal, but it sure felt good.

Frank held me tight, not letting me go. He whispered, "I think I'm falling in loke with you, Mare."

I pulled away from him. "What in the heck is loke?" I asked with a quizzical look.

Pulling me back into his warm embrace, Frank explained: "It's a word I invented. 'Loke' is a feeling somewhere between like and love. I loke you—a lot," he said, his blue eyes twinkling mischievously.

I started to giggle. "You're a funny guy, do you know that, Frank? I loke that in a man."

"I'll take that as a compliment," he said. Suddenly, his voice took on a more serious tone. "Mare, I want you to know that I'm not looking at this as a short-term affair. I care about you and I'm ready for the real thing, do you understand what I'm saying?" he asked.

I smiled at Frank and kissed him again. The real thing.

CHAPTER 21

I met Val at the range the next morning with coffees and bagels in hand. Taking hers, Val said, "You look good, Mel. I take it the date went well—no horror stories this time?"

"I feel good, my friend. In fact, I had a great time AND I was in bed by 11p.m. – just me, Mac and the cats," I replied with an air of moral superiority. Val stood up and saluted me.

"Excellent work, Sarge!" she exclaimed.

"At ease, Wisenheimer," I said.

"So, any inkling that there might be a future with this Frank person?" she asked.

"It's a wee bit early for that call, but I gotta tell ya, he's not like any man I've ever dated. I almost felt like I was in a Capra movie last night—he did everything except show up on his steed and slay the dragon! When I woke up this morning, I wondered If I'd dreamt the whole thing. Then the phone rang, and it was Frank calling to wish me good luck again on my requal."

"So, you didn't dream him up—he's flesh and blood. Hold on to this one, Mel, he sounds like a keeper!" she said. Val was excited for me.

"I don't know what to make of him. The first time we met, I thought he was the date from hell—now it seems like he's almost too good to be true." I sprang from my seat. "Maybe he's an alien . . . that would explain everything!" I cried out, as though I had just proven the Worm Hole Theory of physics.

"Here we go again," Val sighed. My best friend had the patience of a saint when it came to listening to my theories on everything from the afterlife to who broke up the Beatles. I was on a roll; the adrenalin that surged through my body whenever I got into requal mode had started working its magic.

"Val, do you remember Dennis, the officer who worked with us before leaving to work for the Feds?"

"Yeah, I remember him—quirky kinda guy," she replied.

"Well, one day he told me about this theory—I think he called it the "Hollow Earth Theory". He was really into it and said he had the proof to back it up. Anyway, it had something to do with the center of the earth being hollow and that this hollow part of the earth is supposedly inhabited by all manner of giant flora and fauna and, get this, ALIENS! He said the aliens are supposed to look just like humans, only they're perfect beings, and sometimes they come up to the surface to live among us so they can study us. Maybe Frank's one of them!" I exclaimed.

Val stared at me with a queer look on her face. "You're scaring me, Mel. I think you're starting to believe those nightmares of yours! Look, isn't it possible that you finally lucked out this time? Nice, non-alien guys do exist, you know. I happen to be very fond of one myself. You know him . . . his name is George, remember?" she asked as she cautiously gauged the hyped-up expression on my face.

I turned quiet, my automatic response to fear. "That's the problem, Val—I've never lucked out. I've never been with someone who cared about me, just me, not my big boobs or my green eyes. I thought Ritchie was the one and look where that got me. How can I learn to trust my instincts again?" I asked her, sounding as desperate as I felt.

"Maybe the problem is that you never trusted your instincts in the first place. Did you ever think of it that way? Have you ever really listened to them? Right here, right now, what is your gut telling you about Frank?" she asked with a tone of loving impatience.

I closed my eyes for a moment. "It's telling me that he cares about me? That he wants to do the right thing by me?" I answered sheepishly.

Val grabbed me by the arms. "That's the spirit! Stop being so hard on yourself, Mel! Be happy for once in your life and just go with it."

Be happy . . . it sounded so easy when Val said it. We finished our bagels and coffees and headed into the range. I was feeling confident. That night, I called Frank with the exciting news—I was now an expert shot!

"Mare, that's wonderful! Congratulations!" he exclaimed.

"Thanks, Frank. I don't know why it means so much to me, but I feel good about it!"

"You should—you worked hard enough for it! I got some good news today, too."

"Tell me!" I asked excitedly.

"I got an offer to teach full-time in September at Washington Irving Grammar School in Riverdale, not too far from my old neighborhood!" he answered proudly.

"Frank, that's awesome! Hey, I've got an idea. Why don't you come over Saturday night and I'll cook my famous onion-fried chicken, then we can celebrate both our good fortunes!"

"That sounds great—I can't wait, Mare! I'll bring the wine!"

I could barely wait for Saturday myself. I found that I was becoming more comfortable with the idea of happiness, the possibility of it. Luckily, the week flew by and Friday soon arrived. It was the beginning of a new month and I was looking forward to meeting with the Friday Night Dinner Ladies for another exotic culinary experience and accompanying gabfest. We agreed to meet at one of our favorite spots, a Thai restaurant located just down the street from the subway. When I got there, I noticed that everyone was present and accounted for—everyone, that is, except Jaycee, who was away on a cruise with her latest boy toy. We had barely ordered our food when the grilling started.

"So, Mel, the word on the street is you have a new beau," said Gloria, smiling at me like the cat that ate the canary. I shot a look at Val.

"What?" she asked defensively. "You didn't tell me not to say anything."

"I don't know what my soon-to-be-ex-best-friend here told you, but there's nothing going on. I just started seeing him. There's really nothing to talk about at this point," I said matter-of-factly.

Isabel chimed in with her rapid-fire Spanish-accented English. "I dunno, momi! Sure look like you got su'in goin on, si?" Isabel commented as she winked at the rest of the group. The ladies nodded in agreement that, indeed, I must have something going on.

"If it will make all of you happy, I'll ask Madame Clerk here to add the latest tidbits about me and my new boyfriend to the court calendar just as soon as I have some, okay? And that way, the whole courthouse will know my business!" I said as I rolled my eyes.

"Sounds like a plan to me," Carol Anne quipped. With that, our food arrived.

"Let's eat," I urged everyone. "I'm famished!"

Saturday couldn't get here fast enough.

CHAPTER 22

It was very strange . . . I didn't have a single dream Friday night, not even a vampire nightmare; it appeared as though my REM sleep cycle had taken a holiday. Normally, preparing for a day like I had planned for Saturday would have had my subconscious mind hopping from one rabbit hole to another, like a ping-pong ball in a high-stakes game of table tennis. I couldn't remember one night in my life when I hadn't dreamed—I wondered what it meant. I got up, drank a cup of tea and ate some toast while tending to my flock. I loved to sing to my pets, "Mommy had three little lambs, their fleece was white as snow, and everywhere that Mommy went, her lambs were sure to go." They were my biggest fans.

I tidied up the place, but didn't go crazy—I wanted it to look welcoming, comfortable, when Frank walked in. I set the table on the brick patio in my backyard, placed scented candles on the mantelpiece and stacked some wood in the fireplace. Even though it was early summer, a crackling fire went a long way to setting the right mood. I stepped back and appraised my handiwork: very nice, indeed. It was only eleven o'clock Saturday morning and Frank wasn't due till seven but I was already in a balmy state. But it didn't take long for the repressed spirits of my Catholic child-hood to raise their spectral hands to me and warn, "Take heed, Marian Elizabeth Morrison, this is but your second date!" I started to rethink the candles and the fireplace then scolded myself. "Stop acting like a spinster aunt and be the woman you are, for God's sake! You can do this! Remember what Val said: 'Just go with it.'" I resolutely shook off the straight-jacket of turmoil and heartaches past, then set out to prepare a feast, my renown and oft-requested onion-fried chicken with all the fixings. I'd made a brandied bread pud-ding for dessert the night before and Frank was bringing the wine. We were ready for takeoff.

I took one last look around then leashed Mac for his walk. After taking care of a few errands, I stopped into the nail shop to get a manicure—the onion-fried chicken tasted divine but my nails didn't. I'd been a customer of Gigi's Spa and Nail Salon for some years now so they let me bring Mac inside. Like everyone else in the neighborhood, they couldn't get enough of the Macster.

"Oooh, look who here! It the Mac man!" squealed Kim, the shop owner. I let go of his leash and he ran to his friend. Kim picked Mac up and hugged him. "You so handsome! I take you home with me, but I don't want Mommy to cry," she said in her twinkling Korean accent.

"Good morning!" I yelled to everyone above the loud drone of the electric filing machines. The patrons in the shop waved hello. "Hi, Kim! Ready for me?" I asked.

Holding on to Mac tightly, Kim gestured for me to sit down at her work station. "The usual, Missy Mel?" she asked. I had always sported a clear, nondescript nail color. The ded-icated civil servant that I was, I didn't like my nail color to distract from my uniform—that, and the fact I hadn't had any reason to look glamorous as of late. Now, I did!

"How about something different today, Kim?" I mused as I pulled a bottle called Pink Passion from the shelf.

"Oooh, I think Missy Mel got big date tonight!" Kim smiled, the dimples in her cheeks stretching to the size of half dollars from grinning.

"As a matter of fact, I do, Kim," I responded casually. I didn't want to say too much and jinx anything.

Kim put Mac down and tied his leash to my chair. "I so glad . . . you alone long time now—no good. New boyfriend cute guy? What he look like?" Kim asked excitedly as she began to file my nails.

"Hmmm . . . let me see if I can describe him: he's a little taller than me, he's got nice blue eyes and wavy dark brown hair. He's really a sweet guy. I think you'd approve, Kim," I replied confidently.

"Oh, he sound real nice! Maybe he the one for you, Missy Mel?" I was getting asked that question a lot lately.

"Maybe," I answered as I felt a flush of crimson rising to my cheeks.

At five minutes after seven the doorbell rang. I gave one more look in the mirror—not bad, Mel, not bad. I opened the door and invited Frank in. He cradled a bottle of wine in his right arm and held a small box in his left hand. He held out the box to me. "This is for you, Mare. I saw it in a little specialty shop and it made me think of you."

"Frank, that's so sweet," I said as I took the box from him and kissed him hello. His hair was getting longer—it had started to curl around the nape of his neck. He smelled good; his smell aroused me. Frank pulled me to him, kissing me hard. This time I saw Fourth of July fireworks! I heard Big Ben chiming! If I'd had any doubts about his manhood upon our first meeting, I had none now! I began to feel the dormant tug of sex coming alive in my body then abruptly I pulled away from him—I smelled smoke! "Something's burning!" I yelled. Small tufts of black smoke had started to filter into the living room. I sped into the kitchen and turned off the stove – thank God it was only the gravy boiling over!

Frank came running in after me. "Everything okay in here?" he asked with alarm.

"Nothing to worry about," I replied calmly. "It was just the gravy—I guess I didn't inherit the fireman gene!" I joked as I started to clean up the mess. Frank came up behind me, took the towel from my hand and put his arms around my waist, kissing my neck—this wasn't part of my plan to take things slow! I had planned for a delicious meal, good conversation, maybe some hot and heavy necking after the brandied bread pudding. We were moving too fast. I reminded myself of my three-date rule; I needed a diversion. I turned around, our faces almost touching. "Can I open my present now, Frank?" I asked sweetly. He reluctantly moved his arms from my waist.

"Sure, Mare," he replied good-naturedly. We walked back to the living room and sat down on the couch while I opened the box. Inside, nestled on a white satin pillow, lay a delicate silver necklace embellished with the Irish Claddagh symbol.

"I know it's not much, but I thought it was pretty – like you," Frank said.

I stared at the necklace then looked at Frank, tears filling my eyes. "Do you know what the Claddagh stands for, Frank?"

"Yes, I do! Love, loyalty, and friendship—all the things you are."

He took the necklace from its box and tenderly hung it around my neck. I touched the shimmering silver strand and traced the eloquent Celtic symbol with my fingers: a pair of hands holding a heart, a crown sitting atop them. The flickering gold flames that pirouetted in the burning hearth were reflected in the mirrored surface of the necklace's finely wrought links. I thought it the most beautiful gift I had ever received. I threw my arms around Frank, kissing him, breathing him in as if he were my last breath! He took me by the hand and led me to the bedroom. Frank sat me down on the bed then kicked off his sneakers and threw off his shirt. Lying down next to me, he started to unbutton my blouse. In an instant, I felt as though I couldn't breathe—I panicked! Good God in heaven, what was wrong with me?

"Frank, stop!" I implored. "Please stop!"

"Stop now? Why?" he panted. "Do we need protection?"

I put my hands over my face and started crying—I couldn't believe what I was doing! I may have been a thirty-year-old divorcee, but I might as well have been in the back seat of the limo on prom night.

"Mare, what's wrong?" Frank asked worriedly. My tears started to flow like the bad end of a nor'easter. "Talk to me, please?" he begged.

"This wasn't part of my plan. I didn't want to rush into anything with you—it was supposed to be special with you," I sobbed. Frank looked at me wide-eyed. He sat up and glanced around the bedroom. I watched him through a veil of tears as his eyes took in my teddy bear collection, my high school memorabilia, the rosary beads that my grandmother had given me—the very ones her mother had brought with her on the ship from Ireland so long ago. Frank laid back down and gently put his arms around me, stroking my hair.

"Mare, you have to trust me," he said softly. "Please tell me what you're so upset about."

I was comforted by his embrace, his presence. My jerking sobs now reduced to a manageable trickle, I confessed my plan: friendship first, then love, followed by sex. I tried my best to explain the three-date rule. Frank closed his eyes, deep in thought. Suddenly, he jumped out of the bed.

"Frank, I'm sorry! I'm being super stupid. Please don't leave," I pleaded, my tears welling up again.

"I've got an idea—follow me!" he ordered, throwing his shirt and sneakers back on.

"Where are we going?" I asked in puzzlement.

Frank looked me squarely in the eyes. "Mare, are you going to trust me or not?" he asked.

"Yes, Frank, I trust you," I replied, wiping my eyes. I followed him to the foyer. He walked out the front door and closed it behind him. The bell rang and I opened the door—Frank was standing there, wearing a big, goofy grin on his face.

"Hi, Mare!" he greeted me enthusiastically. "Ready for our third date?"

And the rest, as they say, is history.

CHAPTER 23

I was truly in love for the first time in my life, and someone loved me! Thank you, God! I finally understood what others always knew: Frank was IT, the real thing! I thought back to the first time we met, not so long ago. It mystified me, how quickly things could change when you least expected it.

I gazed at the man lying so peacefully next to me, looking almost angelic. A few weeks ago he was just a small, odd-looking person wearing a funny jacket—now he was everything to me.

Frank slowly opened his eyes. "Good morning, Maid Marian Elizabeth Morrison," he said as he tenderly ran his fingers through my hair.

"Good morning, Francis. How are you today?" I asked as I leaned down and kissed him.

"I want to wake up seeing your beautiful face every day, Mare," he answered, returning my kiss.

"I have to be honest with you, Frank, I don't usually look so beautiful in the morning—sometimes I can look downright scary," I warned him. He put his arms around me and held me close.

"No way. Not possible," he replied as he looked deeply into my eyes. "I think I'm falling in love with you, Mare. Does that fit into the rules?"

"There are no rules anymore, Frank. We broke them all last night," I purred contentedly.

"Rrrright! That was awesome!"

"Totally awesome!" I concurred.

"I love you, Mare."

"And I love you, Frank."

When I got into work on Monday evening, the only things missing from my blissful state were the little blue-birds of happiness that had been buzzing around my head all weekend. Oh, they were still there, all right—they were just taking a little rest from all that buzzing.

"Is that you, Mel?" the judge yelled out to me.

"Yes, Judge, coming!" I yelled back as I entered chambers. I greeted his staff as I walked into the large oak-paneled room.

"Good evening, Judge," I sang.

"Good evening, Mel. Sounds like someone had an enjoyable weekend," he observed with amusement.

"Yes, Judge, I did—couldn't have been better! And yourself?" I inquired.

"Good, good . . . the weather cooperated for once. Got in a few rounds of golf. How are we looking tonight?" he asked.

"I checked in with Gloria – the calendar's pretty heavy," I advised him.

"Very well then," he replied, letting out a small sigh. "Let's get this over with."

I walked in front of the judge and into the courtroom. I called the part to order, introduced the judge to the audience, and let T.J. take over the bridge. I sat down by Gloria's desk and let my mind wander, reliving the weekend with Frank; daydreaming wasn't a luxury I usually allowed myself while working. Love changes everything.

"Hey, Mel," Gloria whispered. "Phone call. I think it's your boyfriend!" She raised her eyebrows as she handed me the receiver.

"Sergeant Morrison speaking."

"Good evening, Sarge." It was Frank. "What's a beautiful lady like you doing in a place like that?" he asked.

"I'm keeping the courts safe from perverts like you!" I admonished him. I couldn't stop myself from smiling.

"Well, keep up the good work!" he answered playfully. "I miss you already, Mare."

"Same here," I replied carefully. I knew Gloria was hanging on my every word and I didn't want to give too much away—I hadn't had the chance to tell Val my good news and I wanted her to be the first to know.

"I know you can't say too much at work," Frank acknowledged. "I just wanted to let my girl know I'm thinking about her." His girl . . . Frank's girl. I loved the very sound of it.

"Will you still be up tonight when I get home?" I asked. I usually didn't arrive home from work till about one o'clock in the morning and I knew Frank had a substitute teaching assignment the next day.

"You bet! Talk to you later," he replied. I handed the phone back to Gloria.

"So, Mel, anything new for me to add to the calendar?" she asked coyly.

"The only statement that I am prepared to make at the present time is that he's a terrific guy and I look forward to seeing him again. You may quote me," I answered, then gestured to T.J. to come over to the desk.

"T.J., I have to check out the pen situation. I'll be back in a bit—can you handle this without me for a little while?"

"No problem, Sarge."

"All righty, then. You can get me on the radio if you need me." I went into the back and locked up my guns, then walked over to the pens; after I checked that night's calendar against the pen sheet I could take a break and share my happy news with Val. Since she had switched to working days, we made it our habit to meet in the courtroom that sat opposite the arraignment part before she left for the day so we could catch up with each other. I knocked on the door to the pens. Mike Jackson, the corrections officer in charge there, looked through the door's small wire-mesh window; seeing it was me, he unlocked the heavy steel door.

"Hey, Mel, look at you! Life must be treating you good these days—you glowin', girl!" Mike complimented me as he walked back to his desk. He had a very distinctive walk, like he had a hitch in his giddy-up.

"Thanks, Mike—I'm doing good. How about yourself? How's the family?" I inquired.

"No complaints. Did I tell you that me and the wife bought that place in Pennsylvania I been runnin' my mouth about for the last six months?"

"That's great, Mike, congratulations! The kids are gonna love it there. How's the commute going?"

"Not as bad as I thought. I take the express bus—gets me here in an hour and a half. And Mel, I gotta tell you, it's worth every minute. Now when I go home, I step off that bus and all I'm breathin' in is good old country air!" he exclaimed.

"I'm jealous! Give Lorraine and the family my regards, will you?"

"Roger that, Mel."

So, what's it going to be tonight, boss? Anything I need to know about our guests?" I asked as I scanned the pen sheet.

"Nothin' too bad – looks like the usual Monday night round-up. I noticed one that might get interesting, though," Mike said as he pulled a commitment card off his desk and started reading from it: "Mr. Vincent A. Tyree, a/k/a "Vinnie the Viper". He's a stone-cold bad-ass, alright – just got back into the system after doing 7 years in Attica. He's got this big, bald head so shiny it looks like the chrome on my '69 Chevy; body covered head-to-toe in some real nasty tats and a mouthful of jive and expensive 14K dental work to boot. The man's real jittery, too – he was all hopped up when they brought him in. He's one a them wiry little fellas – you know the type, Mel. It was like trying to get a bobcat into a shoebox when we had to get him into his cuffs – took three of our biggest guys!" Mike remarked with a half-laugh.

I took a good look at the perp's mug shot – Mike nailed it. "Well, either he hasn't learned his lesson, or he just loves our fine accomodations!" I joked. "You know, I'm thinking I might put a double-detail on Mr. Tyree when he goes before the judge – it seems like it's always the little guys that give us the most trouble. Thanks for the heads-up, Mike," I said appreciatively. It was correction officers like him that made our jobs a whole lot easier.

"No problem – and good luck, Mel," he replied as he unlocked the door to the empty courtroom where I was meeting Val. I found her sitting in the jury box reading a paper.

"Look lively!" I shouted. "The chief is in the building!" Val threw down the paper and jumped out of her seat. "Gotcha!" I laughed.

Val gave me a withering look and returned to her seat, picking the paper off the floor. "You know what they say, Mel—payback is a bee-ach," she warned.

"Lighten up, will ya?" I cajoled. "It's only Monday."

"Well, well, what have we here? Our beloved sergeant in a good mood on a Monday night?" She put the paper back down as I slid into the seat next to hers.

"It was wonderful, Val! We didn't leave the apartment all weekend," I gushed.

"You're going for it then?" Val asked hesitantly.

"The whole nine, buddy," I reassured her.

"I can't wait to meet him, Mel—I've never seen you this happy! Come here!" Val said as she gave me a big hug.

"I want him to meet you, too," I replied. "We haven't discussed it yet—you know, meeting each other's families and friends, but you and George are the exception. Maybe we could plan something for next weekend. Frank is still substitute teaching, and we're on a tight budget as far as entertaining, but I'd love to have you and George over to my place for dinner," I suggested.

"I have another idea—why don't you and Frank come over to our house?" Val offered. "We just had it painted and I wanted to get your opinion. I had the living room done in that color you liked so much, 'Scotland Road,' and it came out great. We'll order something in for dinner, that way we can all just relax, maybe even play some charades. What do you think?"

"That sounds perfect, Val. I really appreciate it. I just know you and George are going to love him."

"I love him already, Mel!"

I checked my watch. "Look, I have to get back – the part is about to go up but we'll talk later, okay?" As I rose to leave, Val conferred on Frank her official stamp of approval: two thumbs-up!

The rest of the night moved along like most Mondays until the Tyree case was called then things got interesting, just like Mike predicted. After hearing lively arguments from the D.A.'s office and defense counsel on the merits of the Tyree case, which charged (among other things) a parole violation on a 2nd degree armed robbery conviction, the judge very reluctantly set $500,000 cash bail on the sneering Mr. Viper, thanks in no small part to the brilliant legal maneuvering of his high-profile, sleazebag attorney, the one-and-only Ronald R. Cootey, Esquire! Mr. Cootey informed the court that bail would be paid forthwith. The crew were taking bets on how many of Vinnie's sparkling gold molars would have to be pulled out to pay his bail! Before the judge would adjourn the case, however, he assailed Mr. Tyree (with a sideways glance in Mr. Cootey's direction) with prolonged and heated admonitions regarding his defiant attitude toward the bench, the staff and the world at large. Instead of being grateful for being rescued from another long stint in the slammer, his badass attitude was on full display back in the pens as he was being processed out. He let everyone know just how unhappy he was with his latest legal experience, invoking Mr. Cootey's name as though it was his free pass to trash the system. He threw everyone his middle finger and voiced a few choice words as he was escorted out the door to freedom. I had a feeling that it wouldn't be long before we would again experience the dubious pleasure of Vinnie the Viper's company.

When the part went down, I got dressed as quickly as I could and ran to catch the train (usually, the judge dropped me off on his way home but tonight I couldn't wait to get out of there!). Frank had insisted on meeting me at the twenty-four-hour greengrocer down the street from the subway, just so he could walk me home. As I got to the top of the stairs, I could see him talking to one of the clerks in the store. "Hi, honey!" I called out.

"Hey, Mare!" Frank answered, that beautiful smile of his lighting up his face. We embraced and kissed hello like we hadn't seen each other in weeks. "How was work?" he asked.

"I was in such a good mood that nothing bothered me, not even the sleaziest slimebags!" I answered. "And how did your classes go?" Frank had been teaching summer school recently and found it a bit of a challenge.

"Actually, I was finding it hard to concentrate. While my class of eleven-year-olds was having trouble locating the dangling participial in a sentence, all I could picture was you and I locked in a sweaty, steamy embrace," he growled as he chewed on my neck.

"Aww, you poor thing!" I said, tussling his hair. "Listen, I talked to Val today and she and George would like to have us over for some take-out and charades next Saturday night—what do you think?" I asked lightly, trying to hide the apprehension in my voice. I knew it was a little soon to be introducing friends and family into the mix, but Val was the exception. She'd been through so much with me.

"Sure, why not? I know how close you guys are. But will I have to be on my best behavior?" he questioned playfully.

"Only till we get home, Francis, I promise," I quipped. I never broke a promise!

CHAPTER 24

The following Saturday with Val and George was a happy success—the house looked great and the food was delicious. Frank and George hit it off immediately and wound up teaming against the girls for a nail-biting game of charades. Taking a break in the action to replenish the drinks, Val and I huddled together in the kitchen.

"So, what's your verdict?" I asked, keeping my voice low.

"I think he's absolutely adorable! You're perfect together— it's that simple," Val stated confidently.

"It does seem perfect," I replied dreamily.

"Mel, do you remember my "Couples Theory"? Val inquired.

"Refresh my recollection, professor."

"Let's just say that I see a man and a woman at a party, but I don't know them, so I don't know if they've come alone or with each other. I can almost always pick out the people who are together in successful relationships, even if they're standing across the room from each other. There's just something between two people, like an aura that radiates from them, connects them when they're truly in love," she hypothesized.

"Are Frank and I radiating?" I asked hopefully.

Val made a beeping noise and pretended to wave a Geiger counter over me. "I'd say you're practically nuclear," she exclaimed.

On the way home that night Frank remarked, "I can see why you and Val are best friends. She and George are nice people—solid, you know? I really enjoyed myself tonight."

"I'm so glad," I said, somewhat relieved. "I just knew you'd like them. They loved you!" I paused for a moment. "Thanks for being so understanding, honey—it was important to me that you meet them."

"I know, Mare," Frank replied as he pulled me closer to him, kissing the top of my head.

We got home around midnight. Frank offered to take Mac out for his evening constitutional—they were becoming fast friends. I watched through one of the big front windows as they walked down the street together: my best boy and the love of my life. God is good!

Before long, Frank and I started to fall into a routine: we'd meet at the greengrocer's after I got off work on Friday night, go back to my place, have a light snack then snack on each other. We discovered to our mutual delight that we both loved to cook, so we spent much of our free time preparing the latest additions to our ever-growing recipe collection. Everything seemed right between us, from the kinds of food we enjoyed to the types of movies and music we liked. It was all so different from what went before; we not only loved each other, we liked each other. It was so easy being together.

On Sundays, we would spend a leisurely morning in bed reading the paper, with Mac sleeping between us. Papers done, Frank would put Mac in his doggie bed that was now in the hall outside the bedroom and apologize to him for taking him away from his mommy, then close the door on the outside world in exchange for a couple of hours in heaven. In the afternoon, we'd sometimes hit the bookstore to check the sales bins, or head to the beach on Frank's Harley if the weather permitted. Frank had begun to acquire a nice tan, his pasty complexion a thing of the past.

"I could get used to this," Frank said as we lay in each other's arms one typical Sunday morning. We had been seeing each other for about three months, but it felt like we'd known each other for a lifetime. While we had decided to keep both of our apartments as Frank had to get back to work in the Bronx during the week, he was now spending every weekend at my place.

"Me, too," I added lazily, not wanting anyone or anything to intrude upon our little Eden. Then, through my sex-addled mental haze I remembered something. I propped my head up on my arm. "Frank, didn't you want to buy school supplies this weekend?" I asked. Our summer of love was winding down and the beginning of Frank's new career in elementary education was almost at hand. The new school year was less than a month away.

"Damn, I almost forgot about that. Do I have to go? Can't it wait till next weekend?" he drawled as he nibbled on my arm.

"We've got tickets for the STP concert next Saturday night. I'm pretty sure we won't exactly be jumping out of bed the morning after that one! You might as well get it out of the way—school will be here before you know it. We'll take the car and be done in a jiff. Come on, up and at 'em!" I ordered as I put on my robe. "I'll make some breakfast while you shower." I figured that if we hustled, we could have our mission accomplished in an hour and be home in time to prepare dinner. Tonight, we were going to feast on chicken parmesan with a side of spinach sautéed in garlic—my mouth watered just thinking about it.

"I'm in love with a drill sergeant!" Frank whined comically as he got out of bed. He was preparing for the coming school year as a permanent full-time teacher and had wanted to pick up some extra supplies for his class. Fortunately, the mall wasn't too crowded when we got there, and to Frank's happy surprise he discovered that I was not an aficionado of the mall experience (unlike most women he'd known) and we were done in record time. As we left the stores and headed for the parking garage, I heard a familiar voice calling out to me.

"Hey, Mel, is that you?" I turned to see Ritchie Gianelli walking toward me. There was no mistaking him—as always, he stood out in the crowd, taller than almost everyone. He swaggered up to me, his long legs halving the distance between us. I noticed that he was alone. Ritchie gave me a big hug, kissed me square on the mouth, then stepped back, checking out the new Mel, the Mel that was in love.

"Jesus, Mel, you look incredible! How the hell have you been?" he exclaimed, apparently quite taken with what he saw. I could feel Frank looking at me, trying to gauge my reaction. I was taken off-guard. Let me rephrase that: I felt like I had been kicked in the stomach. I hadn't seen Ritchie since our breakup. Working different shifts made it easy not to run into him at work and everyone knew better than to mention his name around me.

"Hi, Ritchie. I'm good," I answered uneasily, wishing he would just disappear. I looked over at Frank, who was looking at Ritchie, who was looking at Frank. They were sizing each other up like a couple of lions circling each other, trying to decide if the prize was going to be worth the fight. I suddenly realized I hadn't introduced them. With as much aplomb as I could muster I said, "Ritchie, this is my boyfriend, Frank Brennan. Frank, this is Ritchie Gianelli. He works at the courthouse."

Ritchie looked down on Frank—literally. He had at least six inches in height and about forty pounds of solid muscle over him. Frank looked up at Ritchie. As I watched our little drama unfold, I could see reflected in Frank's eyes his insecurities upon meeting my flesh and blood ex-boyfriend.

"Hey, man, what's up?" Ritchie said as he held out his hand to Frank.

"It's a pleasure, Ritchie," Frank replied, ever the gentleman. They shook hands, Ritchie pumping Frank's probably a little harder than necessary. The gesture wasn't lost on Frank.

"Sorry we can't stay and catch up, Ritchie, but we're kind of in a rush to get home," I said, backing away from the train wreck as fast as I could. "Come on, hon," I signaled to Frank.

"It's been great running into you, Mel. You look like a million bucks! Maybe we can catch up some time," Ritchie yelled out with his usual machismo.

"Bye, Ritchie," I called over my shoulder as Frank and I resumed our walk to the garage. "And say "Hi" to Rita for me, okay?" I couldn't resist.

It was a tense walk to the car—Frank was silent on the ride home. "What's wrong, Frank?" I asked. "You're so quiet."

He looked straight ahead, his hands clenching the wheel. "So, that's Ritchie, huh? Big guy—you never mentioned that," he commented.

"Yes, he's a bit on the tall side. Is that what's bothering you?" I questioned.

"Well, geez, Mare, we couldn't possibly look any different!" he retorted in exasperation. I could see where Frank's still-frail ego was going with this—Ritchie was the bigger dog. It hadn't been that long since Frank looked and felt like something the cat dragged in.

"I love the way you look, Frank! Do you think I've been faking it with you?" I asked, the hurt ringing in my voice. "And more importantly, is that all this has been about, looks? Because if it is, let's end this now before the both of us make the biggest mistake of our lives," I cried, suddenly feeling like a huge stone had been laid on my heart.

"God, no, Mare—I didn't mean that, I swear on my life. It's just that you seemed kind of nervous around him," he commented uneasily.

"I haven't seen Ritchie in almost a year, Frank. I was just a little startled, that's all. If we had run into Donna in the mall, would you have been all calm and collected about it? When we first met you didn't even want to talk about her and it was already two years after your breakup," I replied defensively. I turned away from him, staring hard out the car window, my arms knit tightly across my chest.

"I'm sorry. You're right, Mare," Frank said, shaking his head. "I'm such a jerk." He pulled the car into the driveway of my building, switched off the ignition, and turned to me. "I'm not using this as an excuse, but it's kind of a guy thing, Mare. Forgive me, please?" he asked, putting his arm around the cold shoulder I was giving him.

"I don't know," I pouted, still staring out the window.

"Pretty please, Mare? I'll make it up to you, I swear," he promised.

I turned back to face him; he looked like a big kid asking for his favorite ice cream.

"Oh, all right," I answered, trying to sound like I was doing him the favor. Who was I kidding? I couldn't stay mad at him, and besides, Frank was always true to his word. I couldn't wait for him to make it up to me! Later that evening, curled up in each other's arms on my big sofa, I went over the day's events in my mind. Actually, I was glad we ran into Ritchie. After his abrupt departure a year ago, I didn't know how I would react if I ever saw him again, but despite the initial jolt at meeting him so unexpectedly, seeing Frank and Ritchie together calmed my fears. There was no question that Frank was the man for me. "Do you know what you mean to me, Frank?" I asked, holding his face in my hands, not moving my gaze from his.

"Yes, Mare, I believe I do," he replied.

I looked deeply into his azure blue eyes. "You have to promise me that you won't question my feelings for you ever again, do you understand? You're a hundred times the man Ritchie Gianelli is! You're all I'll ever want or need. I love you."

"Ditto, Sarge," Frank said, drawing me close.

That's all I wanted to hear.

CHAPTER 25

It was nearing Labor Day. Frank had received official word in August that he was hired for the full-time teaching position in Riverdale. Work was busy for me, as usual. Frank and I discussed the next big step in our relationship, meeting our families, and it was agreed to take on my family first. We had been a couple for three months now, but had yet to meet or even speak with each other's relatives. Frank and I never seemed to find the time, what with our conflicting work schedules and cramming in as much "us" time as possible on the weekends. The weekends had become sacred to us, and truth be told, we were enjoying our little idyll, just he and I. But now that things were settling down, it was time to take that step. Bonnie and her husband, Finbarr, along with their neighbors, were hosting a Labor Day block party that started on Saturday and ended with a parade on Monday. I suggested to Frank that it would be a nice, casual way to meet the clan and he agreed that it was a great idea. I phoned Bonnie to give her the heads up, then called my mother so there would be no surprises.

"Well, it's about time, Marian Elizabeth!" she exclaimed. "We were beginning to think you were making him up." My mother was making a joke—saints be praised! "What's your young man's name again?" she asked.

Feeling like a great weight had been lifted from my shoulders, I breezily replied, "You can rest easy, Ma. His name is Francis A. Brennan, and he has beautiful blue eyes, just like Dad."

"A fine name. What does the "A" stand for?" she asked.

"That's odd . . . I never asked Frank what it stood for," I answered, somewhat surprised at my lack of foresight in anticipating my mother's predictable interest in vowels.

Mom offered a suggestion. "Maybe it's Aquinas, or perhaps Aloysius?"

"You can ask him yourself tomorrow, Ma, and I hope that I can count on everyone to make him feel comfortable."

"You know better than that, Marian Elizabeth," my mother chided me. We always treat our guests hospitably." She was right, we did—it's the way we were raised. I could have brought home the Creature from the Black Lagoon and without hesitation my family would offer him a place to sit and a cup of tea. I then called Brendan to let him in on the game plan.

"Hey, big sister! Long time, no see! What's this I hear about you bringing some guy to the party?" he inquired.

"You heard right, Brendan, and you can call him Frank," I replied.

"You know, you kind of dropped out of sight, Mel. We were starting to get a little worried about you," he confided. My family had met Ritchie on a few occasions, and they thought he was an okay guy—everyone, of course, but our mother, who had a problem keeping track of all the vowels in his name. Brendan's voice took on a serious tone. "Does this Frank fella treat you right? Would Dad approve?" he asked.

I was taken aback by Brendan's question: what *would* Dad think of Frank? Would he approve? It didn't take me but a second to put his mind at rest. "In spades, little brother, in spades," I answered confidently.

"That's my big sis!" he said proudly.

"Let Hugh know, okay?" I asked. With that done, all my bases would be covered.

"No problemo, sis—we'll see you on Saturday. Bring beer," he ordered jovially.

I was starting to get excited about Frank meeting everyone. Bonnie and Finbarr would be there with their baby, Hugh and Kathleen would be in attendance with their two little ones, Brendan and Bernadette would be there as well, and, last but certainly not least, Mom and Grandma. Mom wouldn't be counting vowels this time! I was hoping that Friday night wasn't going to be too crazy at work—you could never tell how the wind would blow. I wanted to be in top form for the weekend, but when I woke up on Friday morning I wasn't feeling quite like myself. Frank wanted me to call in sick, but, being the trooper that I was, and knowing how hard it would be to get coverage on such short notice on a holiday weekend, I hauled my sorry ass into work. I blamed it on nerves—as the big day was drawing near, I was feeling a little edgy. Frank was wonderful about it, as usual—the calm in the storm.

Friday evening was passing uneventfully enough. I had gone into the small room opposite the pen area that the officers used as a break room. Ray, the second night arraignment sergeant, was sitting at a small table working the crossword puzzle; like most court officers, myself included, he was a wiz at solving them.

"Yo, Ray, what it is," I greeted him as I sat down.

"Hey, Mel, what's going on?" He looked up from his paper. "You look a little peaked tonight—you need a break?" he asked.

"No, I'm fine, thanks. It's been a long day, that's all. Hey, what's my horoscope say?" I asked.

I loved to read the horoscope at the end of the day to see how it should have gone, but almost never did.

"What's your sign?" Ray asked.

"Gemini," I replied.

"Here goes: with Cancer entering your fifth house of solitude and secrets, it would be the wise Gemini who finds a safe haven till the storm clouds pass. This is not the time to be trying new things."

"Perfect timing!" I yelled as I slammed my hand down on the table. "The only time my horoscope comes true is when it's predicting bad news," I rued.

"So, no mas, Mel?" Ray queried.

"I'm introducing my boyfriend to the family this weekend," I explained.

Ray looked amused. "Don't take this stuff seriously, Mel—they just make these things up," he commented, trying to cheer me up.

"It doesn't matter, Ray. I don't really believe in it. Ask me thirty seconds from now what it said and I'll be damned if I'll remember!"

Just then, I looked up to see Ritchie Gianelli walk in the door. Just like I was saying: bad news . . .

Ray shot me a look. "Break time's over. I think I'll head back out now, Mel," Ray said as he slowly got up from the table. "Are you going to be okay?" he asked me as he gave Ritchie a sideways glance.

"Yeah—thanks, Ray. I'll give you a holler if I need anything, okay?"

"You got it," he answered as he left me and Ritchie alone in the room. It had been barely a month since our impromptu meeting at the mall. I looked at Ritchie in astonishment.

"What in the hell are you doing here?" I asked crossly.

"I was down the block so I thought I'd stop by and see if you were around. T.J. told me you were back here," he said as he moved closer to the table. I could smell booze on him.

"You can stay right where you are, Ritchie," I said, putting my hand up like a stop sign. I wasn't nervous this time, just pissed off. He wasn't dealing with a rookie anymore. "What are you doing down the block, anyway?"

"The guys are throwing a stag party for Mike Kramer at Balducci's—he's getting married next week. I guess it brought back some old memories," he reminisced, moving closer in again.

"Give Mike my best—and I asked you to stay where you were!" I ordered, trying to keep my voice in check.

Ritchie backed up, raising his hands in feigned surrender. "No problem, Sarge!" he replied in mock alarm. "What's the matter, Mel? You don't seem very happy to see me."

"How perceptive of you, Ritchie!" I said incredulously. "What gave you the idea I'd be happy to see you?"

Ignoring me, he continued: "We didn't get a chance to catch up at the mall the way we should have," he said as his eyes wandered down to my chest. "So that's the new boyfriend, huh? What's his name again?" The big dog was sniffing around.

"His name is Frank," I answered curtly. I wasn't about to let Richie back into my good graces. "As long as we're playing twenty questions, how's Rita these days? Wouldn't she be upset if she knew you were here checking up on my love life?" Now I was curious . . . what was he doing here, anyway?

"She wouldn't care one way or the other," he replied defensively.

My ears pricked up. "What do you mean, Ritchie?"

"You'll be happy to know we're not together anymore. She went back to her husband," he replied.

Try as I might, I couldn't hide my shock at the news. "Are you serious?" I asked.

"Serious as a heart attack." Ritchie sat down and started doodling on the newspaper as he talked; I didn't try to stop him this time. "I'm surprised you didn't hear about it. She left me about a month ago. She said she'd made a big mistake and that her husband was willing to take her back and start over," he explained with a touch of melancholy in his voice.

"Wow! That guy's going straight to heaven!" I remarked sarcastically.

A dark shadow crossed Ritchie's face; was he feeling remorse for his sins or just feeling sorry for himself? Ritchie Gianelli was not used to losing. I decided to take the high road and hate the sin, not the sinner.

"I'm sorry, Ritchie," I said earnestly. "It's not easy being on the receiving end of that kind of news." Ritchie tried to take my hand. I pulled away from the table and stood up. "What do you think you're doing?" I asked him as he started to move from his seat.

"I want to make it up to you, Mel. I know what I did to you was wrong. I acted like a real shit. I want to set things right. I miss you," he said as he looked at me with his big puppy-dog eyes.

"You're drunk, Ritchie. You don't know what you're saying and I'm only going to tell you one more time to keep your distance," I warned. "Listen to me, Ritchie, there's nothing to make right. It's over between us. I forgive you, okay? Now leave me alone. I'm in love with a wonderful man. I'm happy now."

"Come on, Mel—you're in love with that guy? I mean, he seemed all right, but seriously, you'd pick him over me? Remember what we had? We were hot together, Mel, smokin' hot!" Ritchie exclaimed. Same old Ritchie, cocky as ever, in spite of his supposed heartbreak. He still believed he could have whatever he wanted, whenever he wanted.

"Look, Ritchie, I've got to go now. I've got a courtroom to run. You should be getting back to the party," I said as I started for the door.

"This isn't over, Mel. I'm not giving up that easy," he responded defiantly.

I turned around and took a good, hard look at the man who had once been my everything but was now nothing to me but a bad memory. He looked like a little boy who had just had his bike taken away from him for misbehaving—I had to stop myself from feeling a little sorry for him.

"Ritchie, let me give you some advice: if I were you, I'd move that huge ego of yours out of the way so you can finally give yourself some room to grow up."

As I headed out the door, I heard Ritchie yelling after me, almost threatening me. "You'll see, Mel. This isn't over, not by a long shot!"

CHAPTER 26

It was nearing one o'clock in the morning by the time I got to the locker room to change. I was exhausted. I couldn't wait to get home to see Frank; he would kiss my boo-boo and make it all better. As had become my habit, I called to let him know I was on my way home.

"Hey, baby. How's my girl?" he asked when he answered the phone. I was comforted by the sound of his voice. "How many bad guys did you lock up tonight?"

"Not enough," I replied, thinking back to my confrontation with Ritchie. I had decided before calling Frank that I would wait till I got home to tell him about Ritchie showing up at work. In the time between Frank hearing that story and me getting home, he might begin to imagine all kinds of things, and I didn't want him to worry unnecessarily. It hadn't been that long ago since our encounter with Ritchie at the mall—too close for comfort. "I'll be home soon, hon. I just have to escort the judge to his car."

"You sound knocked out, Mare. Is everything alright?" he asked with concern.

"Everything's fine—just the usual suspects today," I replied casually.

"Do you feel like eating anything when you get home? We've got some leftover chicken noodle soup in the fridge—I can heat it up for you later." Frank knew I usually wasn't very hungry that late in the evening, but tonight, for some reason, I was starving! I must have worked up quite an appetite dealing with the bonehead.

"How about some Chinese?" I suggested.

"Chinese? What's up with that?" Frank asked with a surprised laugh. I normally wasn't a Chinese food lover.

"I'll be damned if I know! Do you mind, love?" I asked.

"Of course not! In fact, I think I'll take a walk and pick it up myself—it's a nice night out there. What does my lady feel like ordering?" he asked gallantly.

"Whatever you're having is fine with me, and how about some munchkins for dessert? The donut store is only two doors down from the Chinese place."

"Sure, Mare, but don't blame me if you have bad dreams tonight!" he replied. Funny thing that he mentioned bad dreams: it occurred to me that I hadn't had one of my vampire nightmares since the night we met.

"You're the best, Francis! I love you."

"I love you, too, baby. Be safe, okay?" Frank worried about me. Despite his initial impression of how exciting my job was, he still hadn't become entirely comfortable with the fact that that I had to carry a gun for a living.

"I will. See you soon," I promised as I hung up the phone.

I sprinted to the judge's chambers. "Are you ready, Judge?" I asked. The judge was giving me a ride home as was our nightly routine. He wouldn't hear of me taking the subway by myself after work in spite of my reassurances to him that he should be more concerned with the person who would try to start something with me.

"Are you kidding, Mel? I've been ready since I got here," he replied, picking up his briefcase. Out of habit, I checked my pocketbook for my house keys. To my dismay, I discovered that I'd left them back in the locker room.

"Judge, I have to run back to the locker room—I forgot my keys. Wait for me!" I admonished him; the old man could be stubborn when it came to following security procedures. I ran to the locker room, grabbed my keys, and made it back to chambers in under a minute. When I got there, the judge was gone. "Damn! I told him to wait for me," I muttered. I ran down the back staircase that led to the parking lot. I checked the elevator at the bottom of the stairs—no judge. When I got outside, I scanned the lot. He had to be out there somewhere—I could see his car was still in its spot. It had become a sore point between us over the years that he insisted on leaving his Caddy on the far side of the lot and away from the booth (he didn't want anyone to put a dent on his precious baby) but it made my job a lot harder security-wise. I walked over to the officer on duty in the booth; tonight, it was being manned by Freddie Brigati, or "Tin Man," as he was known around the courthouse. He had acquired the nickname because of all the medals he wore on his uniform shirt—the guy had earned a medal for everything you could think of. I think he even had a medal commemorating all the other medals.

"What's up, Tin Man?"

"Good evening, Sarge. What can I do for you tonight?"

"Have you seen the old man around? He was a naughty boy and walked out ahead of me – again."

"You sure, Sarge? I haven't seen him out here. You want me to do a search?" he asked.

"No, that's okay . . . I'll head over to his car. He's probably sitting in it right now, wondering what's keeping me. Have a good night, Freddie."

"You, too, Sarge. Stay safe."

As I headed toward the other end of the lot where the judge's car was parked, I heard a man's voice, but it wasn't the judge. This voice was agitated, angry – it sounded like he was yelling at someone. Not knowing what I was going to walk into, I pulled my off-duty .22 Smith & Wesson revolver out of my shoulder holster and sprinted in the direction of the disturbance. With my heart pounding and a trickle of sweat wending its way down my back, I slowed down as I approached the corner of the building. I quietly edged my way along the wall, removing the safety on my gun, breathing deeply and trying not to panic. I stretched out my neck as far as I could to try to get an idea of what was happening. The streetlights that filtered through the tress partially illuminated a harrowing scene: the judge lying face down on the ground and a man standing over him holding a gun to the back of his head. He was screaming, "I'm 'bout to kill your sorry ass, mutha-fucka! You think you gonna make me look like a damn fool, make me look stupid, Mr. Judge-man? We'll just see who's stupid now, cause you about to die!"

I recognized the voice. It was Vinnie Tyree, the repulsive recidivist who had given us such a hard time a while back, the slime ball who walked on bail. I reached for the badge hanging around my neck, trying to keep my gun hand steady. Cautiously stepping toward them, I thrusted my badge into Tyree's line-of-sight to make perfectly clear to him what my identity and intentions were. I shouted the order "Police! Drop your weapon!" The perp smoothly turned in my direction, his bald head glistening, his tats and teeth in full view, his gun still aimed at the judge's head – a real pro. "Drop the gun – NOW!" I screamed, frantically flashing my badge at him, trying to break the laser-like intensity of his deranged stare.

Suddenly, I caught the silvery glint of the perp's gun barrel as it turned in my direction. I quickly dropped to one knee and fired off three rounds. Tyree started to go down, but not before getting off a couple of shots at me. I watched as he stumbled, then hit the ground, the gun falling from his hand. The judge scrambled to his feet, patting himself down as though searching for bullet holes. I heard him cry out, "Mel!" The last thing that I remember was seeing the judge running toward me, screaming for help. I slumped down against the wall, losing consciousness. I was hit.

CHAPTER 27

Ritchie carefully wound his way back to Balducci's. "Who in the hell does she think she's kidding?" he mumbled to himself at the bar as he downed another shot of tequila. He called over to Nick. "Hey, Nick, can I borrow your phone for a sec?" he slurred.

"Sure, Ritchie, but make it quick," Nick admonished.

"Thanks, man." Ritchie took the phone from behind the bar and dialed Mel's home phone number. The answering machine picked up.

"This is the Morrison residence. Please leave your name and number and I will return your call as soon as possible."

He waited for the beep then dropped his bombshell. "Hey, Mel, you know who this is. You can run but you can't hide. I know you still feel it, just like I do. By the way, you looked real hot tonight, baby. See ya soon." The damage done, Ritchie hung up the phone, put it back behind the bar and rejoined the party.

An hour later, the bar phone rang. Nick answered, his face turning pale as he listened. Putting the receiver down, he walked quickly to the back room where Mike's party was in full swing. He looked around the darkened room carefully; he spotted Ritchie at a corner table and gestured to him to come up to the bar. Ritchie walked over to Nick. "Great party, buddy. What's up?" he asked, throwing his muscular arm around Nick's shoulder.

"Someone's on the phone, Ritchie—there's been a shooting at the courthouse. They asked for you."

Richie ran to the bar and grabbed the phone, sobering up quickly. "This is Ritchie. What's going on over there?"

"Ritchie, this is Freddie. You gotta get up here fast, man—it's Mel. She's been shot. It looks bad."

Ritchie dropped the phone and ran to the back room, shutting everyone up. "There's been a shooting up the block—Mel Morrison's hurt. Who's comin' with me?" he yelled. With Ritchie in the lead, the restaurant emptied out. As the officers ran toward the courthouse, they could make out the flashing lights of an ambulance. Approaching the scene, they could see the EMTs working diligently to get Mel secured to the gurney and inserting needles into her arms for the drips and transfusions. There was blood everywhere. A crowd had started to gather outside, staring through the tall courthouse gates, hoping to catch a glimpse of a tragedy.

"I'm coming with you!" Ritchie shouted to the technician above the roar of the sirens from the approaching police cars.

"Who are you?" he yelled back.

"I'm her boyfriend!" He took out his badge and flashed it.

"Okay, get in, but we've gotta get her to the ER, pronto!" the EMT warned. Ritchie jumped into the back of the ambulance as the crew shut the doors and sped away. He watched, unblinking, as they worked to stop the bleeding.

"Where is she hit?" he asked, trying to hide his growing anxiety. He gazed at Mel's face, now covered by an oxygen mask—her head had begun to swell.

"From what we can tell, she took one in the chest – looks like it hit her in the right lung. Another one scored her head pretty good. The head wound isn't life-threatening, but she's got to get into surgery for that lung, ASAP."

Ritchie felt the sting of regret choking in his throat as he spoke to her. "Mel, stay with me, babe. You're gonna be okay! You're tough—the toughest, you hear me?" Ritchie took her free hand and kissed it, fighting to keep his emotions in check. He was surprised at his reaction, didn't quite know what to do with it—this just wasn't like him. Did it take him seeing Mel this way, clinging to life, to realize how he really felt about her?

The ambulance turned into the hospital's emergency entrance only to encounter a throng of police, court officers, and reporters. As the doors swung open, Ritchie jumped down and followed the crew as they quickly disappeared into the cavernous hospital, the popping flashbulbs from the news cameras lighting a trail for them. He followed them until a doctor stepped in front of him, dressed for surgery. He stopped Ritchie. "Are you her husband?" he asked.

"Not yet, but I'm working on it," he answered without hesitation.

"Then you'll have to wait in the lounge for the time being," the doctor instructed. "We'll send word on her condition as soon as it becomes available."

"Doc, is she gonna be okay?" he asked. For the first time in Ritchie's life, his bravado was failing him. He was scared.

"She's lost a great deal of blood, but we're doing everything possible to pull her out of this," the doctor said as he closed the doors behind him.

Ritchie walked to the waiting room and sat down, putting his head in his hands. At that moment, the doors leading from the main corridor flew open, and a large crowd of people streamed in. Ritchie looked up—he noticed a familiar-looking man run to the triage station. It was Mel's brother, Hugh. "Hugh!" Ritchie called out to him.

"Hey, Ritchie, it's good to see a familiar face, man!" Hugh said, hugging him. "What's going on? Where's Mel?" he asked anxiously.

"She's hurt pretty bad, Hugh. From what I've been able to find out so far, she was walking with the judge to his car when some scumbag surprised them. They're trying to piece it together—it might have been an attempted robbery. I was down the block at a party when the call came in."

Hugh looked at Ritchie with red-rimmed eyes. "How can we thank you, Ritchie? I couldn't stand to think of my sister being alone at a time like this," he said.

"I'm glad I could be there for her, Hugh. How's the rest of the family doing? How are they holding up?" Ritchie inquired with a show of genuine concern.

"Not too good, I'm afraid. Our mom's in a bad way. She was always afraid that something like this would happen. We're all kind of reliving a nightmare."

"Is that them over there?" asked Ritchie, nodding in the direction of the large group of people milling about the waiting room. It was becoming a chaotic scene: besides the Morrison clan and what appeared to be about twenty family and friends in attendance, the court brass and court officers had arrived in full force, along with a brigade of fire-fighters, several police officers, and a few priests. The news crews were being held at bay outside. The court brass had assigned two officers to stand outside the doors leading to the operating room suite and a few others to help the family with whatever they needed. A familiar litany arose from the chaos, that of the rosary being prayed. Ritchie walked over to Julia Morrison and knelt down next to her.

"Mrs. Morrison, I don't know if you remember me—I'm Ritchie, Ritchie Gianelli," he said.

Julia glared at Ritchie with an undisguised hostility that was not lost on him. "I remember you," she answered flatly.

"I just want you to know I'm here to help you and the family with whatever you need," he said respectfully.

"I think what we need right now are prayers, Mr. Gianelli, if you'd care to join us," she replied icily. She hadn't forgotten what he put her daughter through. Like a life raft being thrown to a drowning man, Ritchie heard the captain's voice calling to him.

"Gianelli, we need you over here!" he barked over the din of the crowded room.

"Mrs. Morrison, I'm being paged, but if you need anything just let me know," he said as he slowly backed away, seeking shelter from her enmity.

"We'll be sure to let you know, Ritchie," Hugh interjected, trying to diffuse the awkward moment. Julia watched Ritchie's tall, cocksure figure walking away. She finally understood why her daughter had fallen for him—he was a charmer, all right. Then, as if waking from a dream, she remembered the new boyfriend, the one the family was to meet at the block party that weekend. Francis—that was his name. None of them knew him or what he looked like. She felt badly for the poor man, his not knowing anyone— he must be in a state! Maybe Val had spoken with him and he was on his way.

Val was good about those things. Julia went back to her rosary, the presence of the priest nearby a comfort to her. God was going to pull her first-born through this, of that she was sure. She prayed to her husband: "I beg of you, John, my angel in heaven, save our girl. I can't go through this again," she whimpered quietly.

Hugh put his arms around his mother. "She's gonna be okay, Mom. Mel's a fighter," he reassured her, trying to convince himself as well.

Just then, Val came running over. "Hugh, Bonnie, Julia—I got here as fast as I could!" she cried, hugging everyone. Looking around she asked, "Where's Brendan?"

"Brendan is on his way. He's stopping to pick up our grandmother," Hugh replied.

"Have the doctors said anything yet?" Val asked hopefully.

"Not yet, Val," Hugh answered wearily, trying to hold himself together for the family.

Julia looked up from her rosary. "Val, did you call her young man? I think he should be here. We were supposed to meet him this weekend, but God had other plans," she murmured distractedly.

"Sweet Jesus! I was rushing so much I forgot to call him!" Val exclaimed. "Please excuse me for a minute." She remembered Mel had mentioned that Frank was staying at her house that night. She ran to the pay phone and dialed Mel's number—it seemed to ring for an eternity. "Please, Frank, please pick up!" Val pleaded into the echo of the phones' silence.

CHAPTER 28

Frank paid for his order of Chinese food then moved on to the donut store to pick up a dozen munchkins per Mare's instructions. "She's a funny one," he thought to himself as he walked back to the apartment. As he came through the front door, Mac bounded toward him, smelling the potpourri of goodies he'd brought home.

"Sorry, Mac, but this is for Mommy when she gets home," he said. Mac put his little body down on the floor, rolled onto his back and begged for a treat. "Okay, I'll give you a little taste, but you have to be quiet about it," Frank admonished Mac as he slipped his furry friend a small piece of beef. "If Mommy finds out I'm feeding you Chinese food, she'll have my head."

As he placed the packages down on the counter, he noticed the red light blinking on the answering machine. He checked the time—it was almost one-thirty in the morning. Mare should have been home by now. Maybe the judge took a wrong turn and they wound up in Queens again.

"That's probably her on the machine," he thought to himself. He hit the play button; he instantly recognized the voice on the recording—it was Ritchie!

"Hey, Mel, you know who this is. You can run but you can't hide. I know you still feel it, just like I do. By the way, you looked real hot tonight, baby. See ya soon." Frank stood still. Time stood still. The only sound in the room was the ticking of the kitchen clock. He hit the rewind button and played the message again. He thought back to his and Mare's conversation before she left work—she hadn't mentioned anything about seeing Ritchie. He recalled that she'd sounded a little off, that he asked her if she was all right. Why hadn't she said something then? Why hadn't she trusted him enough to tell him about this?

None of it made any sense. "This can't be real," he said aloud as he slowly sat down at the kitchen table. Mac was on his hind legs now, giving Frank a paw. He picked Mac up in his arms, stroking his soft fur, lost in thought. The long tentacles of icy fear that he thought had been rendered invalid upon meeting the love of his life found renewed strength and once again reached into his very soul, wrapping themselves around his heart. The phone rang, startling Frank out of his dark reverie. He stared at it for a while before picking up the receiver. Was it Ritchie again?

"Frank, thank God you're there. Have you heard the news?" Val asked, her voice shaking. At first, Frank couldn't answer her . . . he struggled to find the energy to speak.

"What are you talking about, Val," he asked woodenly, an image of Ritchie the Rock Star drilling its way into his ravaged ego.

"Frank, there's been a terrible accident. Mel was shot coming out of work tonight! She's in bad shape. They took her to Franklin Downtown Hospital and they're operating on her right now. You've got to get over here, fast – do you understand, Frank?" There was no response at the other end of the line. "Frank, do you hear me?" Val screamed into the phone.

"Yes, Val, I understand . . . I'll be there as soon as I can," he answered numbly. Time out of mind.

"Frank! Get here—faster!" she begged him.

"I will, Val, I will," Frank promised as he hung up the phone. He didn't understand what was happening. Mare was shot? While he was proud of the work she did, he'd never been completely at ease with that gun at her side, but she had always reassured him that nothing like this would ever happen. Why her? He knelt down on the kitchen floor; Frank prayed to God to save his Mare and for the strength he needed to face with her whatever else was to come.

He went into autopilot mode; he grabbed the car keys and started running for the front door. At the door, he remembered Mare's most prized possession: her grandmother's rosary. Frank ran back to the bedroom nightstand, put the rosary in his pocket, and ran down the stairs to the car. He drove off into the night like a madman. The only woman he had ever truly loved was lying in a cold hospital bed fighting for her life and he wasn't there to comfort her, to hold her in his warm embrace and make everything better. Frank had broken his promise. He hadn't protected her from the bad guys after all.

Frank swerved his car into the hospital parking lot then ran to the lobby. His eyes frantically scanned the huge room looking for Val, but his view was blocked by the sea of blue uniforms spread out before him. He could see an important-looking man in a business suit being interviewed by the press directly outside the entrance. He looked again carefully—it was the mayor! "Jesus!" he thought to himself. Frank could barely hear himself think above the noise rising from the crowd. He pushed his way through the mass of bodies to the main desk.

"Excuse me, please!" he yelled to the nurse over the clamor. "Can you tell me where Mare, I mean, Marian Morrison is being treated?"

"She is being operated on. We have no further information on her condition at this time," she responded brusquely. Frank looked around in desperation—where the hell was Val? She was supposed to meet him here. He decided to use the chaos to his advantage and walked in the direction of the doors that led to the operating room suites.

A court officer stopped him. "No one is allowed back here except immediate family members, sir." Thinking quickly, Frank said, "I'm Marian's brother, Brendan Morrison—my name should be there." He knew her brother from family photos Mare had shared with him. He prayed the officer wouldn't ask him for identification. The officer checked the list he held in his hands.

"Yes, sir, you're right here. Go ahead in. Your family is in our prayers."

Feeling like a man who had just escaped the noose, Frank answered gratefully, "Thank you, officer. Can you point me in the right direction, please?"

"Straight down the hall and to the left," he replied.

"Thanks again," Frank said as he started to walk down the hospital corridor, his heart beating faster with each step he took. "What if she dies before I get to her?" he thought. He was almost running now. "Please, God, help me," he prayed. After what seemed like an eternity, he made it to the end of the long hallway and turned the corner. He stopped hard, as though he had slammed into a brick wall; there stood Ritchie Gianelli, along with two uniformed court officers. Ritchie looked over at Frank, then murmured something to his friends.

"Remember me?" he asked as he walked toward Frank. His long, tanned arms were wrapped across his chest—this time he didn't offer a handshake. "How'd you get back here?" Ritchie demanded. "Your name isn't on the list."

"What the hell do you mean, what am I doing here?" countered Frank angrily. The two officers started to walk behind Ritchie—he gestured to them to stay back. He got in close to Frank, towering over him.

"Look man, I've got this covered—you can go home now." His voice lowed to a threatening growl. "We'll let you know if we need anything." Ritchie stared down at Frank, challenging him.

Frank had never thought of himself as an irrational person, but at this moment a fury erupted in him – he wanted to kill this man! Ritchie's buddies, alerted to the charged atmosphere, started walking toward him. Frank took a quick step back, then hauled off and belted Ritchie with all the force of a man fighting for his very existence. Ritchie stumbled back, hitting the wall. The officers grabbed Frank by his arms, restraining him.

"What do you want to do, Sarge?" one of them asked. Ritchie, massaging his chin, stepped over to Frank. Frank, struggling to free himself from the officers' grip, looked up at his rival, waiting for what was sure to follow, but not caring. It was over . . . the big dog had won.

"Let him go. I don't think he's gonna give us any more trouble," Ritchie replied scornfully. The officers eased their hold and Frank shook them off.

"Here," he said to Ritchie, pulling Mare's rosary beads from his pocket and throwing them to him. "She'd want these—make sure she gets them," he said, resignedly. Struggling to keep his dignity intact, Frank turned toward the door and began the long walk away from his dream.

CHAPTER 29

The command had provided the Morrison family with an emergency escort that had gotten them to the hospital within an hour of Mel's admittance, as well as an escort for Val, who was considered by all to be a part of her family. Shortly after arriving, the Morrison family was sequestered in a small private room off the main waiting area so that they would not have to endure the noise and crowds during their vigil. Val had declined to go with them, explaining that she needed to be visible when Frank arrived, as she was the only person he would recognize among the throngs of people outside. She waited for him, pacing the floor as she did, anxiously awaiting word of Mel's condition. She looked at her watch: it had been almost two hours since she'd spoken to Frank. "Where is he?" she thought to herself. He couldn't have hit too much traffic this early in the morning.

She decided to get a cup of coffee at the vending machine located nearer to the front entrance of the building to keep a better eye out for him—it would be easy to lose sight of each other in all this confusion. As she took a sip of the hot coffee, she looked through the waves of steam rising from the cup to see a man who looked like Frank leaving the through the hospital's turnstile doors. She called out to him as loudly as she could, but he didn't hear her through the steady stream of noise emanating from the room. As Val put her cup down and started to run toward the door, a joyous shout sprang up from the crowd.

"What's going on?" Val asked the officer standing next to her.

"The doctor just came out—he said Morrison's going to be okay!"

Val looked again at the entrance but the man she thought was Frank was gone. She ran through the turnstile and watched as the dormant city slowly came to life with the rising sun, but the man had disappeared. "What the hell?" Val said aloud, then quickly ran back into the building to join Mel's extended family in celebrating the blessed news.

The Morrison family huddled together protectively in the small waiting room while Mel was being operated on; Brendan and Bernadette had finally arrived with their grandmother. It was a long wait. Finally, after more than five hours into their vigil, there was a knock on the door; Doctor Friedman, the head of the medical/surgical unit walked in, smiling broadly.

"How is she, Doctor?" asked Julia, trying to remain calm.

"I have great news, Mrs. Morrison—your daughter will be fine, just fine! The head wound wasn't serious, just some stitching up there, and we were successful in removing all of the bullet fragments from her lung. It looks like she hasn't sustained any permanent injuries. We'll be moving her to the ICU momentarily. You'll be able to see her soon, but be aware that the effects of the sedation will linger for a while, so it might not be possible to speak with her, but at least you'll see for yourselves that she's doing well," he advised.

Clutching her rosary, Julia made the sign of the cross across her breast.

Shaking the doctor's hand, a relieved and grateful Hugh replied, "Speaking for the family, we can't thank you enough, Doctor." The exhaustion of the day's events was evident on his handsome, worn face.

"Marian is a fighter," observed Dr. Friedman. "But she has a way to go yet—she'll need a lot of TLC when she goes home."

"Not to worry," Julia assured him, regaining her composure. "I'm her mother and I'll be taking care of my daughter till she's back on her feet."

"Very good, Mrs. Morrison. An orderly will be by shortly to bring you to her room."

As the doctor closed the door behind him, all of the terrible worry, uncertainty, and anxiety of the past few hours dissipated into tears of relief and prayerful thanks.

The orderly finally arrived and escorted everyone to the intensive care unit; one by one, Mel's family walked quietly into her room. She was a sight to behold: her head and chest were wrapped in layers of gauze, the needles in her arms attaching her to bags of various colored liquids, her head swollen to the size of a large melon. The only sound in the room was the steady beep of the heart monitor. Julia stepped up to the bed, kissing her daughter tenderly.

"Marian Elizabeth, you always were the hard one, thanks be to God," she said as she choked back her tears.

Hugh put his arms around his mother and grandmother. "We're all here for you, Mel, and we'll be taking you home real soon," he said, trying to be brave for the sake of his mother. Brendan and Bonnie came around to the other side of the bed.

"Hey, big sis," Brendan whispered as he leaned over to tenderly touch her swollen face. "You did it—you took him down! You got the bad guy!"

Bonnie was quiet, tears streaming down her face. She took her Mel's pale hand in hers and squeezed it tightly.

Forming a circle around Mel's bed and clasping their hands together, the family prayed and gave thanks for all their blessings, especially for the gift of life. The clan would again be as it was.

Val ran to the elevator and pushed the button for the fifth floor. As the bell announced its destination, the doors opened to reveal the Morrison family chatting excitedly. Everyone hugged and kissed, emotions running high.

"How does she look?" Val asked hopefully.

"She took a beating, but she's good, Val," Hugh answered. "She's asleep, but you should go and see her when she wakes up. After all, you're part of the family," he said as he put an arm around Val's shoulder.

"Thanks, Hugh," Val answered appreciatively. "Will I see you all later?"

"Of course," he replied. "We're heading home now to get some rest and to clean up but we'll be back later—we want to be here when she wakes up. The doctor is hopeful that it won't be too much longer."

"Okay, guys, I'll see you then," she said.

Val walked over to the nursing station to sign her name on the approved list of visitors and continued down the hall till stopping at room number 525. As Val opened the door she beheld Ritchie Gianelli standing over Mel's bed. She kept her voice down, but her tone spoke volumes. "Ritchie, what in the hell are you doing here?" she hissed. As Ritchie turned toward her, Val noticed he was holding something in his hands.

"Well, if it isn't my worst nightmare," he commented drolly. He hadn't forgotten Val's feelings toward him or her disapproval of Mel's relationship with him. She had always been a thorn in his side. It wasn't going to be as easy to dispatch Val as it had been with Mel's former flame.

For her part, Val had dealt with his kind of macho jerk before, whether they were behind bars or in uniform. She was not a woman to be regarded lightly and took special delight in showing assholes like Ritchie just how seriously she should be taken. Val grabbed him by his jacket collar and pulled him into the hallway with the full force and fury of her anger.

"Maybe you didn't hear me the first time—I asked you what you were doing here! You're not family, your name's not on the list" she said with contempt.

"What's it to you, Val? I have a right to see Mel—we have a history together. I love her," he answered without skipping a beat. He impatiently checked his watch.

"Love her? What a freaking joke! You don't know the meaning of the word, Ritchie. You're just basking in the glow of the melodrama—the big hero! And let me set you straight on something else; you HAD a history with Mel. Past tense! And I'll be damned if your face is the first one she sees when she opens her eyes!" Val moved toward him defiantly, her protective instinct toward Mel fueled by the memories of the days and nights she spent comforting her in the aftermath of Ritchie's abandonment.

"Fine . . . have it your way, bitch. I'm sick of your shit! I'm outta here!" he bellowed, throwing Mel's rosary beads on the cart outside the door.

"Wait just a minute," Val ordered as she stopped Ritchie in his tracks, putting her hand to his chest. "Where did you get these?" she demanded, picking up the rosary from the cart. She recognized it immediately; it was Mel's rosary, the one her grandmother had given her, the one she always kept at her bedside.

"Some guy left them for me to give to Mel," Ritchie answered as he brusquely pushed Val's hand off his chest.

"Some guy? You mean Frank, Mel's boyfriend, don't you?" she asked, her eyes narrowing in anger. "He was here, wasn't he, Ritchie?"

"Yeah, he was here, but he left in a big hurry—maybe he was too chicken to stick around," he replied with a flat laugh.

Val was now sure it was Frank she saw leaving the hospital—his and Ritchie's David-and-Goliath meeting played out in her mind as if she had witnessed it in person. Mel had told her about their encounter with Ritchie at the mall a month earlier and how upset it had made Frank; it all made sense now. Poor Frank . . . she had to get a hold of him right away, before any more damage was done.

"I'd kill you right now if I had the chance, you bastard, but you're not worth wasting the jail time on," she warned.

"Go to hell, Val," Ritchie barked as he strode down the hall.

"After you!" she yelled after him. Val opened the door to Mel's room and sat down on the chair next to her bed; she took in the sight of her best friend lying there so helplessly, her head swollen, blood seeping through the dressing. She tried not to cry, but her resolve gave out. She put her head down next to Mel's and listened to the sound of her rhythmic breathing; it renewed her spirits a bit.

Taking some tissue out of its container on the table next to the bed, Val blew her nose and straightened up in her seat. "Mel, I'm going to find Frank, don't you worry—this has all been a terrible misunderstanding. Whatever I have to do, I'll do it," Val promised as she tucked the light cotton blanket around her friend. "All you have to do is get better. I love you, buddy. I'll see you tomorrow," she whispered as she carefully kissed Mel on the cheek and placed the rosary beads under her pillow.

Mel opened her eyes. At first, she wasn't sure where she was, but then realized she was lying in a hospital bed. The room was dark; the only sound she heard was the beeping coming from the monitor next to her bed. She tried lifting her head but couldn't—it was too painful. Her chest hurt, too. She inspected the tubes and needles in her arms and sniffed the medicinal odor of the room; she touched the gauze wrapped around her head. She was tired and in pain but very hungry—it was her hunger that woke her; she couldn't remember the last time she had eaten. "What's happened to me?" she wondered as she searched the room, trying to get her bearings. It couldn't be good, of that much she was certain. She couldn't stand hospitals. She'd been taken to one when her appendix had burst in the seventh grade and she never forgot that smell, but she fondly recalled the nice nurse who had let her eat as much ice cream as she wanted after the worst was over.

Mel strained to see out the open door and into the corridor. It was eerily quiet. There was only one light on in the hallway and there was no sign of activity. By the look of it, she thought it might be very early in the morning, which meant the breakfast trays wouldn't be coming any time soon. A couple of minutes went by as she lay in the bed, trying to ignore her growling stomach. Then she remembered from her first hospital stay that there should be a call button on the right side of the bed for the nurse's station. She tried to turn over on her right side, but her chest hurt too much. As she slowly lay back down, she was startled to see a priest standing on the left side of the bed. She hadn't heard him enter the room—he hadn't made a sound. He was praying over her, but she couldn't hear his voice. His presence was so comforting to her.

Mel looked up at him and whispered, "Hello, Father." He was a handsome man sporting a full head of white hair, with a short, athletic build and dark brown eyebrows. She couldn't make out the color of his eyes as they were closed in prayer. He nodded his head in acknowledgment of her greeting then continued praying, his right hand making the sign of the cross over her broken body. She closed her eyes as he did so, then opened them to thank him again, but he was gone, as silently as he had come.

"What a nice thing for the hospital to do," Mel thought to herself. "I'll have to remember to thank them tomorrow." Within minutes, her fatigue overtook her hunger and she fell into a deep sleep, dreaming of her breakfast tray.

CHAPTER 30

The clanging of the breakfast carts woke me with a start. "Well, look who's awake! How are we feeling this morning, Miss Morrison? How's our hero doing?" the nurse inquired as she took my pulse and temperature.

"Good morning," I replied, unsure of what the nurse was referring to. "Why are you calling me a hero?" I asked as she hung fresh bags of intravenous fluids to the metal poles by my bed.

"You don't remember? Well, that's understandable. You took a nice hit to your head and that can sometimes cause short-term memory loss. But you'll get it back—it will just take some time. The doctor will be here in a little while and he'll go into more detail with you. Now, let's put a nice clean bandage on that head," she said in her cheeriest nurse voice.

I thought of the visiting priest. "Nurse, I just want to thank the hospital and the staff for arranging to have the priest visit with me earlier this morning. It was a really nice gesture—it did help me feel much better," I said, wincing in pain as the gauze wrapping was peeled away from my forehead.

"What are you talking about, Miss Morrison?" the nurse asked as she dropped the bloodied gauze in the stainless-steel garbage pail and replaced it with a large Band-Aid.

"You know, the priest who comes around to pray for the patients," I said as I went on to describe the good-looking priest in detail.

"The hospital doesn't perform any service like that, dear. Maybe he came by the night you were first brought up here. I remember seeing a couple of priests with your family," she patiently explained.

"No, I swear, I woke up early this morning and he was right here at the side of my bed, praying over me! I would have known the priests that were with my family—I didn't know who this priest was," I insisted. I was becoming frustrated; the nurse wasn't buying my story.

"Well, Miss Morrison, sometimes we dream all sorts of things and think they're real, don't we?" She didn't wait for my answer. "Are you hungry?" she asked, changing the subject. "It's got to be at least two days since you last had a meal," she commented as she expertly drew the metal bed tray across my bandaged torso and placed the breakfast platter atop it. For hospital fare, it didn't smell too bad.

"Could I please have two of those?" I asked shyly. I was starving!

"Why, of course you may. It's a good sign that you're eating so well," she observed.

The nurse put another helping on the tray and placed the buzzer within easy reach of my left hand. "When you're done, just give us a call," she instructed. I enthusiastically nodded my head as I stuffed the food into my mouth, then proceeded to lick the plates clean.

My hunger satiated, I fell into a deep sleep. I dreamed about Frank. I was in my house, going from room to room, looking for Frank but not finding him. I called out to him but he didn't answer. I looked out my back door to the patio; he was sitting on the garden bench holding Mac. Frank looked up at me, his beautiful blue eyes shining with love. Mac jumped off his lap and came running to me. I lifted him up in my arms and he started to lick my face. I was so happy! I gradually awakened from my dream and opened my eyes to find Val standing by my bed, holding Mac close to me while he licked my face. It wasn't a dream after all!

"Val! I'm so glad you're here! How did you get Mac past hospital security?" I asked, lowering my voice to a whisper. I wanted so to hold him but the needles in my arms made it impossible.

"Mel! Thank God you're okay!" she cried, trying not to hug me too hard. "I hid him under my coat! He cooperated the whole time and didn't make a peep!" she said, wiping a tear from her cheek. "God, Mel, you had us scared for a while there. By the way, how does it feel being the hero of the hour, buddy?" she asked anxiously.

"I don't get it. The nurse called me a hero, too. What the hell happened?" I asked as I tried not to scratch my dressings.

"You don't remember anything?" Val asked carefully.

"Not really . . . I remember leaving the building and looking for the judge. And, oh yeah, I remember hearing a lot of yelling. Next thing I know, I wake up here in this getup," I said, pointing at my bandaged head and torso.

"Well, it appears that you surprised a perp who was about to off the judge. Your practice made perfect, Mel. You took him down with a single shot. How does that feel? Great, I bet!"

Did Val just tell me that I killed someone? Even though I was trained for the possibility of something like that happening in my line of work and I took it seriously enough, I sure as hell never expected that I'd actually have to do it. That's why I became a court officer in the first place. If I'd wanted that kind of action, I would've joined NYPD! I was relieved that I didn't remember.

"Geez, Val, I don't know how I feel . . . it's not like I've ever killed someone before. I don't want to think about that right now—it hurts my head. Is the judge okay? How's he doing?" I asked with concern.

"He's fine. He plans on coming in here today for a visit, if that's okay with you. The judge owes you his life, Mel."

"Yikes! How's that gonna work?" I asked, only half-kidding.

Val shrugged her shoulders. "You've got me, kiddo," she replied as Mac began to squirm in her arms. "Listen, I'm gonna get this little guy home, but I'll be back later on tonight, okay?" She seemed to be in a hurry to leave.

"Val, where's Frank?" I asked. "I haven't seen him yet. Was he here when I was still knocked out?"

Val's hazel eyes grew dark; she took a deep breath before she spoke. "Mel, before I say anything, you have to promise me that you'll try to stay calm."

My heart started racing. "What's happened to Frank?" I cried out in alarm. I tried to do as Val asked and not panic but it wasn't working. The beeping on the monitor became louder and faster. She took my free hand and held it tightly.

"Mel, what I've pieced together so far is that he got here soon after you were brought in, then had a run-in with Ritchie and his goon squad. I hadn't gotten here yet so I can only imagine what Ritchie said to him. He thought he was running the show until I found out what he was up to, then I set him straight and got rid of him. Frank had already gone, so I took off like a bat out of hell looking for him, hoping to get to him before he assumed the worst. I'm pretty sure it was Frank I saw leaving the hospital. I ran after him but he was walking so fast he was gone by the time I got outside."

"I don't understand, Val. Why isn't he here now?" I implored, struggling to take in what she had just told me.

"That's what I'm trying to figure out, Mel. I've left him a ton of messages but he hasn't returned any of my calls. I even went by his apartment but he's not answering his buzzer. I think Ritchie gave him the idea that something was going on again between the two of you. I'm sorry. That's all I've got right now," she said apologetically.

A wave of nausea washed over me. "Why would he have believed anything Ritchie said?"

"I don't know, Mel, but I wouldn't be too hard on Frank," she answered sympathetically. "You know how convincing Ritchie can be. He had you fooled once, didn't he?"

My head was pounding; I fought hard against the pain. "What am I going to do, Val? He's the love of my life." I needed my best friend to guide me through the frightening landscape that was opening up before me.

"First things first, buddy. While I try to track Frank down, you're going to get all better so that we can get you home. Between me, your family, and Mrs. Frasier, we can keep it all together, but we want to get you back on familiar ground as soon as possible. And, Mel, I know I'm asking a lot, but try not to worry too much. All you need to do right now is get better, okay? I'll get this mess straightened out," she vowed.

"Thanks, Val. What would I do without you?" I said as we hugged goodbye, Mac wetting my face with his doggie kisses. "What would I do?" I thought as I watched them leave. I lay in bed, wondering where Frank was, what was going through his mind. "How could you not be here with me? I need you, love," I silently cried. There was a knock at the door. "Yes?" I called out weakly. The door opened halfway; a tall, dark-haired man in hospital scrubs appeared.

"Miss Morrison, my name is Dr. Friedman. May I come in?" he asked politely.

"Of course," I answered as I tried to pull myself together. "I'm so happy to meet you, Doctor. I understand that I have you to thank for saving my life."

"Well, it was a team effort, but thank you for the kind accolade," he replied as he moved a chair closer to the bed. "May I call you Marian?"

"You can even call me Mel."

"Very good! Mel, I don't want to take up too much of your time. There is a large crowd of people out there that want to see you, so I'll try to keep this brief. If you have any questions, feel free to interrupt me at any time."

"Okay, Doctor, shoot," I answered. Realizing my gaff, I quickly added, "Sorry, no pun intended!"

Dr. Friedman smiled, but seemed introspective. "Mel, I understand from the nursing staff that you're experiencing some short-term memory loss. Is that true?"

"I guess so. It's just little bits and pieces," I explained. From the pocket of his scrubs, the doctor retrieved a long, metal object that resembled a pen with a small pinpoint of light beaming from the end of it.

"Let's have a look," he instructed as he directed the light into one of my eyes, then the other. "Everything seems to be in order. As is often the case with head injuries, the patient may at times experience short-term memory loss that is bothersome, but rarely permanent. How is the rest of you feeling?" he asked as he gently pressed his hands around my rib cage.

"I am hurting a little," I reluctantly admitted.

"That's to be expected—we had a bit of a time removing all the bullet fragments. As far as I can see, though, you seem to be healing beautifully!" Dr. Friedman declared. "Mel, there's one more thing I need to discuss with you." He faltered for a moment. "Can you remember the last time you had your period?" he asked.

His question took me by surprise; why would he need to know that? I thought hard. "I'm sorry, Doctor, I really can't remember the exact date. I guess it would have been about a month ago. You could set a clock by my periods," I responded proudly.

"Mel, when you were first brought in we ran the usual tests. As is the case with female patients that fall within a certain age range, we check for the appearance of pregnancy hormones. Your sample came up positive," he said, watching me with a steady gaze.

"That's not possible," I replied, somewhat indignantly. After Ritchie and I broke up, I had stopped taking the pill. When it became apparent that Frank and I would become intimate, I told him that I didn't want to take it anymore as its side effects could present complications over time. Frank was very understanding and from that point forward we were extremely careful. Then it hit me: after our squabble in the car the day we ran into Ritchie, we barely made it back to the apartment to kiss and make up—the one time we took a chance.

"Doctor, what are you saying?" I asked, jerking myself back to reality.

"Mel, I would say you are approximately four weeks pregnant," he replied confidently. I closed my eyes and took in his words, letting them flow over me like water. "Are you all right?" he asked.

"You'll have to forgive me, Doctor. That's a lot to take in right now," I answered as I tried to get my battered head around his rather unexpected news.

"There's nothing to forgive. You've been through an awful lot, Mel, but I have to ask for a little more. You inquired of the nursing staff about pain medication. Unfortunately, given your present condition, we are unable to provide that kind of relief, but we can work on a pain-management program that can be of significant help to you during your recuperation."

"Sure, Dr. Friedman. Whatever you say . . . you're the man," I replied lamely, trying to inject some humor into the conversation. Under normal circumstances, his announcement would have given rise to tears of happiness and would have been a cause for celebration. But my circumstances were anything but normal. "Dr. Friedman, could you do me a big favor and apologize to my family for me and explain to them that I'm not feeling up to seeing visitors for the rest of the day. I have a lot to think about, you know?"

"Of course, Mel. Just let me know when you're ready."

"I will—and thanks again, Doctor," I replied gratefully. As the good doctor left the room, I looked out of my window and onto a view of the late summer's afternoon. Amid the green canopy of trees that opened before me, a leaf here and there was just beginning its shimmering red and gold decline into fall. "It's so very lovely, just like a violin's song," I thought as I drifted off to a disquieting sleep.

I was running through the black mists, my heart pounding with the resonance of a familiar fear. The air was tainted with the vampires' rot; the wind howled with their fury. They hunted me with a brutal vengeance. With each step I took, my breathing became more labored until I thought my lungs would burst. The torment had to end, I now knew, or I would simply cease to exist.

I stopped to confront the dark shadows that had haunted me for so many years, challenging their fiendish, glowing eyes, their scaly, ebony-hued wings glinting in the eerie light of their nightmarish world. Their heads turned toward me in unison, their snake-like orange eyes taking in the pitiful sight of the insignificant human standing before them in all of their magnificent maleficence.

"Let's have it done with, then—I won't run from you anymore!" I shouted at the monsters, my voice rising to a fevered pitch. "Go ahead! You can tear me apart and cover this wretched abyss with my blood, but you will NEVER take my soul!" I vowed defiantly. We stood for a moment in hell, facing one another in its frigid, endless, gray nothingness. The soulless ones then took flight, leaving me forever.

I was free.

CHAPTER 31

Any luck, Val?" I asked my best friend, my hopes fading with each day that passed with no sign of Frank. I had been in the hospital four days now.

"Not yet, Mel. Can you remember anything he told you—maybe the name of the school he's teaching in? I could go there right now and, you know, clear the air."

"I've tried, Val. My head hurts from all the remembering I've been trying to do. Dr. Friedman said it might take some time—I guess he was right."

"Hey, did they give you any of the good stuff yet?" she kidded.

"They can't," I replied, trying valiantly not to start crying, but knowing it was going to be a losing battle.

"Why the hell not?" Val looked positively horrified at the thought. "You've got to be hurting like a son of a bitch!"

"I'm pregnant!" I blurted out as the tears spurted from my eyes like a couple of punctured water balloons.

Val lowered her voice. "What did you just say?" she asked as she handed me a wad of tissues and slowly lowered herself into her chair. She looked at me as though I had flowers growing out of my ears.

"I'm about a month along. Dr. Friedman told me yesterday," I sniffled as I blew my nose.

"Holy crow, Mel! You really know how to make the big plays!" she said, shaking her head in amazement. She took my hand in hers. "You mean I'm going to be an auntie?"

"Yes, and Frank is going to be a father."

"Wow! Does your family know?"

"No, I'm telling them today. I wanted you to be the first to hear the news," I answered, somewhat cheerlessly. I tried to talk myself into being upbeat when I dropped the bombshell, but instead I felt sad.

Val knew me only too well. "Mel, I promise you that I'll get to the bottom of this. Do you remember what I told you the night George and I first met Frank?"

I perked up a bit. "You told me that we were perfect together."

"See, you remembered!" Val said encouragingly.

"I do remember!"

"Then hold on to that memory!" Val ordered. "There will be plenty more where that came from when all is said and done."

"Whatever you say, buddy," I replied as I tried to stifle a big yawn. The healing process was turning out to be an exhausting business, especially since I now had to do it under my own steam. How I pined for a painkiller!

"You look tired, Mel. Are you up for any more visitors?"

"I have to tell my mother—I can't put it off. The conversation I never wanted to have with her, God help me," I whimpered.

"Don't they say that what doesn't kill you will make you stronger?" Val volunteered.

"I'm not so sure," I replied lamely.

"It's time, my friend, it's time," she urged. As usual, Val, in her inimitable way, gently pushed me in the right direction.

As Val left the room, she motioned for my mother to come in. Mom walked quietly, almost tentatively, to my bedside.

"Marian Elizabeth, you put quite the scare into us," she said as she bent down to kiss my face. I looked up at my mother; her great beauty had not diminished with the passage of time, but the lines around her eyes had become deeper, sharper than I remembered, and for the first time I noticed a gray hair or two peeking out from her lustrous sable locks. She looked as tired as I felt.

"Ma, I'm so sorry. I never meant to put you or the family through anything like this," I said apologetically. I somehow felt as though I had let them down—I wasn't used to being the one in need.

"My goodness, what are you apologizing for? Why, you saved a man's life!" my mother exclaimed as she broke into her cautious smile. "I couldn't be any prouder of you, Marian Elizabeth! You were always the tough one!"

I tried shifting my weight, then cringed.

"Are you all right? Are you in pain?" she asked anxiously.

"Yeah, Ma, just a bit," I replied a tad sarcastically. "Why wouldn't I be in pain, Ma?" I asked.

"Try not to be impatient with me. I just want to be sure you're all right, that you're comfortable. It has been a trying few days for all of us," she remarked in her no-nonsense way. Same old Mom: no time for self-pity, not even now.

"Ma, is there ever going to be a day when I'm not the tough one?" I wanted desperately to know.

"Whatever do you mean, Marian Elizabeth?" she replied as she sat down, her back as straight as a razor.

"As far back as I can remember, since I was a little girl, you've called me tough. Even now, when I couldn't feel less tough if I tried, when I am more vulnerable than I have ever been in my life, you still call me that. Why, Ma?" I asked, searching her eyes for an answer.

"Well, you were always that way. You were such a tomboy when you were younger—you weren't afraid of anything! I . . . I mean your father and I, we never had to worry about you," she answered carefully, her eyes lingering on her clasped hands. For a moment, she appeared unsure of her explanation.

"Ma, I was only a child! How could you never have worried about me? Didn't you ever think about what I came up against as a kid? I always felt that I had to stand on my own. I can remember feeling that way when I was eight years old, for God's sake. How is it that an eight-year-old girl feels that she can't turn to her mother for help or comfort—or an eighteen-year-old, for that matter?" I demanded with all of the pent-up frustration of the little girl I had suddenly become. I thought back to the bullies I'd had to face down by myself over the years, whether it was to save my tail or one of my younger siblings. I was a runaway train now, but I couldn't stop myself; my anger and want were a long time coming. For the first time in my life, I no longer cared if my mother chose to either set aside her steely composure for an offer of unconditional love, or to walk out the door with her reserve and pride intact. I watched her with a mixture of anxiety and admiration as she got up from her chair and walked over to the window, calm and collected, my verbal onslaught seeming to bounce off her like dandelion puffs skimming the trees on a windy day. How I wished I could be just like her: so self-contained, so sure of her place in the world.

"Marian, Marian . . . I don't know what to say," she replied plaintively. For the first time I could remember, my mother called me by just my first name. Her voice sounded far away, as though coming from another time and place. "You were such a special baby . . . you never cried, did you know that?" she asked as she stared out at the pigeons congregating on the windowsill. "One time when you were very little, I remember waking you up from a sound sleep because I thought you were dead, you were so quiet in your crib! When you started to walk and talk, you were like a gamin, so full of life, always searching, always questioning. I admit that sometimes I didn't know what to make of you. I was brought up to expect that from a boy, not a little girl."

As I listened to my mother's recollections, my grandmother's description of her as a tomboy who loved to climb trees and fought having to wear a pretty dress broke through the cobwebs crowding my mind. In describing my childhood, my mother could have been talking about herself as a young girl. Had my mother simply forgotten those long-ago memories of a carefree adolescence or did she choose not to remember? Had she sacrificed a promising young womanhood and independence on the twin altars of marriage and motherhood?

When I'd asked my grandma what had happened to change my mother so dramatically, her simple explanation was that Mom met Dad and "that was that." I was going to have a baby now. I was scared; I needed answers. I needed my mother.

"But I *was* a little girl, Ma, and then a young woman—I needed you to see that," I said forlornly. "I needed you to help me become a woman, but you didn't. It seemed like you did everything you could to stop me," I whimpered.

My mother turned from the window and looked at me with a softness I didn't recognize. "When your father died," she responded sadly, "my world almost came to an end as well. In a way, the world I knew did end. Your father meant everything to me. I was still a young woman when he passed, not much older than you are now. Looking back, I see that I depended on you too much after he was taken from us. It wasn't fair to you," she admitted as she sat down and took my hand in hers. "Marian, dear, I have a confession to make,

and I pray that you'll find it in your heart to forgive me."
She faltered for a moment.

"Ma, what is it? You can talk to me—I'm not a little girl
anymore," I protested. My heart started racing again; what
dark secret could my saintly mother possibly have to con-
fess to me?

"It is a terrible truth for a mother to face, but as you were
growing older, I was envious of your youth and beauty—
and you were becoming such a beautiful young woman,
Marian! You had the whole world before you," she stated
wistfully.

"But, Ma, no one was more beautiful than you!" I vehemently declared. "How could you have been envious of me?"

"It's not something I am proud of. God forgive me, but
if I am to be completely truthful, I think that perhaps I
didn't want you to have what I had lost. I wasn't ready for
you to grow up, to have the opportunities I never had," she
admitted ruefully.

"Ma, what are you saying? That you regretted getting
married so young? I thought your life with Dad was all you
ever wanted?" I asked in shock.

"It *was* all I ever wanted—and then it was gone. Just
like that. The life I had dreamed of with him, raising our
family, growing old together . . . all gone. But I couldn't
allow myself the luxury of wallowing in my own misery—I
had to think of our children. No, I never regretted a thing.
Our children were the greatest gift he ever gave me," she
reflected. "After all, your father lives on in all of you," she
stated proudly. My mother looked at me pensively. "Marian
Elizabeth, my heart is heavy knowing that I can't get those
years back for you, but if you can forgive me, I promise
that I won't waste another second and I will be the kind of
mother you have always deserved," she vowed. For the first
time since my father died, I saw my mother's green eyes
well up. I crumpled like a rag doll into her welcoming arms,

our torrents of tears washing away the burden of so many desperate memories.

"Ma, I have a confession to make, too," I said as I sat up in the bed, wiping my eyes with the back of my hospital robe.

"Yes, Marian?" she prompted.

"I don't know how to tell you, Ma . . . I feel so stupid," I said. My mother pulled back and contemplated my tear-streaked face. She looked deeply into the green eyes that were so like her own.

"Dear daughter, are you pregnant? Is that what you are struggling to tell me?" she asked.

"How . . . how did you know? Did Val spill the beans?" I stammered in amazement.

"No, no, of course not. Val would never betray your confidence that way," she replied, shaking her head vehemently.

"Then how?" I asked again.

"A mother always knows these things, Marian," she knowingly replied.

"Are you disappointed in me, Ma?" I asked, scrunching the hospital blanket in my hands for comfort.

"For heaven's sake, Marian Elizabeth, have a little faith in me! There's no shame in bringing a new life into the world, no matter the circumstance," she gently remonstrated. My mother paused for a moment. "I know you won't appreciate my asking you this, but I feel I must: is your young man the father of the child?"

"Yes, Ma, Frank is the father," I admitted.

"Well, then, all is not lost. You didn't tell us a lot about him, but he sounded like a sensible boy. He would do the right thing by you and the baby, wouldn't he?" she asked.

"He doesn't know about the baby, Ma. He's disappeared, and I don't know what to do. I have no husband, no boyfriend—I have no one!" I cried into my pillow.

"Now don't be going silly on me, young lady! You will always have your family. And there simply must be an explanation for him not being here with you. Tonight, we'll say an extra decade for the Blessed Mother's guidance on this. My, my, Marian Elizabeth, you're the last person in the world I would pick to be giving up so easily on that young man."

"Well, it seems he gave up on me, Ma," I replied despondently.

"It may look that way now, but don't give up hope—I have a feeling that things will turn around. Marian, dear, here's a thought: if it's alright with you, I'll stay with you for a while once you're settled in at home. You will need all your strength, especially now, and I don't think you should be in that big apartment all by yourself. I was speaking with Dr. Friedman earlier and he told me that with the progress you're making, you should be discharged sometime next week. How does that sound?" she asked hopefully.

"It sounds great, Ma. It will be nice having you there," I replied gratefully.

"It's all set then. And, speaking of the family, everyone's been patiently waiting to see you. Grandma is practically beside herself. Do you want to keep your news our little secret for now?" she asked.

"Yes, thanks, Ma, I think that announcement can wait a bit. I'm still kind of getting used to the idea myself," I answered.

My mother leaned over and gave me a kiss and a wink. The future seemed a little less scary now.

CHAPTER 32

He stared at the newspaper . . . the headline read "HEROINE HEADS HOME". It had been two weeks since Mare's terrible accident and his encounter with Ritchie at the hospital—two weeks since his heart had been irretrievably broken. Before Frank met his Mare, he thought he had become impervious to that kind of feeling; after all, he had lived through the nightmare of being practically dumped at the altar by Donna and her millionaire boyfriend. He had survived that humiliation and gone on with his life, but nothing could have prepared him for this. With Mare, he believed that he had come to know what true love was; it had changed his life. In the space of three short months, he had been transformed from a pathetic excuse of a man to someone who believed that, through his and Mare's love, anything was possible. Now he believed in nothing.

But as Frank looked, for the hundredth time, at Mare's beautiful face shining out from the picture on his nightstand, he slowly rose from the rumpled bed that had become his refuge and shuffled to the bathroom. He looked at his image in the mirror—he looked older and tired. He had stopped shaving and his beard was growing heavier; his hair was becoming long and unkempt . . . he just didn't care anymore. Only a short time ago he had looked forward to his teaching position with eagerness and the happy anticipation of beginning a new career with the love of his life by his side, cheering him on. Now, he plodded through his days looking like a man who had given up on new beginnings—on everything.

Frank opened the medicine cabinet and took out his razor, slowly turning it over in his hand. "Why bother?" he thought to himself. It was Saturday and there was no reason to even get out of bed. He remembered someone once saying that you couldn't outsmart love. Is that what he was trying to do? He looked at the stranger in the mirror staring back at him, dark circles ringing his eyes. The newspaper reported that Mare was leaving the hospital that very day and that a big welcome-home party had been planned for her return. He thought back to the night he heard the news about the shooting, following on the heels of Ritchie's phone message. He had driven like a madman to the hospital, only to find Ritchie standing vigil outside Mare's room. Ritchie then sent him on his way, like a dog with his tail between his legs. He didn't remember the drive home.

He was enveloped in a haze of confusion and desolation that fateful night when he walked into his apartment and heard Val on his answering machine, imploring him to contact her. In a rage of self-pity and despair, he had ripped the phone out of the wall. A couple of days later his landlady, Mrs. Muir, tried to check in on him but he wouldn't answer the door when she knocked. She called out to him, "Mr. Brennan, a woman named Val stopped by today. She said you won't answer your phone or your bell. Is everything alright in there?" He barked at her to leave him alone. He'd felt so hollow, so helpless. He looked again at his reflection in the mirror. "Should I risk it? Should I take another chance?" he brooded. "Maybe I've been wrong about everything. Doesn't Mare deserve that much from me?" he wondered. Frank put the razor to his face and took a giant leap of faith.

Frank pulled a pair of jeans out of a pile of discarded clothes blanketing the floor, dressed quickly, then ran down to the basement garage where he kept his Harley. He glanced at his watch. He figured it was about fifteen miles to Mare's apartment in Brooklyn, so if he rode at a good pace he should make it there in time for her arrival home. As Frank revved the engine, he began to imagine seeing his love again, holding her in his arms, keeping her safe like he had promised. She would be his Maid Marian again, and he, her Robin Hood. The memories of his time with her propelled him on, the bike roaring down streets and over bridges till suddenly, he found himself on the street where she lived. He jumped off the bike and walked a few feet till he saw her brownstone building, gaily festooned with banners and balloons. One after the other they read: "Welcome Home, Hero," "We Love you," "God Bless You, Marian."

A boisterous crowd had assembled, spilling out into the street; an air of excited expectation permeated the scene. Among the crowd he noticed the now-familiar uniforms of firefighters and court officers. As he moved in closer, Frank heard the wailing siren of an ambulance coming from around the block; an eerie feeling came over him. The ambulance came to a stop in front of the building. From where he was standing, he could make out a wheelchair being taken out of the vehicle; he could see Mare's auburn hair peeking out from under a large-brimmed hat. He threw up his arms and screamed, "Mare, Mare, over here—it's me, Frank!" but she couldn't hear him over the cheers from the throngs of well-wishers surrounding her as the chair was carried up the steps to the building's entrance.

The large doors opened wide and she was taken inside. As the last of the jubilant partygoers entered the apartment, Frank saw two burly court officers, guns at their sides, closing the doors and standing guard over the celebration inside. He instantly recognized them; they were Ritchie's goon squad from the hospital! Frank stood frozen in place: at once, he realized that his coming here had been a terrible mistake—a conceit that had clouded his judgment. What else could have fooled him into thinking that, when all was said and done, Mare would throw Ritchie over for him?

Through the tears that had quietly begun to wet his face, Frank took one last look at the house he had once thought of as home and whispered goodbye.

CHAPTER 33

V al approached Frank's apartment building with mixed feelings; if she was successful this time and found Frank she would be ecstatic, but it would take every ounce of self-discipline not to throttle him. It had been three weeks since the shooting and Frank's sudden disappearance, and she had not been able to deliver on her promise to Mel to find him. His phone had been out of order and his landlady had no luck getting him to talk to her. Val was at the point of wanting to break his door down, but Mel wouldn't go there—she wanted Frank to come to her willingly. Val could only imagine the hell he had been going through these past weeks, not knowing the truth, but he had to understand the nightmare Mel was enduring. As bad as things looked, Val would not accept that Frank had given up; she couldn't have been so wrong about him. She located the three buzzers on the outside door of the building and went to press the one for Frank's apartment when she noticed his name was no longer listed on the tenant roll. She rang several times, then gave up and rang his landlady's bell. After waiting for what seemed like an eternity, Mrs. Muir appeared at the door.

"Hello, Mrs. Muir, my name is Val. I don't know if you remember me, but I came by about two weeks ago to ask if you could check in on my friend, Frank Brennan. He's a tenant of yours. I left you my phone number. I apologize for stopping by unannounced like this, but I'm starting to get a little concerned. I still haven't heard from him," Val said uneasily.

"Oh, yes, dear, I remember you. I did try to speak with Mr. Brennan—he was very upset as I recall. He wouldn't even come to the door when I knocked. That was so unlike him—he was always such a friendly fellow. I called you back and left a message. Didn't you get it?" she inquired.

"Yes, thank you for getting back to me, Mrs. Muir. But I still haven't heard from Frank and I noticed his name isn't on the directory anymore. Can you please help me?" Val asked.

"Why, Mr. Brennan moved out, dear, didn't you know?"

"No, I didn't!" Val's heart sank. "When did he move?"

"He left about a week ago. I was so disappointed that he decided not to stay on here . . . he was such a nice young man, a real gentleman. You don't see that too much any-more," she noted.

"Did he mention where he was going, Mrs. Muir?" Val inquired, trying hard not to betray her alarm.

"No, just that he was moving closer to his job. I believe he was starting a teaching job somewhere in the Bronx, but that's all I know," she offered. "I hope Mr. Brennan is all right—the poor fellow looked a fright the day he left."

"Thank you, Mrs. Muir. You've been very helpful," Val assured the old woman. She walked slowly to her car, starting to lose hope for the happy ending she had promised Mel. She opened the door, sat down, and leaned her head against the steering wheel. "I feel like I'm chasing a ghost," she sighed heavily. "God dammit, Frank, what's wrong with you?" she cried aloud in desperation as she started the car and drove away, dreading the latest report she would have to give her best friend.

Val walked into her living room and fell onto the couch like a stone. She removed her sneakers and rested her feet on the coffee table. She was distracted; too much had happened in a short space of time—so much that didn't make any sense. Val heard George come in through the kitchen. She was relieved to see his warm smile as he sat down beside her and kissed her hello.

"Here, babe, you look like you need this," he said as he handed her a cold bottle of beer. George picked up her foot and started to massage it.

"Thanks, hon. You're the best," Val responded gratefully. She sank further down into the comfort of the overstuffed cushions and took a long gulp of her beer. "You're not going to believe this, George. Apparently, Frank moved out of his place last week."

"Christ, Val, this is getting crazy. No forwarding address, I'm guessing."

"Good guess. I don't get it, honey. You met Frank—you saw him and Mel together. You thought the same thing about them that I did, didn't you?" Val asked in earnest.

"Yeah, I did. I thought he was a decent guy, and I love Mel, you know that. They seemed genuinely happy with each other," George observed.

"Then what the hell happened? Mel's lying in a hospital bed after being almost killed, then finds out she's pregnant with Frank's baby . . . don't you think he'd at least try to reach out to her, or to me, to see if she's okay?"

"I understand your frustration, babe, but I can't explain it any better than you can. And while I'm not making excuses for the guy, we still don't know the whole story, and he doesn't know about the baby. I don't know Frank really well, but I think if he knew about that, he'd come around fast enough."

"It's all Ritchie's fault!" Val declared angrily. "He's like a bad case of herpes: he always pops up at the worst possible moment and never stops causing pain and heartache."

"I think Frank got spooked, Val. Didn't you tell me that before he met Mel he was engaged to some hot chick who dumped him for a Wall Street big shot?"

"Yeah, she said he was pretty torn up about that. I think Mel was the first woman he got serious about after that whole mess went down. She said it took him about two years to get back on track."

"Men are babies, Val—everyone knows that. Do you think I'd act any better than Frank if I got it in my head that you were dumping me for some millionaire?"

"You'd better not or I'd have to kill you."

"I know you would, babe, and that's why you never have to worry about me pulling a stunt like that."

"That's a relief!" Val laughed.

"Look, you've gone above and beyond the call of duty trying to help Mel and I'm sure she knows it, so don't keep beating yourself up about it. And you know what else?"

"What? That you love me more than anything in the whole wide world?"

"You know it, babe. But I don't think this story is finished being written. Remember, it ain't over till the fat lady sings. I don't hear any singing—do you hear any singing?" George asked, cocking his ear. He smiled as he pulled Val closer to him. "Come on, babe," George said as he stood and offered his hand to Val. "Let's get some shut-eye. Tomorrow's another day."

Val gratefully took his hand as he led her upstairs. "I'm a lucky woman, George," Val commented as she got into bed, drawing the comforter near.

"I know, babe, I know," he replied with a yawn as he tenderly kissed Val goodnight.

CHAPTER 34

The phone rang on the table next to Val's side of the bed—she quickly grabbed the receiver before George could wake up. She glanced over at the alarm clock, its neon-green glow announcing the time: 12:30 a.m. "Hello?" she whispered.

"Val, it's me! I remembered! I remembered the name of his school," Mel yelled into the phone.

Val quietly slid out of bed, looked over at George snoring peacefully, then crept downstairs to the kitchen.

"Mel, what are you still doing up? You should be getting some sleep—come to think of it, so should I. I have to get up in six hours," she gently scolded her friend.

"Listen to me, Val. I was watching television and got bored so I started flipping channels and I heard the announcer on the public television station say something about their upcoming series on George and Martha Washington. Then it hit me, just like a bolt of lightning! The school is called Washington Irving Grammar School and I remembered that he said it was in Riverdale, near where he grew up. Oh my God, Val, I remembered!" Mel said excitedly.

Val woke up quickly. "Okay, let me think this thing through. It's after midnight so there's not much we can accomplish right now, but I'll call you first thing tomorrow morning and we'll figure something out."

"Don't you have to go to work tomorrow?" Mel asked.

"Let me worry about that . . . I think I feel a cough coming on."

"Val, I'm scared."

"Me, too," Val admitted. "Try to get some rest, Mel. Remember, you're sleeping for two now."

"I'll try, Val, but it's going to be tough—it's all I can think about."

"We've come this far, my friend; we're almost at the finish line. Sleep tight."

"Who am I kidding?" Val thought as she went upstairs and slid back into bed. No sleep tonight ...

Val waited patiently till the hands on the kitchen clock ticked to 10 a.m., then called information to ask if there was a listing for a Washington Irving Grammar School in Riverdale. Damned if there wasn't; Mel got it right! Val dialed the number and picked the option from the menu for the administrative office.

"Good morning. Washington Irving Grammar School; Mrs. Hamilton speaking. How may I assist you?" the official-sounding voice on the line announced.

Val took a deep breath. "Good morning, Mrs. Hamilton. This is Mrs. Adams and I'm calling from the Bronx County Central Jury office."

"How can I help you, Mrs. Adams?" she asked.

"I hope you can, Mrs. Hamilton. Would you be able to tell me if you have a teacher there by the name of Francis, middle initial A, last name, Brennan? He was supposed to have reported for jury duty by nine-thirty this morning but it appears he hasn't checked in," Val asked, crossing her fingers.

"Yes, Mr. Brennan is one of our teachers. Would you like me to have him contact you? I'm sure it's just a simple mistake—he's usually quite conscientious," Mrs. Hamilton replied, a note of concern in her voice.

"Thank you, but that won't be necessary—he may not have received the summons in a timely fashion," Val assured her. "We just wanted to be sure he wasn't playing hooky!" she quipped light-heartedly. "We'll contact him to schedule another date. Thank you so much for your assistance, Mrs. Hamilton," Val exhaled as she hung up the phone. Now what to do? She dialed Mel's apartment and Julia answered.

"This is the Morrison residence. Who, may I ask, is calling?" Julia inquired in her slightly Victorian manner. Val loved Julia's sense of decorum; it evoked a feeling of order and refinement to a world that seemed to become more degraded and unbalanced by the day.

"Good morning, Julia, it's Val. How is our patient doing today?" she inquired.

"Good morning, Val. She's doing very well, getting stronger every day, thank God. Just a touch of morning sickness lately, but other than that, she's been a soldier. How are you? Any good news for us today?" she asked hopefully.

"I found Frank, Julia. He was right where Mel said he was!" Val exclaimed.

"Praise be to God! Our prayers have been answered!" Julia replied with uncharacteristic enthusiasm.

"Well, I don't know about that," Val replied cautiously. "But hopefully, this mystery will be solved by the end of the day."

"Don't worry, Val. Our lord works in mysterious ways," Julia commented reassuringly.

"I hope you're right, Julia. Can I speak to Mel, please?" Val asked.

"Yes, you may. God speed, Val!" she said as she brought the phone to Mel, then quietly closed the door behind her.

"Hey, Val," Mel whispered, her voice signaling her nervousness.

"What up, Mamasita?" Val joked. "Are you feeling lucky this morning?" she asked.

"Was I right?" Mel asked apprehensively.

"Right as rain, my friend! I spoke to someone at the administrative office at the school. I had to lie a bit, I'm afraid. I told them I was from Bronx Central Jury and that I was checking up on a missing juror," Val confessed.

"And they believed you?" Mel asked, feeling proud of her friend for her wily resourcefulness.

"Right, again! Working with lawyers for the past five years has rubbed off on me, I guess," Val joked.

"I don't know how to thank you, Val. What do we do now?" Mel asked as she nervously paced the floor.

"Well, I was thinking that we could take a drive up there before the end of school today and take it from there. Do you think you're up for that?" Val wasn't convinced that even Mel had the strength to take another rejection if Frank wouldn't agree to see her.

"How fast can you get us there?" Mel asked, trying not to jump out of her skin.

"School usually ends around three o'clock in the afternoon. It should take about an hour or so to get there from your house. Can you hold on if I get to your place by one-thirty?" Val asked.

"I hope so! Who's better than you, Val?" Mel asked with feigned ignorance.

"It's been a while since you asked me that question, and I still can't think of anyone!" she laughed, silently praying that Mel would still think of her that way by day's end.

CHAPTER 35

Mel and Val sat in the car in contemplative silence, trying to make sense of the surreal events of the past month. Washington Irving Grammar School stood before them like a sentinel: it was 2:45 p.m.

"It's now or never, Mel," Val prodded reassuringly.

"Wish me luck, Val," Mel said as she looked to her best friend for courage.

"Done! I'm right here if you need me," Val promised.

Mel got out of the car and stared at the walkway leading to the front doors of the school—it seemed a mile long. She slowly made her way to the entrance; she hesitated as she gripped the large bronze door handle, her chest still smarting from her injury. "Blessed Mother, please grant me strength," she silently prayed. She opened the door and resolutely walked in the direction of the sign that read "Principal's Office."

"Excuse me, could you help me?" she asked of the young man sitting at the front desk, who looked to be all of twelve years old.

"Sure," he said as he looked up from his comic book. He stared hard at Mel, as though he was trying to get a tag on her, then asked excitedly, "Hey, aren't you the lady who was on TV—the one who killed that bad guy?"

"Yes, I am, but you can call me Ms. Morrison. What's your name, young man?" Mel inquired.

"I'm Kelsey!" he chirped.

"Who's in charge here, Kelsey?" Mel asked as she looked around the office.

"My mom is—she's the principal. She had to go to the ladies' room and left me in charge, but just for five minutes," he explained officiously. Kelsey's innocent eyes widened. "Wow, Miss Morrison – you're really famous! How'd it feel, getting shot and all?" Kelsey asked with glee.

"It's not something I'd recommend. Listen, Kelsey, I can provide you with all the gory details later, but right now I'd like to know if I can see Mr. Brennan before he leaves for the day. It's kind of important that I speak with him," Mel pressed.

"That's cool. His classroom is number three at the end of the hallway, on the left-hand side. You'd better hurry— the closing bell is about to ring," he alerted her as his eyes wandered back to his comics.

"Good man," Mel said, patting Kelsey on his shoulder. She left the office, picking up her stride as she headed toward Frank's classroom. She broke into a light sweat. "Baby, you're about to meet Daddy," she whispered as she patted her tummy. Just then, the bell tolled the end of the school day and the doors opened to release its grateful detainees. Mel waited for the stampede to end, then stopped at classroom #3 and peaked in – Frank was sitting at his desk sorting paperwork. The late afternoon sun was streaming in through the open window, shedding a golden glow over him. She thought her heart would burst.

"Hello, Francis," she said as she stood in the doorway. Frank turned his head in her direction. His mouth opened slightly, as though he was going to return her greeting, but no words came. The fading tan he'd acquired from their days together at the beach turned ashen.

"Mare? I can't believe it's you!" he declared in disbelief. He stared at her as if she were a vision.

Mel started to walk toward him, then stopped. "It's not like you not to offer me a seat, Frank," she gently admonished him, struggling to keep the waterworks at bay.

Frank jumped up as though snapping out of a trance. "Oh, God! I'm so sorry! Please, sit down." He tenderly took her by the arm and directed her to one of his student's desks. Frank waited until she sat down before taking a desk in the opposite row. They looked at each other across the small aisle; they were both tired, both war-weary.

"You've grown a beard since I last saw you," Mel noticed as she took in Frank's bedraggled appearance. She quickly added, "It looks good on you, very professorial."

"You look good, too, Mare," Frank replied, rather sheepishly. "What I mean is, I'm glad you're okay. What happened to you . . . it was terrible. A nightmare! I followed it in the papers every day, right up to the day you came back to the big welcome-home party." He looked down at the recently polished wood floor, keeping his eyes fixed on an errant scuff mark. In a tremulous voice he asked, "Mare, how did you find me? Why did you come here today? I'm sure it wasn't to check out my new look."

Mel couldn't believe what she was hearing and seeing – he was almost like a stranger to her. This wasn't him; this wasn't her Frank. She knew in the deepest recesses of her heart that she wasn't wrong about him. He wasn't like the all the others.

"Frank, what's happened to you? Don't you still love me? Do you have any idea what I've been going through without you? How can you be so cold?" she beseeched him.

"I'm not cold," Frank answered testily as he shot up from the desk and walked over to the blackboard. He picked up an eraser and distractedly ran it across the chalky surface.

"At least I've come to see you, Frank. I woke up in a hospital bed after almost being killed and you weren't there. I waited every day, every second of every day in that hospital for you to come, but you never did. Why?"

Frank carefully placed the eraser back on the ledge and slowly turned to face her, to be lost again in the green eyes he had dreamt of since the day they first met. "Because . . . because it was too much to lose. I just couldn't bear to lose you, so I gave up. How could I compete with a guy like Ritchie? How can I, Mare?" he implored, gazing sadly at her with red-rimmed eyes.

Mel now knew that Val had been right all along about what went down between Frank and Ritchie at the hospital. She wanted to throw herself at Frank, to smother him with all the love she had been forced to subdue these long weeks without him by her side. She rose from her chair and followed him to the blackboard where she noticed a verse he had written there. Mel recited it aloud:

"The best thing for being sad is to learn," Merlin advised the young Arthur. "That is the only thing that will not fail you. You may grow old and sick, you may miss your only true love; you may see the world around you laid to waste, or know your honor to be devastated by the deeds of evil men. There is only one thing for it then – to learn. That is the only thing which the mind can never tire of, never be tortured by, never fear or distrust, and never dream of regretting. Learning is the thing."

She stared at Frank, his pale face betraying his pain, the light in his once-azure blue eyes now dimmed by melancholy.

"It's so beautiful, Frank . . . and a little sad, to give up on love so easily," she said kindly. Did you write this?" she asked.

"Gosh, no! I'm not that talented. I've been teaching the class about medieval history," Frank explained as he shifted his weight uneasily from one foot to the other. "I paraphrased that from a novel called "The Once and Future King" by T.H. White. I was trying to explain to them that Merlin, the sorcerer, is advising the future King of England about the kind of world he's going to rule when he inherits the throne. I don't know why I put it up there. They're only eight years old—I don't know if they got any of it," he shrugged. Frank looked at Mel as though hoping she could explain it all to him.

Mel thought back to the sage words of advice her grandmother had given her when she had just about given up on finding her soul mate: "You can't outsmart love." She drew closer, her hand caressing Frank's pain-etched face. "Francis, my love. Once upon a time, I promised to be your Maid Marian. Won't you still be my Robin Hood?" she asked softly.

A distant echo of thunder from an approaching storm rippled the air. A strong gust of wind blew through the open window, scattering the papers on Frank's desk. Mel and Frank felt a surge of energy flow through them, electrifying them as they embraced, transforming their despair into desire.

Val sang at the top of her lungs to the song on the car radio—it kept her mind off what was taking place inside the school. It had been over an hour since Mel went inside. She was worried; what if Frank wasn't the stellar fellow she had made him out to be? What if she had inadvertently led her best friend down the wrong road? She wished she had the faith Mel so ardently possessed. She closed her eyes and prayed: "God, I'm kind of out of practice, so maybe you don't want to hear from me, but I am praying with all my might that it all works out for her and Frank. It's time she caught a break, you know? Thanks for listening. Amen." As she opened her eyes, she saw Mel and Frank emerging from the building, strolling arm in arm. "Thank you, God. I'll never disbelieve again," she vowed. Val stepped out of the car as they approached. Mel was simply glowing! Frank had a sappy grin on his face as he extended his hand to Val.

"Val, it's really good to see you again," he said sheepishly.

Val took a step back and gave Frank the once-over. "You knucklehead. I was ready to kill you!" she exclaimed as she punched his arm, followed by a big bear hug.

"Val, I'm so sorry! Mare explained everything to me. Can you ever forgive me for being such a jerk?" he asked plaintively.

"You know, Frank, you really had us going there for a while, but if Mel can forgive you, then who am I not to?" Val replied.

"Thanks, Val, for everything. I owe you, big time—you're a true friend. Listen, I'm taking Mare for a burger. Please join us. Anything you want—it's on me," Frank insisted.

Mel and Val exchanged glances. "That's okay, Frank, maybe another time. I want to get on the road before I hit the rush hour traffic. Will you be taking Mel home tonight?"

"You bet, Val," he assured her.

"All righty, then. Make sure she gets home safe and sound, okay?" Realizing she sounded like a mother hen, Val added, "Will you listen to me? It's just that I've gotten a little over-protective of her lately."

"I understand," Frank replied as he opened the car door for her. "Thanks again, Val. I don't have the words."

Mel hugged her best friend tightly then whispered in her ear, "The verdict is in, Val: there is no one better than you. Case closed."

CHAPTER 36

F rank and Mel walked into the Skipper together, their feet barely touching the ground. They were greeted by a sea of friendly waves and a chorus of "Yo's."

"So, what do you think, Mare? This is where I spent the better part of my formative years, playing darts and drinking beer! It's great, isn't it?" Frank asked rhetorically, happy memories lighting up his face.

"Sure, honey, it's a terrific little place," Mel replied as she adjusted her eyes to take in the darkened, musty room decorated with ragged football banners and tarnished trophies. Pictures of sports legends adorned the yellowed walls; a sign lettered with a single word, "Veritas," hung crookedly from the ancient bar. A smiling waitress sat them at a booth and handed them their menus while explaining the night's specials.

"We'll both have the burger special, medium rare, with raw onions and two beers, please," Frank ordered as he handed the menus back to the waitress.

"Frank, I think I'll take a pass on the onions and beer tonight—maybe just a Coke for me—and I think I'll take my burger well done."

"Okay, Mare. Miss, make that a beer for me and a Coke for my lady with her burger well done. Thanks." As the waitress walked away, Frank put his arm around Mel. "No beer? What's up, Mare? I thought we'd be celebrating tonight. Are you feeling all right?"

"I'm fine . . . just a little tired is all. A beer might put me to sleep," Mel replied nonchalantly. She was dying to give Frank her news, but the neighborhood hangout was not the place she had in mind when she told him he was going to be a father.

"Hey, Cheech, what's up? Playing darts tomorrow night?" asked a large, mustachioed man as he came by the booth, slapping Frank on the back.

"Hey, Sal! How are you doing, man? Yeah, I'll be there— you want to win, don't you? By the way, this is my girlfriend, Marian. Mare, this is my good friend and teammate, Sal."

Sal looked surprised. "Girlfriend? Where's he been hiding you?" he asked jovially as he offered his huge hand in greeting. "Do I know you from somewhere, Marian? You look familiar to me."

"We haven't met, Sal, but you might have seen my picture in the paper recently."

"That's it! You saved that judge from getting killed, right?"

Frank chimed in proudly, "That's my girl!"

"No kidding? Man, that was something!" Sal remarked as he shook his head. "Well, thank God you're all right. It's a pleasure meeting you. Stay safe, okay? Cheech, see you tomorrow night, man," Sal said as he slapped Frank a high five. Mel watched as Sal carefully lowered his hulking body onto his barstool.

"He seems like a really nice guy, Frank."

"Sal? He's the best – kind of like my version of Val."

"I used to work with a guy named Cheech. He told me the nickname 'Cheech' was Italian slang for 'Frank'."

"That's right. Even though my family is Irish, I grew up in a predominantly Italian neighborhood," he explained as the food arrived. "My friends have been calling me Cheech since we're kids."

Mel proceeded to attack her hamburger as though it was her last meal.

"Hey, baby, slow down!" Frank lovingly teased her. "There's more where that came from."

"Sorry!" Mel apologized as she started to wipe an errant drop of ketchup from her chin. "I didn't realize how hungry I was." Frank took the napkin from her hand and kissed the offending condiment from her face.

"Yum . . ." he drawled. "Say, Mare, I don't want to rush you, but do you think we could skip dessert tonight? My place isn't too far from here," he said eagerly.

Mel studied Frank's face, lingering in the calm blue waters of his eyes. "I think that can be arranged, Francis," she concurred.

Frank motioned hurriedly to the waitress for the check, throwing money down on the table before it even arrived. He grabbed their coats, helped Mel on with hers, then hustled them out of the place like their very lives depended on it. Mel wasn't complaining.

The apartment was, thankfully, a quick ten-minute car ride from the pub; Frank and Mel were just about ready to explode. As they entered its small interior, Mel looked around the studio: the place was pretty much bare except for a bed, a dresser that doubled as a night stand, and a single lamp that stood atop a beat-up desk where Frank's collection of books and newspapers were falling onto to the floor.

"It's not much, but it's only temporary—just till my brother sells it," Frank explained apologetically as he watched Mel look around the cramped living quarters.

"It's fine, honey. We're together now and that's all that matters," she answered.

Frank approached his love and slowly drew his arms around her waist, pulling her into himself.

"Can I kiss your boo-boos, Mare? I promise I'll make them all better," he moaned as he covered her neck with his warm, moist kisses.

"Yes, Francis, you may," she cooed.

Afterward, as Mel slept peacefully in his arms, Frank gently stroked her beautiful auburn hair. How could he have been so stupid? He almost lost the love of his life, his soul-mate, and for what – a bruised ego? "Never again," he vowed to himself. "Never again."

CHAPTER 37

Mel stirred and slowly opened her eyes to see Frank's handsome face. It hadn't been a dream after all!

"Hey, baby. How's my girl?" he asked softly.

She loved it when he called her baby. BABY! She forgot to tell him about the baby! "I'm wonderful! Better than wonderful! I love you, Frank."

"And I love you, Mare—more than I can ever express."

Mel kissed Frank, a long, languorous kiss. Frank responded in kind, moving his body over hers, but she stopped him.

"Honey, I'm sorry, but I have to talk to you about something. I was meaning to do it last night, but I guess I got caught up in the moment."

"Can we talk about it later, Mare? There's something else on my mind right now," he commented as he nibbled on her ear.

"No, I've got to talk about it now, Frank. It's really important," she insisted.

Frank let out a big sigh then rolled onto his back, putting his hands behind his head. "Okay, Mare. What do you want to talk about? I'm all yours," he offered.

"Okay, here goes. Do you remember the time we ran into Ritchie at the mall when we were shopping for school supplies?" she asked.

"Sure – how could I forget? I felt like I was being introduced to Mount Rushmore!" he joked.

"Frank, I'm being serious here!" Mel said petulantly.

"I'm sorry, babe. Go ahead, I'm listening," Frank replied as he turned on his side to give Mel his full attention.

"All righty, then," Mel continued as she took a deep breath. "Do you remember what happened after we got home?"

Frank thought for a moment then broke into a big smile. "Yeah . . . that was awesome!"

"Yes, honey, it was totally awesome, but remember how we just kind of threw caution to the wind that day?"

Frank sat up and took her hands in his. "Mare, what's going on? What are you trying to say to me?"

"I'm pregnant, Frank," she announced. He fell silent. "Frank, say something," she pleaded as she anxiously scanned his face for a reaction.

"You're pregnant? From just that one time?" he asked in disbelief.

Mel nodded her head. "Yes, Frank. Dr. Friedman told me the day I woke up in the hospital. When he said I was about four weeks in, it added up. Look, I'd understand if you were angry or upset—I had a bit of a time coming to grips with it myself. I won't have a problem if you need some space to get your head around this," she reassured him. Frank grew quiet again. "Frank, please say something. Please talk to me!"

"So, I'm going to be a father? For real?" he asked.

"Yes, honey, in about seven months," Mel replied.

"I'm going to be a father," he repeated as if in a daze.

"Are you all right, Frank?" Mel was afraid this might be too much, too soon.

He stared at her, this woman who had turned his life around. His heart was about to erupt in heady emotion. "Are you kidding, Mare? I've never been more right in my life! I love you so much! I knew from the first moment I saw you in that restaurant that I wanted to spend the rest of my life with you," he vowed.

"I'm so happy, Frank," she answered as she tenderly took his hand and placed it over her stomach.

"Hello, baby! It's Daddy here," Frank exclaimed as he leaned down and spoke in awe to Mel's belly. He paused, then bolted upright – a look of unease settling over him. "Mare, I have something to tell you, too," he said, his eyes fixed on the wall opposite the bed.

Mel gently pressed him. "What is it, honey?" she asked.

"It's something I should have confided in you from the start. I just didn't know how to handle it," Frank meekly confessed.

"That's okay," Mel reassured him. "You know you can tell me anything. Whatever it is, it can't be any harder than what I just told you."

"I'm not so sure," he replied, as tiny beads of perspiration appeared on his forehead.

"Okay, now you're scaring me. Out with it, Francis!"

Frank turned to look at Mel, apprehension clouding his face. "Mare, I'm adopted," he announced.

Mel's eyes grew wide. "That's it? That's what you couldn't tell me?" she asked plaintively. "Why, Frank? Did you think that would change my feelings for your—just because you were adopted?"

"No, Mare. That's not it – not exactly," he responded diffidently.

"Then what is it, Frank?" she demanded, now becoming alarmed.

Frank returned his gaze to the far wall. "Here's the thing, Mare. I'm not Irish, at least not by birth. I'm Italian.

My birth parents come from a village named La Morra, in northern Italy. My adoptive parents are an Irish couple from the Bronx," he revealed.

Mel lay back in their bed, stunned. After all this, *Frank* was her Italian Stallion!

Frank laid it all on the line for her. "Remember when we first met, how you told me about the problem your mother had with Ritchie and what a hard time she gave you about him not being your own kind? I was so in love with you, Mare—I didn't want to cause a rift between you and your mom so early into things. I was going to tell you before the block party, I swear. I had it all worked out in my head, but those plans got sidetracked for obvious reasons. I'm so sorry, Mare. I should have trusted you enough to know that you wouldn't let it get between us," he apologized humbly.

Mel tenderly studied Frank's handsome face. "Yes, you should have, but then again, if I had trusted you enough to tell you about Ritchie's visit that night, probably none of this would have happened," she observed.

"Oh, I don't know about that," Frank smiled as he kissed Mel's belly. "In fact, in a crazy way, we kind of have Ritchie to thank for some things, right?" he noted.

"That's one for the books!" Mel laughed. "Frank, honey, no more secrets—agreed?"

Frank crossed his heart. "No more secrets, Mare."

Mel nestled back into the safe harbor of Frank's warm body. "Did you ever want to find your birth parents?" she asked.

"Not really, but I'm not discounting the possibility that I might change my mind someday. It's not that I don't under-stand someone's need to do that, but I'm just not one of those people who feels compelled to go digging into the past. I never felt cheated out of anything," Frank replied.

"Did you know you were of Italian ancestry growing up? I would never have guessed you were anything but Irish – and I know Irish!" Mel remarked knowingly.

Frank relaxed a little and reminisced about his child-hood. "My parents were very cool about the whole thing – they told me when I was about five, just before I started school. I guess it felt a little strange at first, finding out I had parents in another part of the world who gave me away. Then the kids in the neighborhood found out and you know how that goes. My dad taught me how to deal with the bul-lies, though; he hooked up a punching bag in the garage and gave me personal lessons. Talk about a tough Mick! I came out of that garage with more attitude than muscles, but he did me a solid. I could always hold my own out on the street. Looking back on it, I can't say it was an easy thing to come to terms with, but I did—in time. It also didn't hurt that I had terrific parents who loved me uncondition-ally—they even moved into an Italian neighborhood so that I could be exposed to my ancestral heritage. But the reality is that I grew up in an Irish-Catholic household with Irish-American parents and relatives, not to mention having these baby-blues and fair skin. I didn't exactly stand out from that crowd," he wryly commented.

"So, that's why your friend Sal called you Cheech," Mel intuited.

"Yup, that's the reason," Frank replied.

"Your parents sound like very special people, Frank. I can't wait to meet them! Is your brother adopted, too?" she asked.

"Funny thing about that. My folks waited a long time to have kids, but for some reason it wasn't happening for them. That's where I come in. Then, a couple of months after they brought me home, my mom got pregnant with my brother!" Frank chuckled.

"By my calculation, that would make you and your brother Irish twins!" Mel observed. "Are you close to each other? I mean, do you get along well?"

"Absolutely! We've always looked out for each other—that's how we were brought up. I think when my parents told Marty about my being adopted he became protective of me, even though I'm the older brother. You know what's weird? Marty's the one with the dark hair and eyes and he gets a tan I would kill for! That's what they call Black Irish, right, Mare?"

"Sounds about right, honey, but I wouldn't lose any sleep over it—you're not too hard on the eyes yourself!" she reassured him.

"If you're trying to sweet talk me into having more sex, it's working, Mare!" Frank enthused.

"I'll tell you what, how does a nice warm bath sound, m'lord?" Mel purred.

"Lead the way, m'lady!" Frank growled.

An hour later, Frank and Mel lay together, overcome by a tidal wave of love's affection, its wake now lapping over them, lulling them in its sensual rhythms.

Frank gently kissed Mel's closed eyes. "Hey, Mare, are you awake?" he murmured.

She wasn't fully awake, but felt him near and pulled him closer. Mel didn't want to open her eyes; she wanted to embrace this perfect peace just a little while longer. After a long, arduous journey, she was finally home.

Frank kissed her soft lips. God, how he loved her mouth, her eyes, her body, the body that now carried and nourished their baby, his baby. This was his family, this was his home.

Mel awoke to the smell of pancakes cooking. She glanced at the bedside alarm clock – it was almost noon! She didn't want to get up – she felt as though she were being cradled in a warm cocoon. Mel thought that was how the baby must feel, and it made her smile. Frank had gotten up before her and had disappeared into the apartment's tiny kitchen. She smelled something delicious and called out, "Honey, what are you up to in there?" Frank walked over to the bed holding a breakfast tray; pancakes piled high, bacon and eggs – the works.

"Thought you'd be hungry, Mare. You're eating for two, now, so I made plenty. I know I worked up quite an appetite last night!" he said with his big, easy grin, his eyes twinkling like little stars.

"You're a sweetie. I am a tad hungry," Mel admitted as she dove right in and ate till she felt like she was about to throw up, which she did, getting to the bathroom just in time. Frank was right there beside her, holding her hair while she barfed up her breakfast. Lying back down in bed, she patiently explained to her very worried boyfriend that there was nothing to get upset about, that what happened was completely normal and the doctor would explain everything to him at their next appointment.

"I'm actually more concerned about your mom's reaction to me being the instigator in all this, Mare. At least she already knows about the baby – she doesn't know about her future grandchild's Italian father," he said uneasily, his brow knotted in concern.

"Don't give another thought about that, Frank. Mom and I are cool, now. Besides, when she gets to know you, she'll love you as much as I do," Mel said as she patted her tummy. "Well, Francis, it looks like we're going to have a bouncing Irish Bambino on our hands in about seven months. By the way, I can't believe I never asked you this before, but what does your middle initial stand for?"

"It stands for Albert," Frank replied. "My parents are huge fans of the Chairman of the Board, and my brother, Marty, is named after another Rat Pack singer – I forget which one."

Mel let out a hearty laugh. The past few weeks had been one hell of a ride!

Frank put the breakfast tray to one side, got down from the bed and knelt before her; he motioned for Mel to come nearer.

"What's going on, honey?" she asked.

Frank grasped Mel's hands tightly in his. "Marian Elizabeth Morrison, love of my life, mother of my child, I know I don't have much right now to offer you, but I promise that I will be a good husband to you and I will be a good father to our baby and that I will love you forever and I will never leave you."

"Frank, what are you trying to say?"

"Will you marry me, Mare?"

"Yes, Francis, I believe I will."

CHAPTER 38

Mel awoke to a quiet, misty spring dawn, the distant darkened storm clouds infiltrating its serenity with sporadic streaks of lighting. She lingered in bed for a while, savoring the stillness of the early morning. She had a busy afternoon ahead of her. For the past couple of months, Mel had been meeting with the Friday Night Dinner Ladies for lunch instead of for their usual dinners; she was now well into the eighth month of her pregnancy and Frank was getting antsy. He insisted she stay close to home for the duration and was adamant about her not being out after dark. Mel didn't even try to get him to see reason; she was still healing from her injuries and she understood his apprehension whenever she was out of his sight. Frank was being so good through it all: the mood swings, the weight gain, the attendant decrease in their once-frenetic lovemaking as her time was growing nearer. He was over the moon with excitement about becoming a father!

Mel would lovingly glance over at Frank as he was grading his papers late into the night after having endured another bout of her moaning and groaning. But he knew his girl: she wasn't by nature a complainer and she must have been suffering so much, especially since she was still recovering from the shooting. He so admired her strength and fortitude—she really was his Maid Marian! The doctor had warned them that it might have to come down to a C-section when she went into labor due to her situation, but Mel reassured Frank that there was nothing to worry about; they would see it through together. When all was said and done, he would always be her knight in shining armor.

Mel met the girls for lunch that day at what had become their favorite spot, Chez Janine. First on the agenda was the viewing of Mel and Frank's wedding album that had finally arrived. They had been married by the Judge on a bright and sunny Thursday afternoon in November, on Thanksgiving Day. The ceremony was held in the garden of their brownstone on the condition that they would be married again in the church when the baby was baptized; that compromise placated Mom Morrison. Mel had worn a stylish cream-colored silk suit, her long auburn hair pinned up in a cascade of baby's-breath, the Claddagh necklace that Frank had bought her glistening against her alabaster skin. Frank thought that she looked just like an angel. For his part, he looked very dashing in his dark blue suit and Aegean blue tie, which brought out the color of his eyes. Mel thought he was the most handsome man she had ever seen.

Mel's best boy, her Mac, was their ring bearer. She had dressed him up in a satin doggy tuxedo replete with top hat and boutonnière. He dutifully trotted down the fieldstone path in the backyard with her to the mum-and-ivy covered arbor, just as she had trained him to do, and he almost stole the show! Julia joyfully gave away her daughter's hand in marriage to Frank, kissing them both; the grace of her gesture moved everyone to tears. The ceremony was followed by dinner in a private room at a tony Manhattan restaurant attended by the Morrison and Brennan clans, and a few close friends. Frank and Mel were seated at the head of the festively decorated table and Frank's brother, Marty, toasted them as the newlywed Mr. and Mrs. Francis A. Brennan. It was during the traditional Thanksgiving turkey dinner that Val and George announced their engagement! Mel was so happy for her best friends – they meant the world to her.

As she basked in the ladies' joyful shouts while they pored over the wedding pictures, Mel felt a big kick in her stomach. She remembered the first time she felt the baby quicken – it happened while she and Frank were exchanging vows. She had stopped the judge mid-sentence to take Frank's hand and place it on her belly – there it was again, even stronger this time! Frank smiled at her in wonder at the miracle they had made together. "Happy Thanksgiving, husband," she whispered.

"Happy Thanksgiving, Mrs. Brennan," he replied. Life, unexpected.

The following month the girls invited Mel to meet them at the courthouse for the walk to the restaurant they had picked for lunch— they didn't want her going by herself as she was so far along now.

She agreed after conferring with Frank; he said it was okay as long as she took a cab from the train – the weather report that morning had mentioned the possibility of showers. That afternoon, Mel stepped out of the taxi and onto the wide sidewalk that loomed in front of the great courthouse; she had not stood inside its marbled assembly since the shooting. She stopped and stared for a long moment, absorbing the building's spare yet elegant art deco edifice that belied its formidable history. It all seemed a bit surreal to her. She waddled up the courthouse steps and squeezed through the turnstile that led to the magnetometers. Mel was greeted at the mags by her old friend and fellow officer, the handsome Steve, who waived her through with a big smile and an even bigger, "Welcome, back, Sarge!"

She turned the corner of the large hallway to her left and, as if on cue, Gloria popped out of the arraignment part and motioned excitedly for her to come in. Mel followed her lead and walked into a sea of people; a wave of cheering and applause arose from the crowd gathered there. She scanned the packed courtroom and realized that it had been decorated for a baby shower! The brass were all in attendance and, one by one, greeted her enthusiastically. Captain Murphy vigorously shook her hand and gave a brief speech announcing that there would be a lieutenant spot waiting for her upon her return to work. The judge, in a rare display of sentiment, hugged Mel and emotionally thanked her for coming to his rescue on that fateful day. Everyone patiently "oohed" and "aahed" while Mel opened the small mountain of presents that awaited her and her baby. She cried as she thanked everyone for their kindness; she was overwhelmed with feelings of love, friendship, and gratitude.

Marian Elizabeth Brennan left her party after a multitude of tearful goodbyes, arms laden with shopping bags full of gifts. What Mel couldn't carry with her, Gloria had gone to the trouble of having delivered to the brownstone. Frank had been in on the party plans all along and arranged to be waiting for her with the car afterward. As Mel approached the courthouse's massive glass doors to meet with Frank, she heard someone call out to her.

"Hey, Sarge, wait for me," Steve yelled as he ran to catch up with her.

"Hi, Steve!" she answered brightly as she noticed Frank pulling up to the curb. He exited the car waving to her and smiling his sweet, goofy smile. She waved back to him, her heart full.

"So, what's this I hear, Sarge? Are you leaving us?" Steve inquired as he helped her down the stairs with her things.

Mel gazed out to the bustling city street below, the wet pavement still glistening from the morning's rainstorms. The sky's lingering gray clouds dotted the horizon here and there, gradually giving way to reveal the faint beginnings of a rainbow.

"As a matter of fact, Steve, I am," she replied. "I'm leaving for a dream."

EPILOGUE

One bright summer's day when I was about ten years old with no one to play with and nothing to do, I decided to investigate the river that marked the western boundary of our town. Up to that time, my parents had forbidden me to go there, but now that I was about to enter the fifth grade, that was no longer a concern. At least that's how *I* saw it. Being the die-hard tomboy that I was, I spent the better part of that summer exploring the river's verdant banks, my only companion being my ever-present bicycle. My mother never seemed to be too concerned about my lengthy absences from the house, even at such a young age. There were a lot of children underfoot, and, I suppose, she welcomed a bit of respite from her maternal responsibilities – which were considerable. Perhaps she thought I could handle whatever juvenile mischief came my way. I have often wondered on what basis she found such faith in me.

I beheld a peaceful refuge at the foot of the riverbank. There, I encountered graceful long-necked swans, rats the size of small dogs, toads the size of small cats, fish I had no names for, and days-old kittens wandering far from their litter and discovering all sorts of mischief in a nearby shed— much like myself. As a child of nature who lived in a New

York City suburb, I thought I had died and gone to heaven the first time I happened upon that river and its denizens, and on one particularly eventful day, I almost did.

I had been exhaustively exploring the flora and fauna of this strange new world for some weeks now. On this particularly hot and humid August day, with the cool, rippling water of the river beckoning to me, I set myself the task of capturing one of the quite large and sometimes badly behaved white swans that I had so admired from a safe distance. While they could be the most elegant of birds, I had occasionally observed them hissing and spitting at each other in territorial rages. Why would I attempt such a feat? I don't know . . . who can fathom the mind of a precocious adolescent? Maybe I was just bored, but it was most definitely a challenge, especially for a ten-year-old city girl like myself. I looked out upon the unsuspecting skein of swans. Then, with a stealth becoming a world-class assassin, I snuck up on my prey and clasped my hands squarely around its long white neck. I got it! Oh my God, I did it – I caught the damn thing! But not for long. Within seconds of my avian abduction, the poor bird started flapping its large wings in protest, squawking within an inch of its life. I let it go and ran for *my* life, with the swan furiously waddling after me in hot pursuit for what I assumed would be a serious beak-pecking as payback for my hijinks.

I ran to the opposite shore, taking quick peeks behind me to watch the swan lose interest in the chase and return to its concerned brethren. As I slowed down, I found myself on unfamiliar ground. I had not explored this part of the river – it seemed different from the other side and somewhat forbidding. The dirt was very wet and muddy, and there was little vegetation or animal life that I could discern. I got a funny feeling in my gut . . . I decided I'd had enough fun for one day. I wanted to go home.

I slogged through the muck with great effort when, suddenly, I felt myself being sucked into the wet ground. In no time, I was up to my waist in a swirling black hole of sludge. I hurriedly looked around for something substantial to grab onto, or else I most assuredly would be swallowed whole by the angry earth. Oddly enough, I wasn't panicked, but I was worried, for as hard as I searched I couldn't find a rock or reed anywhere with which to pull myself out of the ground and I knew I didn't have much time before I was consumed by the river and drowned.

With the mud rapidly inching its way up to my neck, I fervently prayed to God to please help me; what would my parents think when I didn't show up for dinner? No one would know where to look for me. I was picturing the police officers showing up to the house and giving my family the bad news when – literally out of nowhere – a rock the size of a man's fist appeared directly in front of me, exactly an arm's length away! I grabbed onto my small granite lifesaver and pulled as hard as I could. Within seconds, I wrested my small body out of its muddy tomb and dragged myself to drier ground. I lay there for a while trying to catch my breath, covered in slime, my eyes fixed on the puffy white clouds moving slowly overhead. I couldn't make sense of what had just happened to me. When I was being sucked down into certain oblivion by the roiling dank sediment, I had looked everywhere around me and seen nothing, not even a tiny pebble to come to my aid. Had God answered my prayer? Was I the grateful recipient of a miracle?

I got up, brushed myself off as best I could and started the long bike ride home. When I got to the house I entered through the back door, hoping not to run into my mother. If she caught a glimpse of my muddied, disheveled appearance, she would surely want to know what I had gotten myself into this time. How could I explain what had happened when I wasn't even sure myself? I needn't have worried; Mom was at the kitchen sink washing the small mountain of dishes that had already started to accumulate there. I quietly tiptoed behind her, asking God for another miracle – that she wouldn't notice me.

I must have been a very good girl that year, because God granted me yet another wish: my mother didn't take so much as a moment's break from her sudsy daydreams to notice me sneaking through the kitchen and up the stairs to the welcome sanctuary of my bedroom. I propped a chair underneath the door handle to secure it then proceeded to peel the slimy clothes from my body, carefully stashing them in a garbage bag in the closet. I was too fatigued to try to figure out what to do with the evidence of my misdeeds; that was a problem for another day. I dropped onto my bed in exhaustion and fell into a blissful slumber, awaiting dreams of adventures yet to come.

Thank you, God.